Three Strikes, You're Dead

Also by Michael Geller

Three Strikes, You're Dead

✗ ✗ ✗

Michael Geller

St. Martin's Press
New York

Design by DAWN NILES

Library of Congress Cataloging-in-Publication Data

Geller, Michael.
    Three strikes, you're dead / Michael Geller.
        p. cm.
    "A Thomas Dunne book."
    ISBN 0-312-08322-X
    I. Title.
  PS3557.E3793T48   1992
  813'.54—dc20   92-25837
                                                   CIP

First Edition: November 1992

10 9 8 7 6 5 4 3 2 1

Three Strikes, You're Dead

1

They had to be laughing their heads off. They had to be sitting in their two-million-dollar box, with the carpeting and the leather furniture and the museum paintings on the walls, convulsed with laughter and wondering about the look I must have on my face right about now.

I could picture Rex Thompkins, tall, distinguished, with the silver hair and the perpetual tan that was endemic to baseball. He'd be balancing his glass of Chivas between two fingers, and those crinkly lines around his eyes would be dancing as he and Bucky talked about how they put one over on old Slots Resnick.

Bucky Walsh would be belting down a Budweiser, the paper cup lost in his big gnarled catcher's hand. I could just about imagine what he'd say in that wheeze of a voice.

"Geez, Rex, I wish to God I could have a pitcher of Slots's puss when he finds out."

It wasn't as if I hadn't suspected something. Bucky had been my manager a hundred years ago when I played minor league ball for the Mobile Gamers in the Southern League. He could give a hotfoot with the best of them, and as he lit the match on some poor sleeping soul's sole, the corners of his mouth would twitch. Sitting with Bucky in the owner's box at Shea just a couple of days ago, I had seen his mouth twitch that same way.

Bucky had become a scout for the Mets, and he was meeting with Rex, who was vice president and regional head of player development, and how about if I joined them? It was a little strange, but I didn't need much of an excuse to take in a game. Maybe they were going to offer me a contract and a chance to get back into the big show.

Unfortunately, Rex told me, the marketability of an overweight forty-seven-year-old was limited, not that he thought I couldn't still hit.

"You were quite the pheenom, as I recall."

"Hittin' three eighty and change before some jocko cut him down at second breakin' up a DP," Bucky added.

It was .326, but I wasn't about to correct him. It was amazing how the Slots Resnick legend grew with the years. A decade from now they'd have me batting .450, with fifty homers. The truth was I could make contact and I used the whole field. Some sportswriter said I knew how to "find the slots," and the nickname stuck.

After the "jocko" Bucky mentioned did a job on my knee, my pro ball career came to a close. I followed the Irish lineage on my mother's side and became the third generation of male Kellys to join the ranks of the NYPD. This was much to the chagrin of the Resnick faction of the family, headed by my father, Cantor Jacob Resnick.

A few good breaks got me a detective badge, and a few more and fifteen years saw me rise to chief of detectives. When the commissioner's job opened up, every wag in the department figured it would be handed to me. It went instead to Vargas, a political hack from the Bronx clubhouse, who promptly informed me that he didn't care for my "grandstanding" style. I told him where he could shove his shiny new gold badge, and I put in my papers.

Sure, I could have made money. The world is obsessed with security and crime, and those are two areas I know about.

A major retail chain offered me their top security post. A government agency wooed me to train their agents. An industrialist contacted me about being his personal bodyguard. At the very least I would have made triple what I could have had by staying in the department.

I turned them all down. I was getting too old to suffer fools gladly, and I didn't have the tact to hide it. I knew it after the Vargas incident. I realized the best boss for Slots Resnick was Slots Resnick.

Fast-forward a couple of years; a private investigator's license, more than a couple of successful cases that made the papers, a phone call from Bucky, and there I was in the big box overlooking the lush grass of Shea Stadium's baseball diamond.

I was never too comfortable in the world of the movers and shakers. I'm a blue-collar guy, and I don't pretend to be anything else. When you're a cop you get to see a lot of things, move in a lot of circles. The rich and the powerful never impressed me with their riches and power. I've had to look into too many closets over the years, seen too many people like the well-known senator who had a history of coming to New York and exposing himself in the lobby of the Waldorf, and the billionaire financial genius we picked up from the floor of a filling station bathroom, dressed in drag and threatening to kill himself if the sixteen-year-old pump jockey wouldn't come back and live with him.

That's what I liked about Rex. He was to the manner born but never lost the common touch. It tickled me that among the caviar and the other colorful dabs of food arranged on weird-shaped crackers were three hot dogs with chili. Sure I would pay for it later with heartburn, but that's why God gave us Alka-Seltzer.

The bottom line was that they had a prospect by the name of Billy Joe Howlett, who was the second coming of Ty Cobb, playing in a small college in Norville, Colorado. According to Bucky, Billy could hit .350 from either side of the plate, catch a BB in a hailstorm, and steal fifty bases with one foot in a cast. When they told me they were going to pay Howlett a million bucks to sign with the organization I almost fell out of my seat. Hype was one thing, but this was real money.

"You're going to pay the kid a million just to sign?" I asked.

"Well, Billy is a unique case," Rex said. There was something about the way he said it and the look he shot over to Bucky that should have put me wise—that and the corners of Bucky's mouth.

"I figger two years, three the most, and Howlett's out there in the majors. We gonna put Billy in Triple-A ball right out of school. Then Howlett plays winter ball, spends a few months in the Florida Instructional, and then it's the big club," Bucky said.

"That's damn fast to bring a kid along," I told them.

"Not the way Billy Joe has already developed," Rex said, shooting Bucky that same funny look. "Bucky can give us the picture on the field, but before we make a commitment we want to have a little better idea about Billy Joe. That's why we want you to travel down to Norville and give us the complete story on our young prospect."

"We don't need no surprises here, Slots. Kids today come along with a whole bunch of problems, from coke habits to booze to gambling to God knows what else," Bucky said.

Rex nodded. "We want you to do a background check on Billy. We don't expect any problems, but we want to be sure we cover everything before we hold a press conference and announce the signing. We are prepared to make a major investment in the future of Billy Joe Howlett, and we'd prefer to be certain that there's nothing that might come up later which could embarrass the club. Do you think you might be interested, Slots?"

Why wouldn't I be interested in a few days in the Colorado sun, carrying a notebook and wearing a smile? But something was nagging at me.

"Gentlemen, you'll forgive me for being blunt, but why do I get the feeling I'm being hosed? If this Billy Joe Howlett is destined for the Hall of Fame, how come I never heard of him?"

"Because Norville isn't UCLA or Arizona State, or the Dominican Republic, for that matter. You got your scouts today, and they're like your average big leaguer: lazy, overpaid, and know-it-alls," Bucky scoffed. "They sit on their duffs and wait for press releases from PR firms who're hired by the schools to push their players. They wouldn't know a legitimate prospect if one fell in their martini glass. I go out and I hunt 'em down, Slots, m'boy. I'm like those safari guys, beating the bushes and looking under the rocks."

"That brings up another point," Rex said. "Right now, as far as I know we're the only club that knows about Billy, or at least the only club prepared to offer a contract. If word got out that we're interested, it would definitely spark other clubs' interest. One of the things we want to avoid is a bidding war."

"If other clubs aren't interested, why shell out a million bucks?" I asked him.

Bucky laughed and looked down at his beer. "That's just what I wanted to know," he said.

"The answer is that we think that's what the talent deserves. If it were up to Bucky, there wouldn't be a player on the team making more than a hundred thousand."

"What the hell would you pay Babe Ruth, or Williams or Mantle, for that matter, if they came along now?" Bucky shook his head and looked at me with exasperation. "Today any Punch-and-Judy infielder batting two thirty makes over a million. It's ruinin' the game."

"We think Billy is going to be worth it. The bottom line is that Howlett will be putting fannies in the seats. There's a certain something that separates Billy from the other players. I think you'll see it when you get to Norville."

"Yeah, a certain something," Bucky mumbled, bringing the beer to his lips. Was he hiding a smile?

"At any rate, Slots, we'd like you to do your check without anyone finding out. Once we get Billy signed we'll splash it all over the front pages, but until then, do you think you can get around without being obvious?"

"I'll be as obvious as Dolly Parton in a string bikini. In small-town America, every stranger gets put under a microscope." I rattled some ideas around my cranium. "Our best bet is if I pose as a sportswriter from some paper—or better yet, a magazine writer doing a story on Billy Howlett. People like to see their name in print. It could get me close to Billy."

"That sounds perfect. I anticipated that you'd take on the job." He handed me two envelopes. One contained a plane ticket to Denver and directions to Norville, along with a confirmation of a room at the Norville Holiday Inn, the other a check imprinted with the Mets logo for a healthy four-figure retainer.

"This covers you for a week," I said. Actually it was double what I would have asked for, and quite frankly I was prepared to accept a lot less. But what the heck, if Billy could get a mill without even putting on a uniform, I was certainly worth what they were paying me.

"Give us a report in about three days. I doubt if you'll need any more time than that," Rex said.

I white-knuckled my plane in for a landing at Denver-Stapleton Airport, sitting next to a woman who was even more afraid of flying than I was.

"If it's going to happen," she told me, "this is it. The worst is landing. These airports are too damn crowded. Everybody is more interested in the almighty dollar than passenger safety. Do you know that Denver-Stapleton Airport is the fifth busiest in the world? They handle thirty-two million people, two million more than JFK. It's a wonder the planes aren't smacking into one another like bumper cars in an amusement park. Oh Lord, did you feel that bump? That could be the hydraulics. Oh Lord, I hope the wheels came down. I don't think this is a normal descent. Don't you think we're going down too fast? The angle doesn't seem right to me. Oh Lord!"

The cab ride to Norville, which was forty-three miles from downtown Denver, took just under an hour. On a lark I asked my driver, a native Coloradan wearing a Stetson, if he knew a ballplayer named Howlett.

All he could come up with was that Howlett was a pitcher that used to play for the Astros. It confirmed my suspicions that Billy Joe Howlett had to be one of the best kept secrets in sports. I still read *The Sporting News,* and I couldn't remember anything written about this solid platinum, can't-miss prospect. If he was so good, how come nobody ever heard of him? There were kids in high school getting more attention from the press than Howlett, yet here I was doing an FBI-type background dossier for the Mets, who were going to shell out a million plus just to sign him. What was up?

"Without question the best prospect I ever saw," Bucky had told me. "When you get to Colorado, check out the game Saturday night at Norville Stadium. It's Billy's last college game. You'll see what I mean."

I sat in the bleachers of Norville stadium fighting off mosquitos and moths and shifting every six minutes to be sure my butt didn't fall through the two remaining slats in the seat that'd originally had six.

I watched Howlett, a tall lean player, do wonderful things on a baseball field, easily running down balls that should have been in the gaps with long, graceful strides. I saw Howlett stroke the ball into center and right for base hits, and I saw Howlett turn what should have been an easy groundout to short into a hit by flat out beating the throw with blazing speed.

Bucky was right. Howlett was an incredible athlete, far and away superior to the other seventeen men on the field, and Billy certainly had something that was lacking in the other players. Now I knew why Billy was going to be offered a million bucks to sign, why I hadn't heard about him, and why the Mets were being so careful about their new prospect. Now I knew what those looks Rex and Bucky had exchanged meant. Billy Joe's signing a contract to play professional baseball for a minor league team was a big deal. It would rank up there with Jackie Robinson, maybe be even more significant. Billy Joe Howlett was in fact Billie Jo Howlett—a twenty-year-old *woman.*

I wended my way through the tunnel under the stadium that led to the player's locker room. A security guard bought my reporter story and told me Billie would be the last one out. They didn't have separate showers, so she had to wait until all the men were finished.

"What paper did you say you were with?" he asked me, just to make conversation. He was middle-aged and chunky, wearing a blue uniform. This was a moonlight deal for him.

"I'm doing some freelance work. I thought I'd do a feature on Billie Jo Howlett and see if I could get one of the magazines to pick it up."

He nodded. "Billie's good people. Terrific ballplayer, just like her brother."

"I didn't know she had a brother."

"Yep. Jesse Howlett. He was all-everything in basketball, football, and baseball. He got himself killed a few years ago in an auto accident. He hit the bridge abutment near the junction on Ninety-six. That was a damn shame. Some folks say he was liquored-up, but you're always gonna hear that when it comes to Injuns."

"Indians?"

"Yeah, Pueblo Injuns. There's a lot of them here in the state. You find them at the tourist attractions, Cave of the Winds, the Balancing Rock over by Pikes Peak. The Howletts moved here about ten years ago. They lived in a trailer and sold blankets and Injun jewelry along the side of the road. What happened to Billie's mom and dad is another tragedy. That girl's been through a hell of a lot of misfortune." He shook his head sadly.

"What happened to her folks?"

"Raymond Howlett thought his wife was cheating on

8

him, so he did her in with a hunting knife and blew his own head off with a shotgun."

"You know a lot about them."

"That stuff is public knowledge. Everybody around here knew the Howletts. If you don't mind, I got to lock up upstairs. You just wait here until she comes out. It won't be long." He started down the tunnel and then turned. "Say, if you get the story published, send me a copy, okay? Gus Landon. You can send it care of the Eagles."

"Sure," I told him.

The players straggled out in twos and threes. Out of their uniforms and in civvies, they looked a lot younger than they appeared on the field. Some had long hair, one or two sported single earrings. They seemed a likable group, not much different from their counterparts in New York.

I waited another fifteen minutes for Billie and debated whether or not to try and meet her tomorrow. Hell, I was here all ready.

I opened the door and walked into the locker room. It was like every other locker room I had ever seen—or smelled. I walked past the rows of brown steel lockers, each with a padlock. A bulletin board listed practice times for three other Norville College intercollegiate squads. In addition to the baseball Eagles, Norville fielded football, lacrosse, and soccer teams.

I called out a few hellos and got nothing back. The place seemed deserted. I tried again near the shower area with the same result. I was about to leave, figuring somehow I had missed Billie, or maybe there was another way out, when I heard a muffled voice coming from the other end of the room.

Beyond the rows of lockers and wooden benches was a glass-enclosed office with NORVILLE COLLEGE PHYSICAL EDUCATION OFFICE printed on the door, which was open. Billie was there, standing with her back toward me, talking to someone on the phone. The phone had a twenty-five-foot cord, which allowed the woman to pace back and forth. She was still in her baseball uniform, the bill of her hat turned to the side, blocking most of her face.

"You're a bastard! You're a gutless bastard!" she screamed into the mouthpiece, and pounded her fist on the desk. "You do it right now, damn it! If you don't take care of that bitch, so help me, I will. I swear I'll take care of her once and for all!" She slammed down the phone and immediately started sobbing, covering her face with her hands.

It was not the best time to introduce myself, but it would have been worse to have her see me slinking away. I tapped on the open glass door. I did it a few times before she finally looked up.

"Billie, I'm Slots Resnick from New York. I'm a writer, and I've come down here to do a feature story on you which I intend to sell to a major magazine. I wonder if you might have some time to talk?"

It took a moment before it sunk in, and then I could read the expression on her face which could be translated as *Oh shit, not now.*

"Um, come on in." She wiped at her eyes with the back of her fingers.

"Maybe this isn't a good time to talk," I offered.

"Yeah, well. . . ."

"Why don't I see you tomorrow? You can call me. I'm staying at the Holiday."

She nodded. "Yeah, that's not a bad idea. Uh, you know, I haven't had a chance to shower, and uh, well, you know, maybe tomorrow . . . I've got some personal things to work out right now."

"No problem," I said, smiling and backing away, feeling awkward.

Gus Landon met me as I was walking out to the parking lot. "Did you get what you needed from Billie?" he asked.

"Bad time for her. I'll talk to her tomorrow. Can I get a cab out here to take me to the Holiday Inn?"

"Let me change out of this rent-a-cop uniform and I'll give you a ride myself."

"Thanks."

"Not a'tall. I got my stuff on the first floor."

I followed him up to the small office behind the ticket booth that he used to keep his clothes in. I looked out of the window at the now nearly deserted parking lot. A few cars remained; one of those belonged to Gus, the others to maintenance men. A lone figure came into view, walking out of the mouth of the concrete building. It was Billie Jo Howlett, still in her uniform. In one hand she had a duffel bag, which no doubt held her spikes and glove. In the other hand she had a jet black baseball bat. She climbed into a white Mazda hatchback and floored it out of the lot. From the look on her face and the way she punished her car, she was still angry.

I was up early the next morning, and following Gus's advice, I tipped the desk clerk ten bucks and had him take care of the paperwork involved in renting a car. The gray Taurus was a far cry from the candy-apple-red Porsche the finance company and I owned back in New York, but it would get the job done. After checking for messages—Billie hadn't called—I nosed the Ford out of the parking lot and down Bat Masterson Avenue. Norville's city fathers had decided to name the streets after the "famous and infamous settlers of the Old West"; at least, that was what it said in the little booklet of "Norville Facts" I found on top of the TV in the room at the Holiday. I also learned that the Norville Fire Department needed twelve thousand dollars for a new fire engine, that Norville had three finalists in the livestock competition at the state fair, and that the Lou Naples Buckaroo Rodeo would be on Route 324 just south of Adobe.

I made a left onto Geronimo Road and drove a half mile until I reached the Rocky Mountain Diner. There was only a pickup and a van with Michigan plates out front, but inside, seven of the diner's ten tables were taken, as were three of the seven counter stools. I picked the middle-aged couple with the

11

three young children as the visitors from the Motor State. The pickup could have belonged to any one of three farmer types. A couple of senior citizens surrounded by a retinue of kibbitzers were playing a spirited game of checkers in a corner, and the rest of the clientele were nondescript small-town folks hovering over coffees or late breakfasts. It was a little slice of snooper's heaven.

Wearing a big grin and a cloak of affability, I asked the waitress a few questions about that "terrific gal player I saw over at Norville Stadium last night." After I explained about the article I was planning to write, Billie Jo became the topic of conversation in the diner. Even the checker-playing codgers looked up from their game to add a Billie anecdote. There were things I learned from what they said, and a lot I learned from what they didn't say.

Billie's athletic exploits were legendary. She was far and away the finest female athlete ever to come out of the tri-city area comprised of Norville and the neighboring towns of Adobe and Wesville. She was probably the second-best athlete, male or female, exceeded in ability only by her late brother Jesse. He was known as "the Colorado Jim Thorpe" and had an edge on her in basketball and track, but that was debatable, according to my diner sources.

It seemed everyone could cite records Billie had set, as well as her statistics for every sport she participated in. It was only when I asked about her life off the field that I got an uncomfortable silence.

"We don't get involved in a person's private affairs around here," one of the farmer types told me.

"Billie's a terrific young lady, and that's all you have to put in that article of yours," the waitress said.

"I heard something happened to her family when she was growing up," I prodded.

"That trouble was a long time ago. No sense in raking over them coals."

I kept my smile firmly plastered on my kisser, but the atmosphere had suddenly turned cool.

12

* * *

Norville had a library nestled between the Norville Presbyterian Church and a True Value hardware store. They had two rooms, one for "juvenile readers" and another for "adults." There was a "New and Noteworthy" shelf featuring King's *Misery* and *The Eight-Week Cholesterol Cure.* The librarian tried to be helpful: no, they didn't have microfiche. No, they didn't subscribe to any local newspapers. No, she hadn't heard about a murder-suicide involving a resident family named Howlett. Wait a minute, wasn't there some woman who played baseball at the college with that name. Yes they did have a local newspaper. People in Norville got their news from the *Tri City Post,* which covered everything that happened in the cities of Norville, Wesville, and Adobe. The publisher was Dan Shelby, and she gave me his address. "He lives right here in Norville," she said proudly.

I thought I had copied the address wrong until I saw the SHELBY printed on the mailbox. I was expecting a storefront or a little factory; instead, I was looking at a simple frame house with an overgrown front lawn and a variety of potted cacti lined up on the porch rail.

Dan Shelby answered the door himself. He wore what seemed to be the town uniform, jeans and a plaid shirt. His were extra large. He was over six foot, at least two fifty, with a black beard he took care of about as much as he did his front yard. Bread crumbs were evident in the foliage—I hoped they were from this morning's breakfast. I told him my cover story and he welcomed me in with a firm handshake.

"Always pleased to see a colleague," he said warmly.

Just like a New Yorker, I thought to myself. "I didn't mean to bother you at home," I told him. "I asked for your office address."

"Same thing; home is the office, my office is my home. I'll show you." I followed him to a little room off the parlor. The house was messy, but it seemed clean. I would have wagered Dan was a bachelor; I counted six cats as I followed him. Surprisingly, there was no cat odor.

13

"Take a look in here, Mr. Resnick."

The room had a desk, a comfortable-looking black leather La-Z-Boy, and a professional-looking computer-printer setup.

"That's the workhorse. It's a Mac souped up with a 600-DPI laser printer. It takes the place of a whole damn printing shop. I use a publishing program loaded with every font up to 24 points, and a Licht full-page scanner and bingo, I got as good a product as the boys who use lino."

"I have to agree with you," I said, nodding. Sure I had to agree with him. I had no idea what the hell he was talking about. One day I'd have to join the computer revolution. I wasn't exactly technophobic; I had used the FBI's national crime information data base dozens of times. I just never seemed to have the time to learn how the damn thing worked.

"Is this stuff hard to learn?"

"Easy. The more sophisticated the programs get, the easier it is. It's like the phone or the TV; just put it on and you're set," Dan said. He offered me a cup of coffee, which I declined, and then showed me back out to the parlor.

"So who did you say you're working for?" Dan asked when we were seated.

"I'm doing this one freelance. I've had my stuff published in *The Sporting News, Life, New York* magazine."

"Boy, I would sure like to be published in a national magazine. You're here because of Billie Jo?"

"I hear she's quite a ballplayer."

"Better than any man I ever saw, and that's quite a compliment from me. I don't know how you feel about it, Resnick, but I'm not much of a libber. They tell me that you got firemen up there back east that are women."

"That's right. Cops too."

"Well, cops I can understand. They can use them for traffic and parades and stuff."

"They're right on the front line with the male officers," I told him.

"Get out! You mean they bust up fights and run after crooks?"

"That's right."

"Jesus. I'd like to see some ninety-pound filly try to take on a heavyweight like me. That is really stupid. Another thing, if I'm in some building that's burning up, you suppose some woman fireperson is going to sling me over her shoulder and carry me to safety? What the hell are you folks back east thinking of?" he said with a chuckle.

"How about Billie."

"Okay. That's the exception to the rule, and I say more power to her. I got nothing against a female that can do the job. Just don't give any special preference. Billie can do the job."

"You know her well, Dan?"

A fat tabby crawled into his lap and snuggled against his belly. His big hands gently caressed the top of her head and smoothed down the fur on her back. Sunshine was streaming through the open curtains behind him, and another cat, this one black and white, was monitoring the dust with bobbing head movements.

"I guess as well as anybody else around here. I'm the reporter and the photographer and the gossip columnist and every other thing you can think of for the three neighboring towns. I saw her grow up."

"I understand there was a family tragedy in her life when she was a kid."

"It was an unfortunate thing. You thinking of using it?"

"Strictly background. I just want to know a little more about her."

"Okay. This is off the record. Her momma was killed by her father in a jealous rage. Then the bastard killed himself."

"And her brother?"

"That same night her brother found out the news, got himself drunk, then got himself killed in a car smashup. People around here don't like to talk about it. It was a big thing for a while, with some of the major Denver papers coming down to do the story. That was about, let's see, I'd say six years ago, maybe seven. Billie was the one who found her folks like that. She don't remember anything that happened that night, she blocked it all out. I can't see any need to mention it in the story."

"Who took care of Billie?"

"That's the nice thing that happened. Gordon Wallace owned the Shell station next to Ray Howlett's trailer. Gordon took Billie in after he married Patricia Morgan. That's another one of them libbers. She kept the Morgan name, so she's Patricia Morgan-Wallace. Pat and Gordon been the girl's folks. Pat Morgan's one of the wealthiest women in the state. Billie went from a little trailer to the Morgan mansion on Pecos Hill."

"You like Billie, Dan?"

"She's hard not to like. She's got her ways, though. Very competitive. She tells the truth whether you like it or not. Yeah, she turned into a nice young woman."

"Boyfriends?"

Dan smiled. "I don't think so."

"Why not?"

"Not her cup of tea, I guess."

"Of the gay persuasion?" I asked him.

"Yup. Out of the closet, and she'll tell you to go fuck yourself if you don't like it. Is that a problem for you?" he asked.

"Rocks and glass houses," I shrugged.

Dan Shelby laughed. "It's a whole different world today. Everything goes."

I wondered if Rex Thompkins would see it the same way.

2

The desk clerk handed me a couple of messages back at the Holiday, one from Billie inviting me to her home, and another from someone inquiring if I was in. I tipped the kid, who looked like he belonged in a Norman Rockwell painting, a couple of bucks and found out the second caller was a man. Since I didn't know anyone in town, I reasoned my caller must have been Rex or Bucky.

I was wrong. It'd been someone making sure I wasn't around.

My room had been tossed, and not by someone who cared if I knew it. Every drawer had been taken out and its contents dumped on the bed. The two pair of slacks I had brought had had the pockets turned inside out, as did my generic, all-purpose sports jacket. If robbery was the motive, my intruder walked away empty-handed, but not empty-footed: the only thing I could determine was missing was a pair of new black loafers, French Shriners, that had set me back a hundred at Syms.

I called the kid at the desk, who put the manager on, who apologized profusely and offered to call the sheriff's office for me. My pair of shoes wasn't worth the hassle.

I repacked the drawers with my shirts, socks, and underwear, and then I remembered my business cards.

I must have left them in the pocket of the sports jacket. Now at least one other person in Norville knew that Slots Resnick, freelance magazine writer, was Slots Resnick, private detective.

Whoever rifled the room didn't rob hotels for a living. People don't leave valuables in the drawers or on the dresser. The guy hadn't looked in the usual places: the mattress, the soap dish, the light fixtures, and the ever popular toilet tank.

There was a knock at the door. "Mr. Resnick?"

It turned out to be the manager, who carried a complimentary basket of fruit and tsk-tskd in all the right places, with the right expression behind it. I thanked him, told him it was no one's fault, and ushered him out.

I called Billie and waited for the woman who answered to hunt her down. After some wary questioning, Billie agreed to have lunch with me and suggested I come out to her home. I took down the directions to her place, which was about six miles from town.

As soon as I put down the phone, it rang. The man on the other end identified himself as Sheriff Korn.

"Heard you been burgled," he said.

"No big deal, Sheriff. I wasn't even going to report it."

"Big deal to us, sir. We don't have much crime here, and we'd like to keep it that way."

I pictured an older man, about sixty, crisp uniform, Stetson, big .38 on a garrison belt wrapped around a paunch.

"Mr. Olsen called me," he said.

I remembered that Olsen was the name of the hotel manager.

"Be a good idea if you came down and made a list of anything missing."

"The only thing I can tell was taken was a pair of shoes."

"Hmm."

"I really don't plan to be around town too long, so—"

"Like I said, we don't have much crime in Norville, and

when we do, I want to know about it. See, your shoes may not be important to you, sir, but I take it personally when something happens in this town. Today we got a hotel room burglary, you let it go and the next thing is a holdup at Norville Savings. Now, like I said, if you come down to Kidd Street—that's off Main, only a couple blocks from the hotel—we can talk about how you can get those shoes back, and I can nail me a burglar."

"I've got a lunch appointment."

"I'll expect you late afternoon, then."

There was no sense fighting the sheriff. At the very least, he might give me some more background on Billie. "See you later," I said.

It was closing in on noon when I drove the Taurus out of the hotel lot. The sun had beaten down on the car, turning its interior into a sauna. I made a mental note to leave the windows open the next time I parked. I didn't have to worry about having the car stolen; hadn't the sheriff just assured me that there was almost no crime in his burg?

In front of me, heat shimmying off the road gave the distant mountains an ephemeral, Shangri-la look, and every building in the distance was the Taj Mahal.

I was trying to decide if I liked Colorado better than I had the last time I was there, twenty years before. There were far fewer trees, and much less foliage back then. I remembered driving into the teeth of a sandstorm that stripped the paint off my car. More trees, more grass now, but also more Wendy's and McDonald's lining the roads.

I followed the interstate out of town, where it merged into 643, which in turn brought me to an asphalt road. Two miles down this road I reached a turn off with a wooden sign saying CORBIN CORNERS ROAD. This was a two-lane dirt affair, with enough hairpins to stock a beauty school. At night, with no lights, it would be a nightmare.

I was a mile and a half away from Pecos Hill and making a blind turn when I had to jam on the brakes. A man was

19

standing in the middle of the road. He was tall and gaunt, wearing a denim shirt over blue jeans. I could see his long blond hair under his ten-gallon, and his eyes, but not much else. He was wearing a blue bandanna that disguised his face as well as any rubber Nixon mask. Put him back in time a hundred years and he'd be right at home robbing a stage-coach. Right now, he had the business end of a Colt aimed at the center of my forehead.

My move was to pull out my Smith & Wesson N-frame .44 special, put it on my lap, and wait for an opportunity. Unfortunately, my revolver was a bit out of my reach—it was locked in the top drawer of my office desk back in New York. Airlines were ticklish lately about passengers carrying guns on their planes. You had to fill out forms, go to special gates, answer questions from one set of officials before departing, and then answer the same questions from another set upon arrival at your destination. By law, I would have had to report to the local gendarmes the fact that I was carrying a piece, and that would have done wonders for my undercover operation. After all, getting background information on a baseball player didn't exactly call for strapping on a revolver, not in quiet, peaceful Norville.

The man in the blue bandanna ran over to my door and pressed the gun against the window. Behind him, two more men, both with bandannas covering their faces, came out of the trees at the side of the road. They weren't carrying guns, but they looked like hard cases even without the hardware.

"Get out, Resnick! Move!"

I got out and was shoved forward and spread-eagled over the car, my hands resting on the hood. Somebody patted me down and then, finding nothing, punched me in the small of my back.

I made a move to rise and throw a punch, but they were on me in force. The muzzle of the Colt was placed against my temple.

"Don't turn around!" Someone said. "Give me that

thing!" The *thing* he was referring to was a cloth hood, which they placed over my head.

"We going to burn a few crosses?" I asked. It earned me another rap in the small of the back.

Rough hands straightened me up and pulled me along. The gun was still at my head, to discourage any thoughts I might have had about trying to fight my way free. We walked off the road; I felt the dirt change to grass and weeds underfoot.

"Prop him up against that tree and get the car off the road." It was the guy with the gun again. The one who had been pulling me along released my arm. He was probably going to move the Taurus.

"Don't take it too far, I've got to pay for the extra mileage," I said.

I braced myself for the punch, but it didn't come. I was wearing them out, I figured.

"What are you nosin' around here for, Resnick?"

"I write magazine articles."

This time I felt a blinding shot of pain in my right leg as one of my hosts connected with a drop kick. I fell as if I were a seven pin knocked down for a spare. I wouldn't give them the satisfaction of a groan.

"You want to answer that again?"

Looking straight down, I could see two pair of boots in front of me. One pair was dirty tan with oil stains on the toes. I tried to get a bead on the other, but whoever was wearing them stepped over to my right. One of the stains on the left tan boot looked like a cartoon cat. I'd remember that. The other guy's right hand shot up under the hood. He grabbed me by the collar, standing me up. I forced myself to concentrate on his fingers. There was a yellow-brown nicotine stain on the index finger; his thumbnail had a dark black spot at one o'clock. It was the kind of mark you get when you hit yourself with a hammer.

"You got trouble hearin'?"

21

"Fellas, I was about to do a story on Norville's hospitality. Now I'm afraid you've ruined it for yourselves."

This time the kick was to my left leg, with the same result. I went down hard. I tried to fight the haze of pain in order to focus on something that would help me find these guys on another occasion. I was grateful that they were so careful to hide their identities; it meant killing me wasn't on their agenda, and somewhere down the line it might be my turn to do some shit kicking.

"This ain't no kid's game, Resnick. You're a private investigator, and you're not here for your health."

"You're wrong. That's exactly why I'm here. My doctor told me to get out of New York. The climate was killing me."

They didn't like that one either. For a few minutes we played Mexican Christmas and I was the piñata.

They finally got tired, and Black Thumb pulled me up off the ground. I had Cartoon Cat in front of me, and the third goon was behind me now. I wanted to find some way of identifying him, but I wasn't able to turn myself around. He grabbed me from behind and pinned my arms. I couldn't see him, but I could smell him. He wore a heavy, syrupy-sweet cologne.

"Let's try it again. You been askin' questions about Billie all over town. I want to know who paid you to dig up old dirt."

I ached all over. My head vibrated like a tuning fork. I was tempted to tell them the truth, but I doubted they'd believe me. "Go to hell!" I said. My words sounded muffled, like I was talking through a comb and tissue paper. Swelled-up lips and maybe a broken jaw can do that to you.

"Sum bitch!"

If they were angry before, now they were totally pissed. I got pummeled to the point of losing consciousness.

"Okay that's enough. We ain't gettin' paid to kill 'im."

"I'd kill the wiseass heeb for nuthin'."

"Leave off him, I said!"

"Shit, I think he's dead."

"You dead, Resnick?"

I wanted to tell him to fuck himself but it came out a muffled groan.

"He ain't dead, but he's going to wish he was if he don't clear out of here. You haul your ass on the next bus to Denver and then head on back to N'York. Y'here me?"

I couldn't have answered if I wanted to, and all I wanted was to sleep. I wanted to fall down that nice soft black well all the way down to the featherbed right at the bottom.

I tried to move but I couldn't. I knew I had to get up, but it was like being stuck in rubber cement. No matter how hard I tried to make the muscles work, I was pulled back to the ground. After a while, I stopped trying. A thick fog swirled around me, and I drifted off.

I was being pulled again. They were back to finish the job, and I couldn't focus enough to care. One of them said something: "Hector, I found him!" He had a high-pitched voice.

I came out of it in stages. At first there was a painless floating sensation, then a dull ache and dizziness, and then, as if I was breaking the surface after a deep dive, a whoosh of sights and sounds that jolted me.

A brown face, a woman's face was staring down at me. She looked into my eyes and smiled.

"Lie still, señor. I will call someone."

She was gone. I tried to sit up, but a wave of nausea forced me down. I waited for the room to stop spinning and tried again, with the same result. My head was making me an offer: *Keep still and don't move and we can be friends. Try and get up and I'll take you on a carousel ride.*

Another face was peering down at me. "Carla, call Dr. Pierce and tell him to come," the man said, presumably to the Mexican woman who had been there a few seconds ago. "How do you feel, Mr. Resnick?"

"Like I must look. Who're you?"

"I'm Gordon Wallace. You had an appointment with my

daughter Billie, I believe. Carla, our maid, and her husband Hector were coming back from town. He spotted an abandoned car off the side of the road, which I guess was yours. They looked around and found you. What happened?"

"I was jumped." I tried sitting up again and broke out into a sweat with the effort.

"Maybe you'd better take it easy until Dr. Pierce arrives."

He was about forty, with a round open face that probably saw a razor once every two weeks. You could call him handsome, if you liked the pretty-boy look that went out with Tab Hunter and Fabian. He wore his chestnut brown hair in a pompadour. The hair seemed too brown for a man his age, but if it was a dye job, it was a hell of a lot better than the shoe-polish look I had seen on some guys. He stared down at me with blue-gray eyes that looked genuinely concerned.

I made it to a sitting position and then swung my feet off the bed. Gordon put his hand behind my back to prop me up.

"I don't think you should move around too much," he told me. "You look like you've been in quite a brawl."

"I'm okay," I said. I got up and wobbled over to a mirror. My legs were sore but not broken. I assessed the rest of the damage. From what I could tell, I had gotten off lucky. I was aching all over and probably had a slight concussion, but I doubted anything was broken.

It was reassuring to see myself in one piece. Slots Resnick, six two, two ten, silver hair sticking up in a flattop that looked like the bristles of a wire brush. Yeah, it was still me. All features were present and accounted for, except they wore a camouflage of swelling and blue-black welts. I gingerly moved my jaw back and forth. It had been close. It seemed I'd escaped a break, but I wouldn't be chomping down hard on caramels for a while.

"You can cancel the doc," I said, turning around. Gordon wasn't alone. Billie had come into the room.

"I'm glad to see you're up," she said, moving toward me. She reached out and touched the mouse under my right eye.

This was a girl who'd competed with boys and men most of her life. There wasn't a drop of self-consciousness in the way she moved or spoke. "See if Carla can get him an ice bag, Gordie."

"Sure. How about a drink, Mr. Resnick? You look like you need one."

It wasn't what I needed right then, I thought, turning back to the mirror. I needed to keep the peace my body and I had negotiated with each other. I passed.

Gordon patted me on the shoulder and went to round up Carla.

Billie and I were standing looking at each other in the mirror. She peered at me and I peered back. This was the first time I'd seen her up close and out of uniform.

She was almost as tall as I was, with wide shoulders and a long neck, which was accentuated by the V-necked blouse she was wearing over white shorts. Her arms and legs were long-muscled, like a long-distance runner's, not bulky . . . like a football player's. She was a whippet, built for speed, darkly tanned like red hickory under the Colorado sun.

I knew she was twenty. An oval face with the skin tightly drawn over the bones beneath, leaving small hollows under high cheekbones any model would kill for. The Indian blood was evident in her jet black hair, which she wore very short in a boyish cut which was very in with the androgynous types on MTV.

She wouldn't be spending much of her clothing allowance on push-up bras, and you could draw a straight line from her waist to her hips, yet you could tell that with the right makeup and clothes, Billie Jo Howlett could be the next nineties look.

"Have a seat Mr. Resnick." She motioned to a little table and three chairs near the door, a kind of breakfast nook. I wobbled over on rubbery legs, but I was regaining my strength with every passing minute.

"How long have I been here?"

"Carla and Hector brought you in about twenty minutes ago. It's almost four."

I had been lying on the road almost four hours.

"It's a good thing they found you. That road isn't used too much."

"Who did you tell that I was coming out here to meet you?"

Billie looked surprised. Her black eyes, so dark they looked like inkwells, narrowed almost imperceptibly. "I don't think I mentioned it to anyone except Gordon. Why?"

"The three guys who pounded me knew I was coming. They were waiting for me in the road."

"Not necessarily." Gordon walked back into the room carrying a tray with an ice pack and a glass of Scotch and one of water. "As soon as you cut off the interstate, someone who knew this area would know you were heading for Pecos Hill. There are two shortcuts that they could take to pass you and lie in wait. There's the cutover behind the Gant Farm, and old Route Two near the railroad tracks."

"What did they look like?" Billie asked.

I told them what I knew. Billie looked shocked that they had brought up her name.

"I can't imagine who they could be, or why they'd mention my name," she said, shaking her head.

"It doesn't sound like anyone from around here, Mr. Resnick," Gordon piped in.

"Slots'll do."

"Okay then, Slots. We've got a hooligan element, I guess all towns have, but they're more into getting drunk and breaking windows than beating up on people."

"I think we'd better call the sheriff," Billie said.

"I was supposed to see Sheriff Korn this afternoon on another matter," I told them. I didn't want to mention the break-in; it would seem like I was a walking crime wave.

"I've already asked him to drive out here. I didn't think you were up to driving just yet Mr.—uh, Slots," Gordon said.

I was supposed to be drawing as little attention to myself as possible. From the way things were going, I might as well take out an ad in the local paper. The best thing now would be to try to get Billie to talk before the sheriff showed up.

"While we're waiting, maybe I can have that interview with you, Billie." I pulled out a small notepad and the business end of what was now a broken pencil.

"What makes you think anyone's going to be interested in reading about me?"

I gave her a reassuring smile. "There aren't many women athletes around today that can compete on an equal footing with men. That might stir a wide audience."

"All right then, let's do it."

"Would you mind if I stayed?" Gordon asked. He looked at Billie, who turned her gaze to me.

"Fine with me."

Billie's body language showed it wasn't fine with her.

"I would like to get a few quotes from Mrs. Wallace," I said.

"Patricia is at our cabin about twenty miles from here. She's an artist and likes to spend time off by herself, away from distractions."

I nodded. "How do you and your wife feel about Billie's athletic abilities?"

"We're both very proud of her." He put his arm around Billie. "We'd be proud of her even if she wasn't the best athlete in the state. She's the best daughter in the state." Gordon sounded like a used-car salesman.

"How about brothers and sisters, Billie?"

"My brother Jesse died when I was thirteen," Billie said simply.

"I'm sorry."

"It was an auto accident. Jesse was a terrific young man, Mr. Resnick. I should tell you that Patricia and I are Billie's adoptive parents. Her parents died when she was a small child."

I pretended surprise. "I should have figured that," I said to Gordon. "You look too young to have a twenty-year-old."

He smiled his thanks, revealing a set of choppers that belonged in a toothpaste commercial.

"Billie, did your parents die in the same accident as your brother?"

"Well . . ." She threw a glance at Gordon, who rushed to her aid.

"Billie doesn't like to talk about it. You understand, don't you?" I got the smile once again.

I nodded. Slots Resnick was Mr. Understanding. I posed questions about Billie's high school and college careers, and got a rehash of what I had heard in the diner.

"You've done well in baseball against men in both high school and college. Do you feel you could compete on a professional level?"

"I'm good enough," she said matter-of-factly. "But it won't happen."

"Why not?"

"The owners of baseball teams are mostly men. The scouting structure, the coaches, the managers, the players themselves are men. They hear about a woman athlete and it makes them think of their little sisters tagging along after them on the playground. I've set records on every team I've been on. If I were a guy, there'd be scouts here from every organization, begging me to sign. Do you know how many pro teams have come to see me play, or asked to see my tapes, or responded to the letters Norville College sent out? Not one," she said disgustedly.

"It's discouraging," Gordon agreed.

"I would think there's a big financial incentive, though. How many more women would watch the games if there were a female player?"

"Look Mr. Resnick, a woman ballplayer would have to be at least twice as good as the men, with acceptable looks, and be willing to put up with all the sexist bullshit and phoniness. She'd have to be Miss Goody Two Shoes, a Miss America in spikes. That's not me."

"That sounds a little angry Billie," Gordon said nervously.

"That's because I am angry, Gordon." There was an edge to her voice.

"Well I don't think that Mr. Resnick is looking for that angle in his article. Am I right, Slots?"

"I don't give a shit what he's looking for. The reason I'm willing to talk to him is so that people might find out how the male-dominated society keeps women down. Is that a problem for you, Slots?"

They both turned to me, Billie looking daggers and Gordon flashing his American Dental Association teeth.

"One of the things I like about my job is that I get to ask the questions instead of having to answer them. You know what might be a good idea; all I've seen of this place is this room. How about someone giving me a tour?"

"I'll be happy to. I'm sure Gordon has something to do."

"I think I'm being asked to mind my own business. Very well, my dear." He pecked Billie on the cheek. "See you later, Slots."

I wanted to separate Gordon from Billie. He would run interference and would mother-hen her past every one of my attempts to get to know the real Billie. At this point I didn't know what to make of the blue-ribbon prospect. I could deal with the feminist rhetoric; after all, she was twenty years old, and having all the answers was a birthright of youth. It takes at least three or four decades before any of us really appreciate the depths of our ignorance. Her sexual preferences were her business. The fact that she was cocky was okay too in my book. I don't know any successful athlete who doesn't believe in himself or herself. It goes with the territory.

The negatives, the other side of the scale was the Billie Howlett I'd seen on the phone the night before. Not knowing what her outburst was about left me at a disadvantage, but it was something that was in the back of my mind. Professional baseball players had to deal with adversity. If you lost your head, or had a quick fuse, you didn't last long in the big show.

If Jackie Robinson had had "rabbit ears," a baseball expression meaning hypersensitivity, it would have taken Afro-Americans another five years to break the color barrier.

What also concerned me, and I know it would concern Rex, was Billie's tragic childhood experience. Having her father murder her mother and then commit suicide, and then losing her brother the same night, gave Billie a lot of baggage to carry through life.

The Morgan mansion, as Dan Shelby called it, turned out to be quite an eyeful. It was surrounded by four finely manicured acres, and adjoined tennis courts, a swimming pool, and a half-mile racetrack where Gordon and Patricia broke and trained the horses they bred.

Billie walked me through the barn and introduced me to Mr. Potato, a ten-year-old stallion whose services brought the farm twenty-five thousand per live foal. A tough job, but somebody had to do it, I told Billie. She laughed, and we walked along the fifteen or twenty stalls, Billie stopping to talk to and touch each horse. Here was a different Billie Jo, one very relaxed and at ease, obviously attached to the animals and comfortable around them.

"Who named him Mr. Potato?" I asked as we left the area.

"One of the grooms Grandpa Morgan had back then. He's not the brightest horse in the world. He's got the IQ of a potato. That's what makes them good runners, though. The smart ones just run fast enough to get by. When they get ouchy they protect themselves and pull up. The dumb ones haven't the sense to stop before it's too late. Mr. P. ran a race with a hairline fracture. He was lucky Grandpa felt the heat in the leg and took him out of training. The vets in Ocala saved his life."

We walked back to the house, eighteen rooms cocooned inside red brick, with a glazed concrete circular drive, sprawling rough stone porch, and black and red mosaic flooring. On the porch, green and red canvas chairs fronted a yellow cane table, on which a thick copy of *Breeder's News* lay open and folded to an article about "bleeders."

Inside, past the polished-teakwood-and-lead-glass door, was the wide cool-looking hall, paneled in blond mahogany. A dark-skinned man, about sixty, wearing a sombrero, was on the way out carrying a green flower box. Billie introduced him as Hector, Carla's husband.

"You're the man who found me, then."

He nodded, and his weather-beaten face broke into a smile, one that made me think he didn't understand English.

"Bueno," he said, bowing self-consciously.

"Thank you. I want you to know how much I appreciate your helping me." I caught myself raising my voice, as if by speaking louder I could make Hector understand me. Carla appeared from one of the rooms and started speaking to her husband in staccato Spanish, obviously translating what I'd said. He answered her and looked at me.

"Hector says he is happy to see you walking and hopes you feel better soon."

"I'm okay," I said. I ached, and I knew it would take a while before the bruises and contusions were gone, but all in all it could have been much worse.

Billie led me into a medium-size, pleasant living room furnished with a red leather chesterfield and a couple of wing chairs. There was a heavy filigreed mirror on one wall, a walnut coffee table in the center of the room, and a baby grand and bar opposite the door. A large bay window looked out over the grounds.

"I'll give you another chance to have that drink," she said.

"Make it Scotch and water."

I watched her maneuver among the bottles, glasses, copper pitchers, and silver ice buckets. She poured me a few fingers from a bottle whose price was what I paid for my first car.

"Same for me, Billie."

We both turned to the doorway, where the man I figured

to be Sheriff Korn was standing. A second later, Gordon followed him in.

Korn was nothing close to my mental picture. He was wearing a brown uniform with a huge Smokey the Bear hat, which he took off and placed on a chair. If they ever needed somebody to play Huck Finn, Sheriff Korn was straight from Central Casting. He was freckle-faced and tow-headed, with a red mark on his forehead where his hat had rested. Except for a patiently tough expression and a silly handlebar mustache he probably grew to make himself look older, he looked for all the world like a gangly teenager wearing his father's clothes.

Billie handed us our drinks. I noticed she took a mineral water for herself. She exchanged a warm smile with the sheriff.

Korn and I eyed each other like two boxers getting the ref's instructions. "Tough day for you, Mr. Resnick," he said flatly.

His voice had the heavy raspiness of a smoker's, and as if on cue he reached into the pocket of his uniform shirt and pulled out a pack of Marlboros. He didn't offer, and I was glad. My willpower after ten months of abstinence would have been sorely tested.

"I've had better."

He made a production out of lighting his cigarette, flipping open the top of a gold lighter with a showy wrist flick.

"How you been, Billie? Your dad tells me the season's over at the college."

"That's right. I'll be looking for a job come September."

"No offers?"

"She got a call from a professional woman's team," Gordon told the sheriff.

"Yeah. Softball." She made a face.

Korn settled himself into one of the wing chairs. He took a sip of his drink and made an appreciative grunt, brushing a speck off his shirt sleeve. He took a deep drag on his cigarette. He brushed back the top of his hair. He was a guy who liked to be the center of attention.

"Trouble seems to follow you around, Mr. Resnick. Have

32

any idea why folks would want to rearrange your features?"

"You're the sheriff, you tell me."

He thought that over, giving me a long stare. "Mr. Wallace, Billie, I wonder if you'd be kind enough to allow me to speak alone to Mr. Resnick."

"Sure, Sheriff," Gordon told him. "C'mon, Billie, let's give the sheriff and Mr. Resnick some privacy."

They went out of the room closing the door behind them. Sheriff Korn stood up and came over to where I was sitting.

"Maybe you and me better get right down to it, Resnick. I'm a plain man, and I like to lay things right out on the table. I been sheriff here for the past three years. If the people see fit to vote me in for another three years, I'll be happy to serve. Before you poked into my town I got an occasional speeder, a few habitual drunks, maybe a little juvenile vandalism on Halloween. You're in town a couple of days, we got a burglary and an assault back to back. How do you figure that?" He stood in front of me, hands on hips, and placed his boot on the armrest of my chair.

I had seen this type before, bantam roosters with inferiority complexes using their badges to strut and posture. Bullies in uniform.

"You know, Sheriff, if I was in your place, I'd be interested in the perpetrators and not the victim."

"Is that what you are Mr. Resnick, a victim? I was wondering what the hell you were. See, I spoke to Dan Shelby, who said you wrote magazine articles. I asked Dan to do me a favor and make some calls to friends of his in the magazine publishing field. You know what, Resnick? Nobody ever heard of you."

"Really? Maybe Sheldon didn't ask the right people."

"That's not what I think."

"No?"

"I'm kind of curious how you got interested in Billie in the first place. I heard you were out at Norville Stadium and the diner asking all kinds of questions."

"Why don't you tell me your theory, Sheriff."

33

Korn smiled. "You think you've got an easy mark here, don't you Resnick? Well, whatever you and your friends have in mind, it just isn't going to work."

"My friends? The people who broke into my hotel room and knocked me around are my friends?"

"The way I figure it, they had more sense than you. They didn't want to go along with your scheme. Maybe you tried to strong-arm them and they didn't take to it."

"What's my 'scheme'?"

"The Wallaces are wealthy. I know how you people think. You hear about a family like the Wallaces, you look around Norville. To you this is a Cracker Jack box of a town with a million-dollar prize. What was it going to be, a robbery? A kidnapping?"

I leaned back and took a deep breath. I'd thought Rex had overpaid me for this job, but maybe I was wrong.

"It never got that far, Sheriff. When the boys heard that Norville was Sheriff Korn's town, they decided they'd get out fast. One of them was in such a rush to get out of my hotel room that he picked up my shoes by mistake and left his. That's why they ambushed me, by the way; the guy wanted his shoes back."

"This is a joke to you, isn't it, Resnick?"

"No Sheriff, you're the joke. Save your Bogart routine for the locals, and get your foot off the arm of my chair before I break it off and shove it where you keep your brains." I said it quietly, more a statement of fact than a threat.

It seemed to shake him. I saw his Adam's apple bob in a big swallow. People didn't talk to the great Sheriff Korn like that.

"Tough guy," he finally said, but he backed away from my chair. His hand rested on the holster of his gun. "Maybe I ought to toss your butt in our jail."

"If you're going to arrest me you better have a magistrate's warrant. If you don't have that, you better be able to show that a felony or a misdemeanor was committed in your presence, or you have reason to believe that I committed a felony."

He thought about that. "You're a jailhouse lawyer, huh? I heard about guys like you. You draw hard time and you study the lawbooks to wriggle out of your sentence."

Maybe he saw the look in my eyes and had more sense than I gave him credit for. At any rate, he turned on his heel, picked up his hat, and strode to the door.

"My advice to you is to get out of Norville. I'll be watching you Resnick!" he called over his shoulder. Ever the actor, he exited by slamming the door behind him.

I hauled myself out of the chair and stretched my aching muscles. As long as I was moving I wasn't too sore, but the stint listening to Korn had tightened everything up.

There was a knock and Billie poked her head in. "I just saw Jack leave in a huff. Is everything okay?"

"Do they allow marriage between brothers and sisters in this state?" I asked her.

"No. Why?"

"I'm trying to figure out how your friend Sheriff Korn got that way."

Billie laughed. "Jack's harmless enough."

"This guy was elected?"

"Well . . . his dad, Jack senior, was our sheriff for the last twenty years. When he passed away, people sort of voted for Jack junior out of respect for his father. I mean, it's not like the sheriff here actually does anything. We really don't have any crime." She looked at my battered puss and stopped herself. "Well, anyway, we usually don't have *much* crime."

She walked me down the hall to the front door. There was a painting I hadn't noticed when I came in. It was a large piece, four feet by six, of a horse and a foal standing in a green pasture at either daybreak or sunset. I wasn't an art critic, but I didn't have to be to know that the artist had more than a little talent. The name on the bottom right corner was P. Morgan.

"Your mother?"

"Stepmother," she corrected me. I thought Gordon had told me that he and his wife had adopted Billie Jo. I let it pass.

"She's very talented."

"Yeah, she's good at that," Billie said. The implication from her cold, bitter tone was there was plenty she wasn't good at.

I smiled. "Family problems. We've all got them."

Billie shrugged. "Patricia can be a pain in the butt. We had a disagreement before she went up to the cabin. I'll straighten it out when she gets back." She suddenly realized that she was talking too much, particularly to a magazine writer. "It's no big deal." She smiled.

"Sure. Look, speaking of pains in the butt, I've certainly been one for you and Gordon."

"No, I—"

"You've been very gracious, and I really appreciate it. I also need a little bit more for this article. What if you join me for dinner tonight and we can just iron out a few loose ends."

"I would like to, but—"

"Please, I insist. Maybe you can point me in the direction of a good restaurant. I'm still trying to digest that Rocky Mountain Diner coffee."

"I already have plans, with a friend."

"Great. Bring your friend along."

"Well . . ."

She was wavering. "Come on. I'll be leaving in the morning, and this will give me a chance to get to know you better."

She thought about it. "I guess it's okay. To tell you the truth, I feel a bit guilty about what happened to you on the road. I have no idea why those thugs would bring my name up."

"Good. If that's what it takes to get you to join me you have my permission to feel as guilty as you want."

"There's a place Ramona and I like—Ramona's the friend I mentioned. It's Mario's, in town, off Cochise. If you like Italian."

"My favorite food. Let's make it at seven thirty," I said.

36

3

There's a thing called "cop memory." Ask cops their anniversary or their kid's birthday, and chances are you'll get a blank expression, but they can remember a felon whose picture they glanced at in a post office six months before.

I was sitting in Mario's waiting for Billie and Ramona and a guy sitting at the corner table was setting off all kinds of alarm bells in my head. He had that button-man look, big gold chain, heavy gold pinky ring, Porsche glasses with an amber tint. I figured him for fifty, grey hair at the temples with a weight lifter's upper torso that was now melting into fat. The when and the where hadn't come back to me yet, but I knew he was from New York.

He saw me looking at him, and he stared back. Mario's was practically empty. It was a cozy family restaurant, with red and white checkered tablecloths, a big mahogany bar backed by a smoky mirror and tended by an acne-faced consumptive, a jukebox filled with oldies, and a hazy aroma of booze competing with garlic.

The edge of his mouth shifted a half inch, which I guessed was his best shot at a warm smile. He followed up that opening by getting up from his table and walking over to mine.

"Mind if I join you?"

I made a motion toward a chair, curiosity getting the best of me. "I'm expecting some people," I said.

"Well, just until they arrive. What are you drinkin'? Let me buy you a brew." He turned around and called out to the bartender, who snapped to attention like a Gestapo colonel. "Couple of Coors here, Barry."

"So what are you doin' in Norville?" He said, turning back to me.

"Looking around."

He nodded. "You figure on lookin' around long?"

"A while."

"Well, I don't think you want to stay around too long. This isn't a good town to look around in. Not much to see here, in my opinion."

"Maybe you ought to keep your opinion to yourself." We matched stares.

He twisted his pinky ring and hunched his shoulders. "Hey come on, chill out. I'm just trying to be friendly."

"I've got too many friends all ready. It takes me a whole afternoon to write out my Christmas cards."

"See, I bet it was that kind of attitude that made someone want to smack your face and leave you with those bruises."

He moved back in his chair to let Barry set down the beers. "I'm going to take a guess that you're from back east, am I right? I figure New York or Jersey. I'm Mario Santamaria. I own this place. So who beat you up, pal?"

"I nicked myself shaving."

"No kidding! You ought to go for electric. You can get yourself into trouble using a blade."

"So I've been told."

"Can I give you some advice?"

"Do I have a choice?"

"Order any dish with shrimp. I just got them in a little while ago, and they're fresh and delicious. Enjoy your beer."

He lumbered off toward the kitchen and left me staring

38

into my beer, trying to get a make on him. For all the tough-guy bluster, Mario seemed nervous.

Billie and another young woman walked in. I waved them over.

"This is my friend Ramona," Billie told me.

"Pleasure to meet you."

She was much shorter than Billie, with heavy black liner under her eyes and too much red stuff on her cheeks. She was wearing a black shorts outfit that probably would look better if she were five pounds thinner. Her hair, black as her clothes, looked greasy to me, but what do I know about style? Billie was fresh-faced and natural-looking. She was wearing some blush and a drop of lipstick, but side by side the two of them were like a before-and-after picture of how to apply makeup.

I called Barry over and ordered drinks for the women. Ramona wanted white wine, and Billie ordered a vodka tonic. I stuck with my Coors.

"What's wrong with you now?" Billie asked Ramona.

There had to be some kind of invisible body language that I missed.

"Nothing."

"Don't tell me 'nothing.' "

"I thought we agreed that you weren't going to drink."

"Oh, come on!"

"Forget it."

"She has this crazy idea that I can't have a drink without getting drunk," Billie told me with exasperation.

"All it takes is one drink and she gets stupid and loud."

"Bullshit!"

"Look, don't ask me if you don't want me to tell you, okay?"

"Okay."

They sounded like an old married couple.

"You're a magazine writer," Ramona said, turning her gaze to me.

"That's right, freelance."

Billie got up and walked over to Barry at the bar.

39

"She can't handle liquor," Ramona confided to me. "She makes a damn fool of herself and then she makes me promise not to let her drink and then she gets mad at me."

I nodded. There was something about this Ramona that wasn't quite right either. As she spoke to me, her eyes wandered all over the place, as if she was having a petit mal seizure, or taking a trip in her brain.

"Okay, I cancelled the vodka and got a Coke instead. Are you happy now?"

"You can do whatever you want," Ramona said, shrugging.

I tried changing the topic, and we settled on the Norville Eagles. I told Billie how impressed I was with her performance.

"I'm glad the season's over," Ramona said. "She's so involved with baseball she hasn't any time for anything else."

"I guess you must feel the same way," I prodded Billie.

"I could play baseball twenty-four hours a day, every day," Billie said simply.

"That's true. That's why she has no friends," Ramona chided.

"The guys on the team are my friends."

"Oh please. You're a freak show for them. When it comes down to it, the only person who gives a damn about you is me."

"Ramona, stop."

"Well it's true!"

Mario poked his head out of the kitchen and looked around. He seemed surprised to see me with Billie and Ramona. He walked over with a concerned look on his face.

"Good evening, folks. Billie, Sheriff Korn's on the phone. He says he has to talk to you."

"What do you think he wants?" Ramona asked her.

Billie shrugged.

"He says it's important," Mario said. "Take it in the kitchen."

Billie got up and followed him out to the kitchen.

Ramona and I stared at each other. The silence was starting to get uncomfortable.

"You and Billie know each other long?" I asked, trying to make conversation.

"What's your game, Mr. Resnick?"

"Pardon me?"

"What do you really want from Billie?" Her eyes were darting around again like the steel ball in a pinball machine. "I don't believe for one moment that you're interested in Billie's story. Did Amanda hire you?"

"Who's Amanda?"

"Oh puh-leese. Spare me the wide-eyed innocence. You can tell my dear mother to stay out of my life once and for all."

Before I had a chance to answer Billie burst into the room and came running to the table. Her face was drawn. "There's been some kind of accident at the cabin," she said. "I think Patricia was hurt badly. The sheriff wants me to meet him there."

"Can I help?" I asked.

"I'll drive you right over." Ramona said, rising. "We don't need your help, Mr. Resnick." She put an arm around Billie's waist.

"It sounded serious, Ramona."

"We'll be there in a few minutes. Don't worry sweetheart."

"I'm sorry, Slots," Billie said.

"Just go on. I think I know what I want to say anyhow. I hope everything's okay."

They went out, and I heard the squeal of burning rubber as Ramona pulled her car out of the parking lot. I didn't know Billie Howlett very well, but what I did know of her I liked. This was a talented kid who was trying to make it in the face of enough tragedies to stock a midday soap opera. The fact that she was able to lose herself in sports was something Ramona and others didn't want to understand. I wondered about her and Ramona. The weird little Ramona was controlling and jealous, but she obviously worshipped her friend. For

41

some reason she viewed me as a threat to Billie. She thought I was working for her mother.

Mario came back to the table.

"Did you want to order?" he asked.

"Some other time," I told him. I felt his eyes burning a hole in my back as I walked out the door.

There were the three dudes that had played tennis with my head; there was Mario, Ramona, and Sheriff Korn. Who said Slots Resnick didn't know how to make friends?

A wind kicked up from the north, and with it a fireworks display and great peels of thunder . . . then came the rain. It was the kind of rain that made you wonder if God had finally gotten fed up with all of us and decided to try it again with a new cast. I dashed the thirty feet to my car amid magnesium-flare lightning and peals of thunder that sounded as though you were standing underneath a Brunswick pin setter. Back at the Holiday and without me asking, the kid on duty said he'd send up some extra towels. I squished my way upstairs, slipped out of my clothes, and dried off with the one bath towel with the green Holiday Inn logo and two postage-stamp-size wash-cloths.

In a stupid way I felt pretty good. I had taken a beating— "caught a beat'n," as they say on Baxter Street—and come out of it in one piece. In fact, the swelling around my face had gone down quite a bit. The hood they had put over me acted like another layer of skin, which cut down on cuts, and just maybe my bones and hide were a lot tougher than I thought.

I know it's a failing, but I'm not a turn-the-other-cheek kind of guy. I had a few ideas about how to track down the Three Stooges, but I was willing to wait until I finished my background check on Billie. I'd wrap that up tomorrow. It would be in Rex's lap how he wanted to deal with Billie's alleged sexual preference, and how her head might have gotten messed up by her family's deaths. I fell asleep wondering whatever happened to the kid with the towels.

It wasn't the thunder, but it was pretty loud. The little

fold-up alarm with the glow-in-the-dark face was showing 3:15. The knocking on the door started again, this time with a voice behind it.

"Let's go Resnick, open up!" I recognized the dulcet tones of Sheriff Korn.

"Go away!" I said, still half asleep.

"C'mon Resnick, this is the sheriff. I want to talk to you."

I waddled out of bed, trying not to trip over the blanket I had wrapped around me. I just about got the lock unbolted before Korn came barreling in.

"Couldn't this wait?" I asked him.

He was wearing the big-brimmed hat and a yellow rain slicker with knee-high black rubber boots.

"Nice outfit," I said.

He sneered at me. "Get dressed."

"Why, you want to take me dancing?"

"Shut up, Resnick. I've had about all I'm going to take from you."

His hand moved to the Colt underneath his slicker. It was a good argument that didn't leave much room for rebuttal. I dug out a pair of pants and a shirt, stepped into my still-wet shoes, and asked the Sheriff what the hell was up.

"You'll see," he said cryptically.

Fifteen minutes later I was sitting across the desk from him in his office. It was a small dank room broken by a portable divider, which probably shielded another desk and chair. The main piece of furniture was a large gun cabinet. A ceiling fan was revolving very slowly with a perceptible click each time it made a full turn. Behind the sheriff there was a steel door with a thick glass porthole. Long ago someone had lettered the words CELL BLOCK in bold red paint on the door, but somewhere along the way the C and the O had flaked off, leaving ELL BL CK.

The sheriff leaned back in his swivel chair and tossed some Polaroids onto his desk. "Take a look!" he ordered.

They were not for the squeamish. A woman in her mid-forties had gotten her head smashed in. The pictures showed

43

her sprawled on her back, her lifeless eyes wide open. There were a half dozen graphic head shots, which clearly showed that the blow had been delivered to the upper left side of her forehead. The force of the instrument used left a furrow that extended down through the forehead to the eye cavity. Streaks of blood radiated down from the injury, covering her nose and cheek.

You never got used to seeing pictures like this. Somehow, because the victim was a woman, it disturbed me more.

"Patricia Morgan-Wallace," I told him, handing him back the photos.

His hand hung in midair. "How did you know that?"

"Relax, Sheriff. I was with Billie at Mario's when you called. She thought Patricia had had an accident."

"Who said it wasn't an accident?" Korn asked, trying to be cagey.

"Sheriff, this kind of injury you don't get from walking into a door. The woman is in pajamas, lying on a wood floor, so one could hazard a guess that this didn't happen in a car crash. Then there's the fact that you got me up at three in the morning and dragged me down here."

"Maybe you know too damn much. How come before you got here we didn't have any trouble, and a couple of days after you show up everything started happening?"

"You're blaming me for that woman's death?"

"Let's say you're a prime suspect. I'm going to hold you until I'm satisfied you're clean," Korn said, jutting out his chin. It was all I could do to stop myself from slugging him.

He took out an ink pad and a print form from the desk drawer. "I want to get a set of your prints," he told me.

"You're making a mistake, Sheriff."

"Just put your fingers on the pad, Resnick." I let him roll my digits on the ink pad and press them on the paper. "You can put your valuables in here." He handed me a large envelope. I took out my room key, my wallet, and a handful of change. After thumbing through my credit cards, Korn

44

counted the one hundred thirty-two bucks in my wallet. He wrote the figure down on the envelope and had me sign.

"Very professional," I told him.

"Stand up, Resnick. It's going to give me great pleasure to lock you in the slammer."

"Good. Maybe I can finish up my night's sleep in the cell block." I went with him to the metal door.

Korn didn't have much of a sense of humor. "You're going to be sorry you ever set foot in Norville."

"Well I'm sorry I ever laid eyes on you. Are you really going to put me behind bars?"

"That's right."

"You never searched me. Suppose I decide I don't want to go to jail. Suppose I'm carrying a snub twenty-two, the kind all the professional hit men use."

"I didn't have to search you. I watched you get dressed, remember."

"Did you watch me every second? Can you be sure I didn't put something in my left sock?"

Korn jumped back and whipped out his Colt. "Stick your hands out in front of you Resnick. Do it now!"

I smiled as he cuffed me. I got a kick out of pulling the twerp's chain. He kept the gun on me as he patted me down.

"Bullshit artist!" he sneered.

He shoved me forward to one of the three cells in the "block." They were really more like chicken-wire cages than cells. All three were empty. A tribute to Sheriff Korn's reputation as a fearless lawman, no doubt. The cell itself was clean, with a commode, a sink, and a small cot. There was the scent of ammonia in the air, and although they weren't four-star accommodations, I'd spent time in worse spots, like a hotel in Cleveland that stole *my* towels.

Korn slammed the door and locked it.

"About breakfast; make it bacon and eggs, home fries, light toast with margarine—I'm cutting down on choles-terol—orange juice, and black coffee. I'd appreciate a wake-up at nine, nine thirty the latest, and don't forget *The New York Times.*"

"Screw you, Resnick. When your prints come back and I match them to the ones we lifted at the crime scene, you're going to be singing a different tune."

"Gee, Sheriff, you're right. That's what's missing in here, music. Pipe in some country stuff: Anne Murray, Kenny Rogers, anything by Willie Nelson or Alabama. And Sheriff? Fresh-cut flowers."

When I woke up, the sun was streaming through the window bars, casting long polelike shadows on the opposite wall. It took me a couple of moments to recall how I'd wound up there, and then I noticed the cell door was open. Not only that, but the steel door leading to the Sheriff's office was also slightly ajar, and damned if I didn't smell bacon and eggs and fresh-brewed coffee.

Okay, I admit I'm not the most trusting person in the world. Visions of me sticking my head out of my cell and Sheriff Korn blowing it off screaming "Jailbreak!" flashed into my brain. On the other hand, Korn was a jerk, but that didn't make him a murderer.

"Hey Slots, you up yet?"

The voice sounded familiar, but I couldn't place it. I got up and walked into the sheriff's office.

Dan Shelby was standing next to the room divider, a large skillet full of sizzling bacon and eggs in his hand. What I'd figured was another desk and chair behind the divider turned out to be a small refrigerator and a stove. Dan had a white apron tied around his ample girth and he was ambling over to the sheriff's desk, where there were two plates, orange juice, and coffee.

"I couldn't get the fresh flowers," he said, putting bacon and eggs onto the plates.

"Close enough," I told him. "What the hell are you doing here? You run the town newspaper and double as jailhouse chef?"

"I'm a special deputy, assigned as of last night on account of the Wallace murder. Dig in 'fore it gets cold."

"Sheriff Korn know about this?"

"Hell, it was his idea. Kind of trying to make up for the fact that he made an ass of himself. He sure was embarrassed when he found out who you were."

"How'd he find out? The prints couldn't possibly have come back yet." I sipped a little of the coffee. It was the way I liked it, strong and hot.

"He called Denver about having the crime scene investigating section get right down here, and he mentioned he had a suspect. When he mentioned your name, the fellow on the other end thought Korn was joking. His name's Captain Greeley, and he worked in New York about ten years back, under your command. He told Jack that he was holding the best cop in the country, and that if you weren't out of jail in five minutes, he'd personally ride into Norville and kick Jack's butt." Shelby laughed, the thick black beard bobbing up and down. "So anyway, I got the call to come down here, be sworn in till the termination of the case, and give Jack a hand. It also gives me an inside angle when I write the story for the paper."

"How do you put up with the little snit?"

"Jack's not so bad, once you know him. He's trying to fill some pretty big boots. Jack senior was a fixture in these parts. Put in twenty or so years, and did one hell of a job. He was a close friend of mine, and I guess I kind of feel I owe it to him to look after the boy."

I wolfed down Shelby's cooking and felt a lot better about Jack Korn and the rest of the world. "So where is the boy wonder?" I asked Shelby.

"He's up at the Morgan cabin. Denver's had a rash of murders in the last couple of days, and they can't send a team down for at least a day or two."

"Too bad. The first twenty-four hours is crucial."

"Yeah," Dan said. Something was on his mind. "Y'know, I guess Jack couldn't come right out and ask you himself. He

47

kind of hinted that I . . . well, you have to understand that a homicide here is very rare, and quite frankly, um . . ."

"You're telling me the sheriff is over his head on this one."

"Well, that's about the size of it. I'd say so."

"Any particular reason why I should get involved?"

"Well, the sheriff and I figure you might want to find out who stole your shoes and shellacked you out on Corbin Corners Road. He also figures that whatever you're in town for has to do with Billie, and since it was Billie's adoptive mother that got killed—"

I held up my hand, cutting him short. "Just give me directions to the cabin."

There was a big smile on Shelby's face. " 'Preciate it, Slots. I'd be happy to drive you up there myself."

He told me that it was a favorite spot of Patricia Morgan-Wallace's even when she was a child, and no one, not even Gordon, went with her when she felt she needed a retreat.

"How about answering a question for me?" Shelby asked.

"Shoot."

"Why *are* you in Norville? Did you have some idea something was going to happen to the Wallaces?"

"I'm a private detective working on a case. I'd like to tell you more Dan, but I can't do it without my client's permission."

"I understand. Can you tell me who hired you, then?"

"Nice try."

"Okay, if I take a guess will you tell me if I'm right."

"No, but take a guess anyway."

"Amanda Bernard."

"That would be Ramona's mother."

"Correct. Did I hit the jackpot?"

"No, but you're the second person who came up with three lemons. Why Amanda Bernard?"

"Sorry, Slots. I have to protect my sources too."

"I get it. You'll show me yours if I show you mine. How

about if I take a guess. Mrs. Bernard is none too happy about her daughter Ramona's relationship with Billie."

"Bingo."

I thought that over. "Ramona doesn't look like the type that would respect her mother's wishes."

"There's another angle. Amanda happens to be the Wallaces' attorney."

"So she has to tread softly. How did Patricia and Gordon feel about Billie and Ramona?"

"Pat is—I mean she *was*—hard to read. Very much a public person who never really showed what she felt inside. Gordon wears blinders and smiles a lot."

"I've noticed. I've got one more thing to ask you."

"Hang on, Slots. This started with me trying to get something from you. It hasn't worked out that way," the big man protested mildly.

"Hang in there with me and maybe you'll wind up with a Pulitzer. Tell me about Mario Santamaria."

That surprised him. His head snapped back as if he were slapped.

"Mario? What in heaven does Mario have to do with this?"

"Maybe nothing. Indulge me while you think Pulitzer."

"He's a solid citizen who came to Norville about ten or eleven years ago. His wife Rosa is blind; some say she has the gift of second sight. I don't believe in that myself." He shrugged. "I don't know what to tell you. He makes a great clam sauce." Shelby shrugged again.

I thanked him for his help, and after we'd cleared up the breakfast, we went out and climbed into his Jeep for the drive to the cabin.

49

4

Patricia Morgan-Wallace's cabin was a half hour out of Norville. There was a quick drop in the temperature as Dan followed the winding roads up a steep mountain. Driving in that part of the country is a study in contrasts; you go from arid plains, narrow canyons, and deep valleys to moderate-size mountains. The cabin was a couple of hundred feet off the dirt road. We parked the jeep next to the sheriff's car and hiked the rest of the way.

I'm a Lower East Side New York City boy. When I hear *cabin,* the picture that pops into my head is Abe Lincoln's place, lots of rough logs on top of each other, iron potbellied stove, big oak table and chairs, hurricane lamps, and a blazing fireplace.

Patricia's cabin was made of wood, Douglas fir and ponderosa pine, but that's where the similarity between it and Abie's place ended. It looked more like a Swiss chalet or a ski lodge imported from Aspen than a cabin. It was a big building, seemingly carved into the side of the mountain, supported by oak stilts under the porch. A stone stairway made out of the mountain itself seemed to be the only way to reach the cabin. The stairs actually went up the mountain another fifteen yards

51

past the house to the peak. Dan was huffing by the time we reached the door.

The view from the porch was magnificent. We looked down on a green forest, lush grasses, rough gray and tan boulders, the blue slash of a stream, a field of yellow and red columbine worthy of Van Gogh. Off to the side was Shelby's Jeep and Korn's cruiser, looking out of place in a landscape that except for the cabin and road hadn't been changed for thousands of years.

The door was ajar, and I followed Dan right in. It was a loft-size room with a cathedral ceiling. A fifteen-foot-square skylight flooded the room with a blaze of sunlight, which poured down on the thriving yucca, Bonsai, and other house plants that filled the place.

Jack Korn sat straddling a wooden chair. He was staring down at the chalk outline of Patricia's body, deep in thought. If I thought for a moment I was going to get an apology and a thank-you-for-coming from Korn, I was mistaken. He barely nodded hello to me, which was fine as far as I was concerned.

I gave the chalk marks a quick glance, and then I looked more carefully. Something was very wrong! The polaroid had shown her on her back, but the chalk outline was of a body lying on the left side.

"Did somebody move the body?"

"We had to turn her over to take the pictures," Korn said.

It wasn't a joke. "You mean to tell me you touched the body before the medical examiner and the crime lab showed up?"

"They didn't get here till early this morning. I still don't know when the crime scene investigating section is going to show up."

"Korn, you're a moron," I told him. He winced, but he kept his mouth shut.

Dan Shelby cleared his throat. "I'm going to wait in the Jeep. Give me a call if you need me."

Korn waited until Dan was out of earshot. "Take it easy Resnick. I just wanted to check if the murder weapon was under her. I would have looked like a horse's ass if the lab boys found a wrench or something. It wasn't a big deal."

"You were trying to solve this on your own. It was a stupid thing to do. You never move the body or even touch the body. If you ever do find the murderer, a good lawyer could use this information to put a doubt in the jury's mind."

"I'm not worried about that. When I catch him it's going to be airtight."

"Airtight. The only thing airtight is your brain."

"I don't have to take your crap, Resnick," he snarled.

"I thought you invited me out here."

"I invited you to collaborate with me. If you don't want to, get lost."

"With pleasure!" I turned toward the door.

"Just one thing. I know when you came to town you seemed to be real interested in finding out everything you could about Billie."

"What of it?"

"I've got something to show you. I found it this morning after they took the body away. I think you might be interested." He walked into the kitchen, and after a moment's hesitation I followed him.

"Y' see, Slots, even without your help I got a jump on this case. I think that's the murder weapon on the table. I found it under the porch. The fact that it was under there means it was protected from the rain last night. You look close, you can see some bloodstains, a couple of hairs stuck to the wood. You know whose it is?"

"Why don't you tell me."

I knew of course before he said the name. I remembered it from Saturday night. It was Billie's black bat, the one she'd tossed into her car after storming out of the stadium—filled with anger—and after I'd overheard her telling someone on the phone "If you don't take care of that bitch, so help me, I will."

"If you take a look on the handle, you'll see a B.H. scratched into it. That's Billie's bat, and that's the murder weapon."

"It's a bat all right, and those are her initials. I wouldn't go further than that."

"I guess I'll talk to Billie about it," he said. He reached down to pick up the bat.

"Don't touch it, Korn! You shouldn't have taken it from the place you found it. Call up Denver and have the crime lab boys pick it up, or if they're busy, ask them to send a size thirty-six Saran roller. That's an evidence bag for bludgeon instruments. You got that, Sheriff?"

Korn nodded and wrote it down in a small notebook he drew out of his shirt pocket.

"You tell them you want a blood, hair, and fiber workup. How tall was Patricia?"

"I don't know. About five two or three. Why?"

"Your killer was at least four inches taller than Patricia, right-handed, and strong."

"How do you know all that?"

"The Polaroids show a single blow was delivered to the left side of Patricia's forehead at a down-slanting angle. That would mean a right-handed, fairly tall person who had the strength to do all the damage with one hit. Patricia was standing looking at the person and didn't seem to be trying to defend herself, which meant she probably knew her killer. She was also comfortable enough not to feel threatened, in spite of the fact the killer was holding a bat."

Korn nodded. "Everything points to Billie Howlett."

"Don't jump, Korn. It's all circumstantial. Last night you had *me* in jail as your prime suspect."

"I made a mistake. You want me to apologize, okay, I apologize. I need your help. This murder fell into my lap. It's not like it's just anybody who got killed; it's someone from one of the richest, best-connected families in the state. I can't even pass it on to Denver, because it's totally my jurisdiction, and their top guys are stuck on a triple homicide. I don't want to screw this up. I figure you're a law officer, whether you want to admit it or not. You were taught just like I was to assist a fellow officer. You have an obligation to help me out here."

The only obligation I had was to my client, who in this case was Rex.

There was a white telephone on the wall next to the door; I went over to it and dialed Rex's number.

Rex picked up after three rings. Because of the time difference, the executive was just starting his day.

"We got some trouble," I told him. I explained how the little lark of a background check had developed into a full-blown murder case. Rex did most of the listening, asking a pointed question now and then. There was a long pause while he sorted it out. There could be a flood of negative publicity coming out of this case; I could understand it if Rex told me to scratch the mission and jet back to the Apple.

"There's a lot at stake here," he said finally. "I think we should see it through. If Billie is guilty, let's find out; if she's innocent, let's clear her name and sign her. Stay with it, Slots. Do whatever you have to do to get to the bottom of it. Do you have any strong feelings one way or the other?"

"I do, Rex, but I'd rather keep them to myself for now."

"Understood."

I sent regards to Bucky and walked out of the kitchen. The sheriff wasn't in the big room but the outer door was open.

I found Korn looking down at the terrain from the porch.

"Consulting with your client?" he asked me with that touch of superiority in his voice.

"Maybe."

"You in or out, Slots?"

"I know I'm going to regret it, but for the moment anyway, I'm in. But on my terms only."

"What's that supposed to mean?"

"I handle the investigation my own way. You follow my orders."

"You're out of your mind."

55

I shrugged. "Suit yourself."

The little wheels started turning in the sheriff's head. "Suppose I go along; nobody has to know that you're running things, right?"

"Right."

"I'd get the credit for solving the case?"

"I don't plan to run against you in the next election, Jack."

He thought about it for about a second. "Okay, I'll do it," he said. "Where do we start?"

"Who's your telephone carrier for this area?"

"Pacific Bell."

"Get to them and have them give you the phone records from the cabin, and while you're at it, get the outgoings for the phone in the Norville Stadium locker room. There's got to be a real estate office around town."

Korn nodded.

"See if they have a reverse phone directory. If not, see if you can get one from Pacific Bell."

"I'll get right on it. Then I'll talk to Billie."

"Stay away from Billie until the medical examiner calls you with the time of death and the exact cause of death. For all you know, she might have been dead before the blow was administered, and it turns out this isn't a murder after all. It wouldn't be the first time someone was framed for murder when really death was by natural causes. Lesson one: take nothing for granted."

"I'll remember that," he said with a touch of sarcasm. It was a marriage of convenience for Jack, and although it served his purposes to have me guiding him through the minefields of a murder investigation, he didn't have to like it.

"Good. Now I'll have Shelby drive me back to the hotel so I can pick up my rental car and take care of some things on my own? How long before all the reports find their way back to your desk?"

Korn shrugged. "I don't know. It depends on how many other cases the—"

"I thought you told me the Wallaces had connections all through the state."

"Well, they do."

"Fine, then call the governor's office and tell them to turn up the heat on Denver. I'll meet you in your office at six tonight. By that time you should have everything."

"I'll try."

"Don't try, do it!" I said enjoying, Korn's discomfort.

One thing you could say for Norville, it didn't tax your brain when it came to making consumer decisions. There was one gas station, one diner, one supermarket—A&P—one hotel, one movie theater—the Rivoli—one hardware store, and one all-purpose pharmacy with the down-to-earth name Joe's Drugstore, into whose parking lot I nosed the Taurus.

Joe's was a good-size store containing six well-lit aisles of school supplies, sundries, grooming products, and over-the-counter medications. The rear of the store was devoted to filling prescriptions. The pharmacist, a white-haired gent with bifocals, was leaning on the counter and reading a magazine. I walked over and asked him about men's colognes, and without looking up he cocked his head to the right. I followed and found myself in front of a cosmetic's counter and a gum-chewing teenage salesgirl. Among the perfumes, nail polishes, foundations, and moisturizers was a tray of men's cologne.

I introduced myself as an associate of Sheriff Korn and said I needed to check out the smells of different colognes.

"You mean you want me to open them up so you can smell them?" She said it louder than she had to.

The way she said it somehow made it sound perverted. I could see middle-aged female shoppers shaking their heads and young mothers shooing their children away from the strange man.

The pharmacist put down his magazine and ambled over.

"What's the problem Shirley?" he asked. He was wearing a name tag that said JOE, and I wondered if he possibly could be the Joe of the store's name.

"My name is Resnick," I said, extending my hand and getting a lukewarm shake. "Sheriff Korn and I are checking into something, and it might help us if we can identify a certain cologne."

"He wants to smell the colognes," Shirley explained.

"No problem. Just gather up all the samples and let the gentleman have a sniff," Joe said.

I thanked him.

"No trouble a'tall." He went back to his magazine.

She poked around in the showcase and brought out ten spray samples which she placed on the counter. Shirley obligingly sprayed the first five on separate tissues and smelled the colognes along with me. They were either "cool," "bad," or "yechh," according to her. The sixth bottle we tried was called Buster. Its label had a bare-chested guy playing tenor sax, with two scantily clad woman staring hungrily at him. The pitch was "Buster, when you're tired of playing around."

They say the sense of smell does the most to trigger memory, and Buster brought me right back to Corbin Corners Road. It was the same syrupy-sweet smell I'd caught on the guy who held me from behind as his pals pummeled me. I checked out the price tag. It was a steep forty bucks for three ounces.

"Do you sell a lot of these?" I asked Shirley.

She shrugged. "I'm not here all the time. You can ask Joe."

I carried the bottle of Buster over to Joe, who peered up at me over his bifocals.

"Find what you were lookin' fer?"

"I got the cologne, now I need the man."

Joe balanced the bottle in his hand. "This is a new one. We just started carryin' it."

"Expensive."

"Got to have a couple of expensive ones. People come in ask fer the most expensive stuff you got. They don't care that it smells like goat piss. That's your snobbery factor at work. I had a couple of bottles of this."

58

"That's the only one left. Can you recall who bought the other one?"

"You got a lot of stores in this state. Lots of stores carry this brand."

"Yeah, but I know this guy was in town and this must be the only store in Norville that carries Buster."

Joe nodded. "Let's see. Hmm. Yeah. Maybe I can help you at that. About four days ago a fella come in. Maybe late twenties or early thirties. Can't really recall anythin' about him. He came in lookin' fer a cologne, said he wanted somethin' new, and the strongest I got. I mentioned Buster to him and he said he'd try it. That's about all."

"Was he with anybody?"

"Nope, he was by himself, though I did get the impression there was someone waitin' fer him outside. Hold on! Now I remember. He had on this denim jacket, lots of stars and spangles on it. I asked him where he got it and he told me he had it fer the rodeo. Yeah, that's right. He was from the Naples Rodeo over by Adobe."

That made sense. They could have been three rodeo roustabouts looking to make some extra money by roughing me up. My man with the cologne might be a stable hand looking to hide the heavy scent of the horses he took care of.

I found out from Joe that the rodeo was a yearly event that took place every fall. Lou Naples was a local boy who went to Hollywood in the fifties and got in on the Western movie craze just a little too late. Lou appeared in a couple of Westerns with his idols Gene Autry and Roy Rogers and was even a regular on Rogers's TV show along with Trigger and Bullet. He got together with some friends and they pooled their money in order to start their traveling rodeo, which netted them a good living for the next thirty years.

I thanked Joe for the information and paid him for the bottle of Buster cologne, which I carefully wiped with my handkerchief and placed in a bag.

"I thought you didn't like the smell," Joe said, ringing up the sale.

"I've got a friend that might like it," I told him. "Do you know Mario Santamaria?"

"Yep. He's the fella owns Mario's."

"Any chance I can get somebody to deliver this over to him?"

"Tommy, my delivery boy, can take it over this afternoon."

"Let him tell Mario it's a present from Slots."

"Okay, present from Slots." Joe nodded.

Joe said to take Route 324 just a few miles. I made a wrong turn, and when I finally found the right road, it took me almost an hour to skirt Adobe and find the Naples Rodeo on the Applegate Farm.

The rodeo was housed on a flat piece of grazing land that Applegate leased to Naples for the three-week stint. The site was active with men fixing the wooden structures and pounding in stakes for new tents. It was the usual kind of thing that went on during the day to prepare for the performance that would go on at seven thirty in the evening, and to accommodate show changes for both the animal and human cast members.

I avoided the parking lot, reasoning that the Taurus would be too obvious among the vans and RVs. The thing I had going for me was the element of surprise, and if one of my three chums saw the Ford, it was as good as taking an ad out in the paper that I was around. I found a spot down the road and pulled the car up onto the shoulder and then hiked back the hundred feet to the rodeo entrance.

The rodeo itself was set up like a big wheel. The outer circle was composed of trailers and vans with the gold Lou Naples logo on the doors: a cowboy in chaps holding on to the reins of a bucking bronco with one hand and clutching his Stetson in the other. I figured the big vehicles acted as mobile barns for the animals. The next ring was made up of bright-colored tents, same logo, which promised "artifacts and genuine antiques of the Old West." At the very center was the main building, a large roofless wooden structure where the actual rodeo would take place. Next to it stood what I was looking for, a screened-in gazebo with a sandwich sign outside that said COOKY'S CHUCKWAGON.

A quick look inside told me that except for a heavy girl scrubbing down the grill, it was empty. It was possible that my boys might walk in, but I figured it was worth risking it to get the information I needed.

"We're closed," she said, turning her head when she heard the screen door open. She was one of those girls of whom people say, "She'd be so pretty if she would only lose some weight."

"I was hoping you might help me out with some information," I told her. "I met this fellow who told me to look him up if I wanted to bring the kids to the rodeo. I was riding by and thought I'd say hello, but damned if I can remember his name." I gave her the million-dollar Resnick smile.

"They all come in here one time or another. What's he look like?"

I gave her the description Joe gave me. "He wears this denim jacket covered with spangles and stars—"

"Oh, you mean Hank Brand."

"That's it."

"Hank is over on the trailer row. Just make a right when you walk out of here and follow the fence. I don't think he's back yet, though. Lou sent him over to Adobe to pick up some hardware. The rain washed away a couple of tents. Hank's trailer has a big H.B. painted on the side. He says he put it there so when he's drunk he can find his way home. Hey, if you find him, tell him Gayle wants to see him about straightening out his tab."

"Will do," I told her, and walked out. I found Brand's trailer a few minutes later. It was a Land Cruiser, vintage 1975, connected by an umbilical cord to an equally ancient red and white Impala. I knocked lightly on the door. There was no answer, and it was locked tight.

Brand did have his initials painted on the side, and that

gave me an idea. A man so worried that he'd be too drunk to find his way home would also be worried he would lose his keys. He would hide another key . . . where? There was a tattered doormat; I knew the emergency key would be underneath it, and it was.

From the outside of the trailer and the beaten-up Chevy, I was expecting a mess inside. Surprisingly, it wasn't as bad as I thought it would be. I guess if you live in one of those cramped things, you almost have to put everything away and be neat. It was one room with a fold-down bed that doubled as a couch. There was a little table next to the bed with a half played game of solitaire layed out on it. I walked into the nook of a kitchen, opened the pint-size refrigerator, and helped myself to an apple and a can of Stroh's. I kept an eye out for Brand returning as I went through the trailer, looking around. There wasn't much to find, except that his medicine chest was stocked to the brim with different colognes. The guy must have some kind of olfactory fetish.

I didn't have to wait long. Brand came walking down the path from the opposite direction from which I had come. He was carrying a bag of groceries, which he balanced on his knee while he fished around in his pocket for his keys. He put the key in the lock and opened the door.

I didn't give him a chance to walk in. I grabbed him by his hair and his collar and hauled him across the trailer, ramming him head first into the opposite wall. The groceries went flying out of the bag, and Brand crumpled to the floor like a deflated balloon. He tried lifting his head, groaned, and fell back. I wanted to take the fight out of him but not knock him unconscious. I poured what was left of my Stroh's into his face, and he came around. The beer smell competed with the stink of Buster and came out on the short end. I noticed the son of a bitch was wearing my shoes.

"Hello, Henry," I said. "Remember me?"

He shook his head and tried to focus. "Oh shit," he said. I hoisted him to his feet and tossed him onto the bed.

"I didn't do nothin', man," he whined.

I slapped him hard with the back of my hand. It snapped his head back and left a red welt on his cheek. "You don't talk unless I ask you a question."

He nodded.

"I want the names of your two friends. You have one chance to tell me straight out. You say the wrong thing, I'm running you into the wall again. Understand?"

"I don't know their names," he told me.

I grabbed him by the back of his pants and the front of his jacket and slammed him into the wall again. There was a loud crash as he bounced against the aluminum frame. The trailer shook, and glasses and plates tumbled out of a built-in closet and shattered on the floor.

Brand was moaning on the floor, holding his shoulder. "You're gonna kill me, man," he said, gasping for breath.

"Maybe. Let's try it again. The names of your buddies. I have all day, and I really enjoy this game."

"I'm tellin' you—"

I lifted him up again. He was tall and thin; he couldn't have weighed more than one forty or fifty.

"Please! Please! No more!"

"I'm waiting," I said quietly.

"Look, Resnick, I'll tell you the truth, but you're not gonna like it."

"Try me."

"The two guys are the Lukas brothers, Marty and Roy. But you can't touch them."

"What's that supposed to mean?"

"They're gone. I swear it man. They took off this morning. They had a fight with old man Naples and they quit. They might be halfway to Vegas by now. That's the truth, Resnick, I swear on my mother. Jesus, Resnick, let me get to a doctor. You broke my shoulder, man."

I put my hand on his shoulder. It was dislocated, not broken. I pushed down slightly, and he screamed in agony.

"Who hired you?"

"My shoulder, I need a doctor. Please," he whispered.

63

"Who hired you?" I repeated. I pushed down harder.

"Ramona Bernard."

"Ramona? How do you know Ramona?"

"I don't really know her. She's a friend of Roy Lukas's. She gave Roy and Marty and me fifty bucks each to break into your room. She told us she'd give us another fifty each if we scared you into leavin' town."

"Why?"

"She's crazy over Billie. She thought her mother hired you to find out some dirt and break them up. She's a crazy dike, man. Who knows how those bitches think. I didn't really do nothin'. It was Marty and Roy. I just held you, man."

"Shut up!" I thought about it. It made sense, especially in light of the way Ramona had spoken to me at Mario's.

"Who killed Patricia?"

"I don't know Patricia."

"Maybe I'll start on the other shoulder. You'll have to eat your food with your feet."

"No, man. I swear, I don't know nothin' about anyone gettin' killed. I *swear*, Resnick—you got to believe me, man! All we did was rough you up. I mean Roy and Marty roughed you up a little, I just took care of the car and held you. None of us were involved in killin' anyone. I swear it, Resnick. I swear it."

I believed him. I took Brand's belt and tied his hands behind his back. He screamed as I moved his shoulder around, but I wasn't going to go easy on him. I pulled the Shriners off his feet roughly and pulled his wallet out of his back pocket.

"You're gonna rob me too?"

I took two fifties out of the cowhide wallet and tossed it on the bed.

"Oh, man I'm dying in pain," he moaned.

"Not yet. I'm going to check on your story about Marty and Roy. If you're lying, I'm going to come back and finish the job."

"You'll see I'm tellin' the truth."

I checked it out with Gayle in the gazebo. "Those Lukas

64

boys were bad news," she told me. "Good riddance to them. By the way, did you mention that tab to Henry?"

"Yeah." I handed her one of the fifties.

"I got to give you change. It was only sixteen bucks he owed me."

"He said you should keep it," I told her.

5

It was late afternoon when I got back to peaceful Norville. I parked in front of Mario's restaurant and walked in. The restaurant was empty, as I'd expected that late in the afternoon, and the fellow Mario had identified as Barry was polishing the silverware.

"We open for dinner at five," he told me.

"Where's Mario?"

"He's in the kitchen. You want him?"

"Just tell him it's his friend Slots Resnick."

A few moments later Mario emerged, with Barry just behind him. He looked at me with a good deal less than pleasure. He held a good-size meat cleaver in his right hand.

"Take a walk, Barry," he growled.

"I didn't finish putting—"

"I said take a walk!"

Barry nodded, jammed his hands into his pockets, and walked out, leaving Mario and me facing off like gunfighters. After a few long seconds of staring at each other, Santamaria went behind the bar and poured himself a shot of bourbon. He didn't offer me any, but he did put the cleaver down as he drew the glass to his lips.

"What's the story with you, Resnick? You looking to bust my chops or something?"

"I'm looking to be friendly, Mario."

He reached under the bar and pulled out the bottle of Buster cologne I'd had Joe send over. "What the hell is this? Some kind of joke? Is this supposed to have some meaning that I'm supposed to figure out?"

I smiled. "Mario, you're much too suspicious. It's just a little gift, since you and me got off on the wrong foot. After all, you were kind enough to ask about my bruises, kind enough to give me some advice about my stay in Norville."

"Don't horseshit me Resnick!" He put down the glass and hefted the cleaver. "Just understand something, pal: I can take care of myself. You try and push me, I'll push you back ten times over."

I knew him. I knew his voice and the way he carried himself. I knew him from New York and the mob. I knew him from maybe ten years ago or more, but I couldn't for the life of me place him or come up with his real name.

"So what the hell are you staring at, Resnick?"

"You've got an attitude problem, Mario. You're going to chase away business with that chip on your shoulder."

"Here's news for you, Resnick: I don't want your business. I don't want you snooping around this restaurant no more. In fact, I ever see you again, I'm gonna enjoy taking you apart. Now take this shit and get out of here." He put the Buster bottle on the bar and slid it over to me.

"Don't think an apology is going to get this gift back for you," I said, carefully lifting the cologne by the cap. "I'll see myself out, thank you."

An hour later I was in the sheriff's office with Dan Shelby. Korn had driven to Denver to get the lab reports, and Shelby was looking in Korn's supply closet for the fingerprint powder.

"Is this it?" the big man asked. He pointed to five bottles of the stuff on the top shelf. There was enough powder to do all of East L.A. Korn had white, black, red, gray, and silver. Generally you used either white or black, depending on the color of the surface you were lifting the prints from. Light colors were for dark surfaces, and dark colors for light surfaces. I chose the white powder and dusted it liberally over the cologne bottle I had given Santamaria.

"How come you hold it so far away from you?" Shelby asked me.

"I'm allergic to the stuff. Fingerprint powder is carbon-based, made from lampblack, graphite, or willow charcoal, with a filler that stops it from clumping up. There was this one case where I did a lot of dusting; I was living on decongestants even a month later."

The powder is designed to adhere to the salt in perspiration that makes the fingerprint. I got two good prints of Mario's index and middle finger on one side of the bottle, and a perfect thumb print on the other side.

"Is that from Pat's cabin?" Shelby asked, handing me the tape I pointed to.

"No, but it may have something to do with the case." I used the tape to lift off the prints, and then I transferred them to a latent fingerprint lift card Shelby took from the same shelf where he'd found the powder.

"This is the first time I ever saw that done," Shelby told me. "Isn't there some kind of spray they have now?"

"Yeah, it's called ninhydrin. The only trouble with it is that it's toxic. It's good for taking prints off paper, cardboard, and wood, but if you get a whiff of it, you're going to be good and sick. I'll stick with this stuff, it's bad enough. Is there anyplace around I can find a fax machine to send this out on?"

"I got one in my office you're welcome to use. Does the sheriff know what you're doing?"

"Right now there's nothing to tell him, Dan. This is a hunch of my own. If it amounts to anything, I'll be glad to let you both in on it." I wrote out a number on the back of the card and handed it to Shelby. "Do me a favor and fax it out to this number; I'll call my friend and let him know it's coming. I'll wait here for Korn."

"Should I wait for an answer?"

"No. Even with the best of luck it's going to take hours to match the prints. Send them out and come back."

I waited until Shelby left before I called Elmer Robinson. Elmer would be sticking his neck out for me, and I didn't want anybody, including Shelby, to know who I was asking the favor of.

First I called his office number, and I would have bet the ranch that he wouldn't be there. I would have won the ranch. The second number I had was the contact number. No matter where Robinson was, he would be paged after the contact number was called.

After the first ring a computer-generated voice said, "Your area code and number." I punched in the number on Korn's phone and hung up. Twenty seconds later the phone rang. There was no sound on the other end.

"Elmer, I don't know what the code word is today. The last time I spoke to you it was Capricorn. In case you haven't guessed who this is, it's Slots."

"It's still Capricorn," the familiar deep voice said. "It's been Capricorn since 1987 when Nancy Reagan got the director caught up in all that astrology shit. What can I do for you Slots?"

"I need a favor."

"If I got it, you got it, my man."

"You still doing the Pizza posse."

"You better believe it. Every time they look at themselves in the mirror, they see my black face right over their shoulder. I'm around so goddamn much some of the button men think I'm an honorary mafioso. We really got the families on the run now, Slots. I say in five years all the dons gonna pack their bags and run back to Sicily. So what you need, man?"

"I want you to do a print match for me. I'm faxing you a latent card. Feed it to Big Bertha and get me a make and

70

model number. I can't place the guy, but I'm sure he's one of the boys."

"Where's he out of? Chicago? Detroit?"

"Don't laugh, Elmer—Norville, Colorado."

"Slots, this ain't a put-on, is it? I mean, Colorado isn't exactly a hotbed of criminal activity. What's this guy's gig, cornering the abalone market?"

"If I wanted to hear sarcasm, Elmer, I would have stayed married. I *know* I know this guy from somewhere, and it's driving me nuts."

"I know the feeling. I'll be in the office in an hour, and I'll start the ball rolling."

"I don't want you taking any heat on this."

"I'll handle it."

"Thanks, Elmer. I really appreciate it."

"You got to be kiddin', man. You got me here. If it weren't for you, Slots, I might be behind bars myself instead of puttin' the bad guys there. You call me anytime, and when I come back to New York I want to catch a game at Shea or maybe a fight at Stillman's with you."

"You got it."

I gave him the number at the Holiday and told him that he could call anytime during the night. Just then Korn walked in, with Shelby following.

"Talk to you later," I said.

"Who's on the phone?" Korn wanted to know.

"I called a friend of mine."

"If it was long distance, you pay for the call."

"You can send me the bill, Sheriff."

"You bet I will." It was the cocky Jack Korn all over again. "I guess I won't be needing your help after all, Resnick. He placed a folder of reports on the desk.

"Really?"

"Yeah, really. I got the reports, and it was just the way I figured. Patricia Morgan-Wallace was killed by a single blow to the head from the bat belonging to Billie Howlett. Everything matches up."

"Nothing left to do now but arrest her," I said.

"That's right. The phone company records say that a call went out of the Morgan cabin to the Norville Eagles locker room at 10:40 P.M. just about three or four hours before what the medical examiner fixed as the time of death. I'm figuring that Pat said something to Billie on the phone that set her off and she drove up to the cabin and killed Patricia," he said smugly.

"You mind if I look at these, partner?" I asked, picking up the phone records. I checked the outgoing calls from the locker room first. There was one that had occurred after the game, right around the time I'd overheard Billie talking on the phone in the office. The notation next to that number was *Morgan Mansion*. About six minutes before, there had been a call from the cabin to the locker room. Korn had used the reverse phone directory and written down *locker, Billie.* I noted one other call that went out from the cabin before the call to the locker room. Korn hadn't bothered to check that. The call to Billie fit his scenario, and that's as far as he wanted to go.

The ME's report supported what the sheriff had said: Patricia Morgan-Wallace had been killed around midnight, and the murder weapon was the bat.

"So Billie got a call from her mother, got into an argument, drove up to the cabin and killed her," I said.

"That's how I see it."

"What was the argument about?"

"Well, I—"

"Do you have any witness putting Billie at the scene of the crime? Where's your motive?"

"He's right, Jack," Shelby told him after some thought. "Gordon can afford the best lawyers in the country. If you don't have a witness or a motive you don't have much of a case. It's all circumstantial."

Korn brooded. "So what the hell do we do now? Maybe we should get over to the mansion and question her." He looked at me for approval.

"Bad idea for you to go, Jack. It might be better if I went alone." I saw that raised his hackles, so I took a conciliatory line. "Think about it a minute, Jack. If I go and see her, sort of pay my respects, she'll have her guard down. If it's you, both she and Gordon are going to get defensive and clam up. You're not going to get a thing out of them, and the case could drag on past the next election."

"He makes a good point," Shelby said.

Jack wasn't thrilled. "We'll try it your way. If it doesn't work, I'll go over there myself and do it my way. And I warn you, I want to know every detail of what happens, Slots."

"No problem." I picked up the reports. "I'll need to look these over. I'll return them later."

The ride out to the mansion was without incident. I noted the spot where Brand and his friends waylaid me, and I knew I had to be grateful that the beating hadn't been worse.

I used the door knocker and waited. It was Carla who answered. She was wearing a black mantilla, which she clutched to her neck with her left hand. Her eyes were red and puffy.

"I have to speak to Billie," I told her.

"She won't see anyone now."

"Please tell her it's Mr. Resnick. It's very important."

She hesitated. "You will have to wait out here."

I cooled my heels for a minute and a half, and then Carla returned.

"I am very sorry. She cannot see anyone now. Perhaps tomorrow. You understand, I'm sure."

"If I can't speak to her now, Sheriff Korn will come out here, and she doesn't want that. Please tell her it's urgent."

"I'm very sorry, señor, I can only—"

"Let him in. It's all right Carla," Billie said. She was standing out of my line of vision to the right, behind the door. "Thank you, Carla, you can go to bed now. Gordon won't be back until very late, so don't bother with his supper."

"Bien, Señorita Billie."

73

I followed Billie to the living room, where I'd met Korn the day before.

"Gordon is away?" I asked.

"He's in Denver, trying to get the medical examiner to release Patricia's body so we can bury her."

"I'm sorry about Patricia," I said.

"Thank you. . . . It was a terrible shock."

Billie didn't look terribly shocked, or grief-stricken, for that matter. She was wearing a pink terry robe over silk pajamas and slippers. There was a magazine on the coffee table, folded over in the middle where she'd marked her place when I'd knocked on the door.

"What did you mean, Jack Korn would want to talk to me?"

"You don't know?"

"I don't read minds," she said impatiently.

"He thinks you killed Patricia." I watched her take that in. There wasn't the slightest twitch.

"Oh. Is that what you came to tell me?"

"You don't seem surprised."

"Look, Slots, thanks for warning me. A lot of people knew that Patricia and I didn't get along. If Jack thinks I killed her, he's wrong."

"I'm glad to hear that," I said.

Her eyes narrowed. "What's this to you? I thought you said you were leaving Norville."

"I was."

She glared at me. "I suppose you're going to do your magazine story on this," she said sarcastically.

"You have it wrong, Billie. I'm worried about you."

"I don't need your help. Please leave!"

"I think you do need my help. Korn has your bat—it was the murder weapon. He knows Patricia called you just a few hours before she was killed. All he needs is a motive to build a case around, and maybe I can give him that motive. I was in the locker room, and I heard you on the phone. You told someone if they didn't take care of her, and right away, you'd do it yourself. I saw you storm out of the Norville Stadium parking lot. You had your bat with you. You also told me that you and Patricia had an argument before she went up to the cabin."

"You son of a bitch! You're trying to blackmail me."

"No, I want to help you, but you've got to level with me."

"Get out of here Resnick!" She went behind the bar, bent down, and came up with a .357 Magnum in her hand. "I want you out of here now!"

"I'm on your side, Billie. Put the gun away."

"You're a liar. Amanda hired you to dig up dirt on me. You're a private detective. Ramona told me about you."

"Did Ramona tell you how she knew? She financed that beating I took."

"I don't believe that."

"I am a private detective, but I'm not working for Amanda Bernard."

"Sure."

"I was hired by the New York Mets."

"You must think I'm an idiot. Why would the Mets want you to spy on me?"

"A lot of baseball clubs hire detectives to make sure their prospects will hack it in the bigs. The Mets were interested in you, they're still interested in you. If you want, you can call Rex Thompkins or Bucky Walsh in New York."

Billie's hand holding the gun dropped to her side. "I know who Bucky is. He's a Met's scout . . . I can't believe this. They were thinking of giving me a contract?"

"A contract with big numbers and a chance to be in the big show in a couple of years. I don't think anyone is going to want to wait for you to get out of prison, though, so I suggest you cooperate with me."

Slowly she put the gun back behind the bar. She touched the bottles and the glasses, deep in thought. Finally she looked up, and the fight had gone out of her. "Do you want a drink, Slots?" she asked.

"No thanks. You go ahead."

"I don't drink."

I thought about Ramona and the way she warned Billie not to drink. She said Billie got stupid and loud and made a damn fool of herself.

"Slots, have you told the sheriff what you heard?"

"No, not yet."

"Good. It's not what you think. You didn't hear me talking about Patricia; I was talking about Amanda Bernard, Ramona's mother."

"And you were talking to?"

"I was talking to Ramona. She was waiting for me here. She was practically living here with me, but she kept trying to keep things cool with Amanda. She'd spend a couple of nights with me and then run home. You heard me telling her that she was going to have to tell Amanda once and for all that we wanted to be together. I was saying that if Ramona wouldn't do it, wouldn't take care of it, I'd call her mother and tell her myself. It had nothing to do with Patricia."

"There was a call from the cabin to the locker room."

"I did speak to Patricia. She always called me after a game to find out how I did. We spoke a couple of minutes and that was it."

"You said you and your stepmother had differences."

"She didn't approve of Ramona. We argued about it constantly."

"And Gordon?"

"Gordon was more understanding. He would talk to Patricia and calm her down."

"Is that why she took off Friday morning? She didn't like the idea that Gordon agreed with you about Ramona?"

"Gordon doesn't necessarily agree with me, he just wasn't so adamant as Patricia. She didn't like that. She always expected him to back her up. She was used to everybody agreeing with her and doing what she said. If she didn't get her way, she would rant and rave and then run off to the cabin."

"Saturday after the game, where did you go?"

"I came back here."

"Ramona was with you?"

"Yes."

"She spent the night?"

"Yes."

"Where was Gordon?"

"I didn't see him. He might have been sleeping."

"What happened to your bat?"

"The last I saw it, it was in the car. I never took it out. I swear, Slots, I have no idea what happened to it. I only noticed it was missing this morning. The car wasn't locked; anyone could have taken it. You're sure it was my bat?"

"According to the report, yes."

"Do you think someone is trying to frame me?"

"That's very possible."

"Slots, I didn't do it. What can I do?"

"Did anyone have a grudge against Pat?"

"I don't know of anyone."

I didn't know if I believed her or not. Some of her story rang true; there were other parts that didn't pass muster. It was nothing you could put your finger on; it was just based on the intuition that comes after a couple of decades of hearing people's stories.

"You're sure you're telling me everything?"

"Yes."

"I want to talk to Ramona. Can you set that up for me?"

"I'll call her, and I'll give you her address."

"Tell her I'm helping you, but don't tell her more than that."

I watched Billie make the call and mentally made a note of the number. I'd check it later against the list Pacific Bell had given Korn. Billie held the phone to her ear for a minute, and then said, "She must be out with Amanda."

"I'm going back to the Holiday. Talk to her and ask her to call me in room two-seventeen."

"What about the sheriff?"

"For the time being I've got him on a leash, but I can't promise that's going to last. My advice to you is to keep quiet

77

and not discuss the case with anyone. It wouldn't be a good idea for people to know what I told you about the Mets."

"All right."

"How is Gordon taking . . . what happened?"

"He's very upset. He couldn't even talk about it. I feel bad for him."

"No tears from you though, Billie."

She looked up at me. "All the crying in the world won't bring her back. I've tried that, with my own flesh and blood. Patricia was good to me, but it was Gordon who made her adopt me. It was Gordon that really cared about me. I didn't hate Patricia, but I knew she resented me. I can understand that now. I can understand that she wanted Gordon for herself, and she had to share him with a bratty kid like me. When she couldn't have children of her own, she resented my presence even more."

"She didn't have to take you in."

"She was madly in love with Gordon, I'll give her that. She knew how much it meant to him, so she gave in to his wishes."

"Gordon must be very fond of you."

"He was always kind to my family; we lived next to his service station. He was friendly with my father. He used to help us with money for groceries. You don't know Gordon, Slots. He's just about the kindest, most generous man in the world. There isn't a person who would ever say a bad thing about him. We even argue about it every now and then, because all he can see is the good in people. Patricia's killing is just about going to destroy him."

When I got to the hall, Carla seemed to appear as if by magic. She walked me to the door and locked it behind me after wishing me a good evening.

I propelled the Taurus back toward town through an ocean of pitch black ink. My brights were only able to cut through twenty feet of the road ahead. People who lived in the country always tell you that country roads are the safest in the world.

"You don't get that glare from all your lights you city folk have all over the place. You don't hear 'bout any big accidents out here in the country."

I had just made it past Joe's Drugstore when I became aware of the white Cadillac Sedan De Ville that was following about a half block back. I made a turn down Doc Holliday Boulevard and checked in my rearview as the Caddy followed suit. I tried turning again on Main, and the Caddy made the turn right after me. I hung a sharp left that took me out of the Caddy's line of sight. Then I parked, got out of the car, went behind a tree, and waited.

Following the script, the Caddy came around the corner. It slowed immediately, and then parked behind the Taurus. The vanity license plate read A.B. ESQ.

The driver seemed to be looking around, trying to figure out where I'd disappeared to on such a deserted street. The Caddy's door opened and a woman stepped out. She walked over to the abandoned Taurus and peered in.

I walked up behind her and tapped her shoulder.

She whirled around. She was maybe five nine, with auburn hair and a strong, not unattractive face. She was wearing a black skirt, a black blouse, and a bright yellow blazer.

"You startled me!" she said.

"You were following me, Ms. Bernard. I'd like to know why."

"How do you know my name?"

I pointed to the caddy's plate.

"I didn't know if you were Slots Resnick. We don't get that many strangers in town and I had an idea of what you looked like from Ramona. I was on my way to see you at the Holiday Inn when your car came by. I thought I'd follow you and see if you were going to the hotel."

"What did you want to see me about?"

"Just to tell you to stay away from my daughter. I just happened to be on the extension when I heard Billie telling Ramona that she needed an alibi for Saturday night. I don't want Ramona involved in this. I certainly don't want her to perjure herself for Billie."

"Are you saying that Ramona wasn't with Billie on Saturday."

"She was with her for a few minutes after Billie came back from her baseball game. Billie got drunk and had a fight with Ramona. My daughter got disgusted and left. She spent Saturday evening in my house, and I will swear to that."

"What will Ramona swear to?"

"I'm telling you the truth, Mr. Resnick. Ramona will tell you the same thing."

"I would like to talk to her."

"That's not possible, I'm afraid. I've advised her not to discuss this case with anyone, particularly you, Mr. Resnick. I understand you have a vested interest in proving Billie Howlett's innocence."

"My vested interest is in getting to the bottom of Patricia Morgan-Wallace's murder."

"Well then, look no further than Billie Howlett."

"You're very certain."

"Yes, I am certain. Don't forget, Mr. Resnick, not only was I Patricia's lawyer, but I was also her friend and confidante."

"There are some people who would say you're angry at Billie over the relationship she and your daughter have."

Amanda laughed. "Good Lord, that lesbian thing again. Mr. Resnick, Billie Howlett is no lesbian, and neither is my daughter. The problem with Ms. Howlett is she's got an overactive heterosexual drive. Don't believe what you've heard."

"I've seen them together, Ms. Bernard."

"Yes Mr. Resnick, so have I. Ramona idolizes Billie, but that's as far as it goes. My daughter is a devoted friend, maybe too devoted. She's not Billie's lover. Why don't you talk to Mr. Santamaria about Billie? She seems to spend a lot of time at his restaurant."

"I'm not good at riddles, Ms. Bernard. Why don't you help me out."

80

"All I'm saying is Billie seems very fond of Italian food. Her appetite picks up when Mario's wife, poor, blind Rosa, isn't around."

"Why would Billie want to kill Patricia?"

"Why? The oldest reason in the world: greed. Patricia called me from the cabin and told me she wanted Billie out of her will. She was cutting the girl off without a penny."

"When did she call you?"

"Saturday night. I understand that was the same night she was killed."

"Just for the record, what's your phone number?"

She told me. It was the number the first call from the cabin had gone out to on Saturday night, according to the phone company records; the call before the one to the locker room.

"What did Patricia tell you?"

"She simply instructed me to be prepared to draft a new will, and she said she was just about to call Billie and let her know."

"Why did she want to drop Billie from the will?"

"Ask Billie. I have nothing more to say. I am giving you warning: stay away from Ramona. She's got nothing to do with this."

"Did you happen to hear anything else when you accidentally listened in on your daughter's call?"

She picked up my skepticism. "It's a mother's job to protect her child," she said stiffly. "I could have hung up, but when I heard Billie's tone of desperation, I listened to find out what was going on." Amanda looked me in the eye as if daring me to find fault with her.

"Did you know Ramona hired a man by the name of Hank Brand and a Roy and Marty Lukas to rough me up and chase me out of town? She thought I was working for you."

"That stupid little bitch! I was wondering about the bruises on your face. I would hope you wouldn't press charges. I know the Lukas brothers, they're the dregs of humanity. I warned Ramona to stay away from them."

She reached into her bag and pulled out a checkbook. "You're a stranger in town, and I'm sure the prospect of going to court and trying to prove an assault case, what with legal expenses and the time involved, wouldn't exactly appeal to you. Therefore I am prepared to make you a cash offer to put the unpleasant incident out of your mind. Would you accept five hundred dollars?"

"No."

"All right then, a thousand. I'll send you a release and—"

"I don't want your money."

"Fine. For the record, though, I offered a settlement that you refused. I expect you'll testify to that when the time comes."

"Tell me why Patricia wanted Billie out of the will and we'll call it square."

"You're serious?"

"Very."

"Very well, then. Patricia found out that Billie was stealing from her. There was the matter of some twenty thousand dollars taken out of a checking account. It wasn't that Patricia couldn't afford it; for her, that was small change. But she was irked by the fact that she had taken this girl in, done everything for her, and this is how she was repaid. That's why she went to the cabin after confronting Billie about it. I understand there was a terrific fight, and Gordon had to be the peacemaker and referee. Patricia felt Gordon was sticking up for his little angel, and that enraged Patricia even more. At any rate, it must have worked on Patricia all the time she was at the cabin, and she finally decided she had had enough. She told me, and I quote, 'I gave that little whore a roof over her head and food on the table, and she repays me by stealing. I want her out of the will.' "

"Billie said she argued with her stepmother over Ramona."

"You can believe what you choose. You might want to have a chat with Mr. Silk at Norville Savings. Good night, Mr.

Resnick. Don't forget our bargain." She turned, got into the Caddy, and drove off into the night.

Amanda Bernard didn't strike me as the most honest person in the world—she herself said she would do anything to protect her daughter. Did that include lying, saying Billie had stolen her mother's money when she hadn't? I checked the phone calls from the sheet again. The timing tended to support Amanda's scenario, although you could make just as good a case for Billie's version. First came the call at 10:20 to Amanda's house. According to Amanda, Patricia says that she's discovered that Billie stole from her, and she wants Amanda to change the will, presumably on Monday morning. At about 10:30 Patricia calls the locker room and tells Billie she's been disinherited. At 10:40 Billie calls someone at the Morgan mansion, possibly Gordon, in an effort to have him reason with Patricia. If need be, Billie says, she'll take care of it herself. That was the call I overheard. Billie storms off with her bat, and then in the next three hours or so someone takes Billie's bat, drives up to the cabin, and clubs Patricia to death. Any way you looked at it, Billie Howlett was in big trouble.

6

The night man at the desk called me over and told me there were two messages. The first was from Sheriff Korn, asking me to call him as soon as I came in. He'd have to wait until tomorrow. The second message was just a phone number. That would be Elmer Robinson. I didn't want Elmer's number to come up on my room bill, so I beelined it to the lobby pay phone. I passed on my phone card for some reason and filled the sucker up with dimes and quarters and waited for the operator to put me through to Washington.

"This is a gag, right Slots?" Elmer said. "Where did you get those prints?"

"I took them off a cologne bottle this afternoon. What's the story?"

"Your guy must be Jesus Christ, 'cause he's the only man I know who can come back from the dead," Elmer said.

"Let's hear it, Elmer."

"The prints belong to Bruno Piazza."

"Piazza's been dead for fifteen years."

"What do you think I'm telling you, man?"

It *was* Bruno Piazza. His face had been changed, probably by plastic surgery. His eyes were different, and his nose, which had been broken, had been straightened out. Maybe the jaw was different now too.

"What gives, Slots?"

"I'm not sure, but I've got an idea and it isn't pretty."

"I'm not much for dealin' with the dead, Slots my man, so as far as I'm concerned, I don't know nothin', and I don't want to."

"I always said you were smart, Elmer."

"In fact, I'm not even on the line anymore. See you in the big city, Slots." The phone went dead.

Bruno Piazza had been a contract hit man for Frank Scuzzy. When Scuzzy's boys went up against the Matera family, all hell broke loose in New York. The upshot was that Scuzzy got control of the numbers and sharking business in the South Brooklyn territories, and Matera could keep the drugs and prostitution. It was an agreement no one liked, but it meant peace, and that's what the dons wanted. One piece Scuzzy agreed to on a secret handshake with Joe Matera was that his main torpedo, Bruno Piazza, had to be hit. Piazza had gunned down Joe Matera's brother-in-law in front of Joe's wife's sister Theresa and their kids, which was a violation of protocol in this type of business. Andrea, Joe's wife, was driving Joe crazy for revenge, and if Bruno wasn't out of the way, Joe wouldn't have any peace, and that meant Scuzzy would have no peace. The whole deal revolved around Bruno getting offed, and Scuzzy agreed to it. It was easier to find another shooter than to blow a multimillion-dollar deal. The problem was that Bruno got wind of it. Before Scuzzy could have him killed, Bruno went to the feds and agreed to testify against Frank Scuzzy.

Scuzzy put out a hundred-thousand-dollar contract on Bruno, but it didn't do any good. Bruno testified against Scuzzy about a murder Frank committed when he was just getting started. Bruno got immunity and the Witness Protection Program, Scuzzy got ten-to-twenty in the big house. Once behind bars, Scuzzy became even more enraged at Bruno's ratting him out. He upped the price on Bruno's head to a half million bucks.

Three months later, Bruno was being taken to his new quarters in Chatsworth, California, when the van transporting him was blown to smithereens. Bruno and the FBI agent with him were killed. Bruno had to be identified from dental records. The talk on the street was that a then small-time thug named Peter Grassi bought his way into the garage where the van was parked and rigged an explosive to go off when Bruno turned on the ignition. Grassi collected a half million and made his bones in the brotherhood at the same time. Grassi went on to control a big piece of Matera's action when Joe got busted on tax evasion. That at least was the theory. The reality was that Bruno Piazza was alive and well, thank you, in Norville, Colorado, and all bets were off concerning the rest of what had transpired fifteen years ago.

I checked my watch. Mario would still be at the restaurant. It was time to find out where Mario fit in Patricia's murder. I lifted the receiver.

"Mario's."

"Let me speak to Mario, please."

"Mario, it's for you."

In the background the jukebox was playing Lee Greenwood's version of "Wind Beneath My Wings," which was released long before Bette Midler did it in *Beaches.*

"Yeah?" I recognized Mario's voice.

"We have to talk."

"Who is this?"

"Resnick."

"I've got nothing to talk to you about."

"Let's talk about Bruno Piazza," I said.

There was a long pause, but Mario's voice sounded strong when he finally answered. "Yeah, maybe we should talk at that. I'm closing up in an hour. Come around the back—and come alone." He hung up.

* * *

The back door of Mario's was open. Through it was the kitchen, which consisted of a long butcher-block table, an industrial stove and refrigerator, lots of stainless steel cookware, and Mario himself scrubbing dishes in a large sink. There were shelves full of cans of olive oil and tomato paste with solemn-looking Italians gazing out from their labels.

Mario wiped his hands on the white apron he had wrapped around his middle and nodded.

"You come with anyone?" he asked, walking to the door and looking out.

"No."

"How'd you get here? I don't see your car."

"I walked."

"Yeah, that's good." He closed the door and locked it. "They say walking's very healthy for you. Sit down, Resnick. I take it you've got something on your mind." He nodded at some stools pulled up to the butcher block, and I stayed close to him until he sat down.

"So what's with this name you mentioned—what was it, Piazza?"

"Bruno Piazza."

"Is that supposed to mean something to me?"

"It should. It's your real name."

He laughed. "Too bad nobody told that to my mother and father." His expression turned serious, and he leaned toward me. "I don't know what the hell you're talking about, pal. I know who I am. I got my school records, my baptismal certificate, my business records. What kind of gag are you trying to pull?"

"Stop bluffing, Bruno. I know you've got a drawer full of history, compliments of the Witness Protection Program, but I got something better—your prints off that bottle of cologne."

That shook him. He sagged like a sack of potatoes.

"I've been dreading this for fifteen years," he told me in a voice a little above a whisper. "For ten years I've been waiting for someone to come walking through that door and blow me out of the water." He glared at me. "I'm not going to make it easy for you."

He stood, reaching under the apron, but I was waiting for him to make the move. I clipped him on the rise with my full weight behind the punch. If I had connected on the point of his chin, it would have been a knock out. As it was, I caught his right cheek, and the force of the shot swept him off his chair. I was on him before his head could clear. I held him down and grabbed the .38 he had tucked into his belt under the apron. It was a S&W Bodyguard with an extended frame, which formed a shroud over the hammer.

I got off him slowly, the gun leveled at a spot in the middle of his forehead. "Get up!" I ordered.

"You going to shoot me Resnick?"

"Think about it, Bruno. If I wanted to cash in on Scuzzy's contract, I could have blown you away a half dozen times. I didn't need to walk in here and discuss it with you."

"You weren't sure," Bruno said gingerly, sitting back down on the stool.

"Don't kid yourself. The plastic job isn't that good."

He sighed, and rubbed his cheek where I hit him. "So if it's not the half million, what are you doing in Norville? I recognized you the moment you came in; Slots Resnick, big-time chief of detectives out of New York. You want to tell me what you're interested in out here in the Old West?"

"I'm working on a case. I'm in business for myself now, and I was supposed to do a background check on Billie Howlett. It turned into a murder case when Pat Wallace got clubbed to death."

"You telling me you weren't tracking me down?"

"I'm telling you I wasn't here for you."

"You saying you popped into my restaurant by chance?"

"It was Billie's idea. I had no idea you were alive. When I saw you, some bells went off, and I got curious. I faxed your prints to Washington, and they came back Bruno Piazza."

"What else do you know?"

"I can figure it out. You cut yourself a different kind of

deal with the government. They rigged the car for you and told the world you and an agent were killed in the blast. For once, they did a pretty good job."

He gave a half smile. There was some pride in his voice. "That's because it was my idea. I wouldn't open my mouth in court unless they went for it. I knew Scuzzy wouldn't rest until he nailed me. My brother does special effects in the movies; he handled the technical stuff. The agent, Dave Krane, he never existed. They fabricated a whole background, with pictures and a family and everything."

I listened to Bruno's explanation, and it just raised more questions. There was a piece missing. The whole reason for the Witness Protection Program was to encourage people like Bruno to come forward without fear for their lives. If the feds admitted to the world that while in their protective custody, Bruno had been killed anyway, why would anyone take the chance and agree to be a government witness?

"I know the feds, Bruno."

"Do me a favor, Slots. I've gotten used to Mario; it's my name now. Bruno died fifteen years ago, as far as I'm concerned."

"The feds don't like to embarrass themselves, not unless they can get a bigger pay off," I said.

"Maybe we ought to just leave it right there."

I thought it over. It had to be a sting operation: it was a way to infiltrate the mafia.

"It comes back to Peter Grassi," I said finally. "Grassi collected Scuzzy's money and shot up the ladder in the mob—except he was really an undercover cop, and Scuzzy unknowingly financed the operation for the government."

"You're a smart guy, Resnick, I'll give you that much," he said grudgingly.

"Let's see how smart you are, Mario. What can you tell me about Patricia Wallace's murder?"

"You think I had something to do with it?"

"Most people would have a hard time killing a human being. Cops shoot someone in self-defense and they wind up on a shrink's couch for the next ten years. The VA hospitals are loaded with soldiers who are carrying around the ghosts of people they killed in war. You don't have any problems like that. You killed people for money, no remorse, no self-doubt. I wouldn't rule you out as a suspect. At the very least, you've been around here long enough to know the players, and you can point me in the right direction."

"Speaking of pointing, how about putting that pea shooter away." He nodded at his gun in my hand.

I emptied the bullets out of the chamber and handed it back to him. It was at that moment that I knew I'd made a dumb mistake. He reached down under the table and came up with another gun, a snub .22. I had told Jack Korn that hit men all carry a spare gun in their sock, and here I was forgetting my own warning.

"Old habits die hard. How many more do you have hidden away?"

"Shut up! Put your hands behind your back."

I brought my hands behind my back, and Mario bound them with rope he took from his pocket. Mario, it seemed, had been well prepared for our chat.

"Mario, this doesn't make any sense. You know I'm not after the contract money. I'm not going to blow your cover."

"I'm tired of running, Resnick. I'm tired of looking over my shoulder for guys like you. Maybe what you told me is true, but things happen. One day you'll be down on your luck, and you'll need some money real bad, and the next thing, you'll remember old Mario out in Norville. I'm a half-million-dollar asset sitting out here in Colorado. I can't go through the rest of my life wondering when you're going to cash me in. Do you understand that?"

It turned out to be a rhetorical question, because he slapped a piece of tape over my mouth before I could say anything.

He pushed me forward to a door at the back of the kitchen. Through it was a staircase that led to the basement. I hesitated for a moment and felt the sharp stab of the two-inch gun barrel being jammed into the small of my back. He pushed again, and I almost lost my balance, but I managed to negotiate the stairs on my feet. At the bottom he turned on the lights, and it didn't make me feel any more secure.

In front of us was a walk-in freezer. It looked as impregnable as any vault in a major bank. He opened the door, and a stream of frigid air gushed over me. Inside, the light went on, illuminating the row of hanging meats on steel hooks and the boxes of frozen vegetables and seafood.

I tried bracing myself to prevent him from dragging me inside, but without the use of my arms I was pretty helpless, and he was able to get behind me and half carry, half throw me in. At this point the gun was no threat. Getting shot to death was preferable to being frozen solid. I tried kicking, but the floor was slick with ice, and I went down.

"Look, if it means anything, I don't particularly like doing this to you. It's Rosa, see. Somebody's got to take care of Rosa, and if anything happened to me, she'd be lost. I can't take that chance," Mario said.

The door closed and the lights went out again. I heard the click of metal on metal as he locked the freezer from the outside. As quickly as I could, I struggled to my feet. I slid on the icy floor over to the door. I tried throwing myself against it, but it didn't give a fraction of an inch. Turning around, I groped until I felt the door's metal handle. I knew he had locked it from the outside, but I tried again and again, hoping that I could spring the lock. Nothing happened. I knew there had to be a light switch on the inside so I pressed myself against the wall until I felt it. I nudged it with my shoulder and the light went on. It was a single bulb on the ceiling. Any thought that I could use the heat of the bulb for warmth was discarded. I looked around me. One of the hooks used to hold the meat was on the floor. I wriggled over to it and got the hook between my bound wrists. It might be possible to cut the ropes using the hook, but then what? I couldn't think of that now. I had to do something and attacking the ropes with the hook was the only thing I could come up with.

I could still move my legs, but I knew I would have to keep pacing. Already the cold was numbing my toes and the exposed parts of my face. I was trying to keep my fingers moving to keep from losing the feeling in them.

I worked on the ropes until my hands shook so much that the hook fell to the floor. I couldn't pick it up, my fingers were frozen. I knew I should continue to move, to jump up and down to keep my circulation going, but it was becoming too painful. I sank to the floor. The realization hit me that no one knew where I was. Mario would open the freezer in the morning and dispose of my frozen carcass in any number of delightful ways, which I didn't care to think about now. What pissed me off most was that the bastard would get away with it. Slots Resnick would disappear and that would be it, unless Elmer decided to follow up on my call, and why the hell should he? Best to leave sleeping dogs lie. Best to leave sleeping Brunos lie.

I was past feeling cold now. I was just numb. My mind was wandering. I wanted to sleep. I wanted to drift off and sleep, but a part of me was screaming that I had to do something. The line from Little Caesar came into my head: "Is this the end of Rico?" Is this the end of Slots? Don't fight it. Drift off. Drift off into the good night. Death comes not with a bang but with a whimper. Not even a whimper, just a grunt behind a pennysworth of glass tape. I fought to keep my eyes open, but it was no use. I was floating to a warm place in front of a fire . . . I was a moth in front of a flame. Icarus falling into the sun. Cold became warmth and warmth became cold, and soon there was nothing left but to fade to black. . . .

I wasn't dead—I was too cold for that. My body was quivering like a six-foot tuning fork. I tried to move, but my hands were pinned by a couple of tightly wrapped blankets. A sweet-faced middle-aged woman wearing sunglasses was kneeling beside me, gently patting my cheek. Around her neck was a heavy wooden crucifix which dangled onto my face.

"Are you awake, Mr. Resnick?"

"What . . . ?"

"Don't try to talk now, dear. Mario, hurry!"

She was looking at me without really seeing me. This had to be Rosa, Santamaria's blind wife that Shelby had told me about. I wasn't in the freezer. They had carried me upstairs to the restaurant, and I was lying on the carpeted floor next to the bar. I felt a hand slip under my back, propping me up, the blankets were loosened.

"Drink this," Mario said, putting a steaming cup to my lips. "It's coffee with a little brandy. Sip it slowly."

The heat radiated through my body. In a little while, the shaking revved itself down, and my teeth stopped chattering.

"Are you all right, Mr. Resnick?"

"Yeah," I growled. "Change of heart, Bruno?"

"What Mario did was unforgivable, Mr. Resnick," Rosa said. "I'm sure he knows that and is very sorry. I think you should tell Mr. Resnick how sorry you are."

He stared at her and then back at me. "I'm sorry, Slots." He finally said unconvincingly.

"Mr. Resnick, are you okay?" Rosa asked, concern in her voice.

I tested out all my moving parts and decided they were in adequate working order. Except for a little freezer burn on my butt, I was in passable shape.

"I'll live," I told them.

"When Mario told me what he did, I made him rush right back here and get you out. I don't know what the man was thinking. Praise Jesus we got here in time."

"I was just trying to protect—"

"Mr. Resnick, that's not my husband talking. That's not the man who will be saved by our Lord."

"Here we go again," Mario grumbled.

"We are good people, Mr. Resnick. We firmly believe in the teachings of our Lord. I told Mario that if you chose to reveal our secret, it is the will of God. His will be done."

"I don't intend to betray you. I told Mario that, and the next thing I knew I was turning into an ice cube."

She sighed deeply. "Mr. Resnick, would you indulge me for a moment and allow me to feel the palm of your hand."

She reached out and I let her hold my hand. I thought she was trying to see if I'd thawed out, but she had something else in mind. She lightly touched the lines of my palm with her fingertips. Whatever she felt must have pleased her. She released my hand, smiling broadly.

"Yes, I could tell from your voice, but I wanted to be sure. You're a man of good character, a man who can be trusted. Do you hear me, Mario?"

"I hear you, Rosa," he said patiently.

The expression on her face turned to one of concern. "There's some disturbing news you have to tell us, isn't there Mr. Resnick? Someone has been hurt badly, perhaps killed."

I looked at Mario.

"When Rosa lost her eyesight, she acquired the gift of second sight," he said. "She just knows things. Tell her why you're here."

"I'm investigating the murder of Patricia Morgan-Wallace."

"Oh Lord no!" Rosa cried out. She clutched her crucifix tightly. "How did it happen?"

"Someone went up to her cabin and clubbed her to death late Saturday night or early Sunday morning."

"Mario, why didn't you tell me this?"

"I didn't want to upset you."

"You knew her well, Mrs. Santamaria?"

"She had come to see me Thursday night. I warned her. Oh, if I had only *insisted* she get protection."

"Why did she come to see you?"

"For advice," Mario said. "Are you all right?" he asked Rosa.

Rosa's shoulders were hunched, and she was slowly rocking back and forth. She rose. "I need a moment to be by myself," she said. She went toward the bathroom. Mario tried to take her arm, but she pushed him away. "I'll be fine. I just need some time to think."

"She's upset," he said, noting the obvious.

"This hasn't been an afternoon jaunt in the park for me either, pal. What do you mean, people come to her for advice? What kind of advice?"

"I told you, she has the gift. She tells people things they have to know." He didn't seem overly impressed.

"You believe in psychics?"

"Look Resnick, Rosa can be one big pain in the ass. But there's something to this second-sight stuff. I've seen too many strange things not to give the lady her due."

"Has she always been blind?" I asked him.

"No, she had an accident just before we came out here. She fell down a flight of stairs and got a blood clot on the optic nerve." He seemed to be wrestling with something. "No, that's not the truth," he said finally. "I promised myself, no more lies. I was a bum, Resnick, a no-good bum. I'd get a snootful and beat up on anybody who got in my way. This one night, Rosa got in my way. I don't even remember it. All I know was that my hands were all bloody and Rosa was in the hospital fighting for her life. She won that battle, but she lost her sight. I'll tell you something else that I have to give her credit for: in all this time, she never once brought it up to me, never said one word to me about what I did to her. I guess you can say I owe her. I'm trying to pay my debt. I take all the shit she has to offer, and I smile and come back for more. From morning till night she's a nonstop broken record about me changing my ways and being a good Christian. She thinks I can still be saved. Between you and me, Resnick, if I have to spend the rest of eternity with her, I'd rather go to hell. But I owe her, because I caused her blindness, and now I got to take care of her.

"I put you in cold storage because without me around, who knows what would happen to her. I took away her eyesight and that's been on my conscience. I can't leave her to make it by herself."

"So what's the real reason you got me out?"

"The truth?" he shrugged. "I don't know. Maybe all that

96

Bible thumping *is* sinking in. Who the hell knows, maybe Bruno Piazza really did die fifteen years back. I'll tell you this, there was a time I could have locked you in that freezer and had a good dinner and never given it a second thought."

Our eyes locked. For the moment I bought his explanation.

"Was Patricia a steady customer of Rosa's?" I asked.

"She wasn't a customer. Rosa doesn't charge money. She says God works through her, she's an instrument of the Lord."

"Sorry. How often did she see Rosa?"

"I'm not really sure, maybe once or twice a month. Whenever there was something troubling her."

"She came to see me Thursday evening," Rosa said, coming out of the bathroom. She came and sat down at the table with me and Mario. "She was very upset. I sensed a great betrayal. I felt it the moment she walked into the room."

"Who betrayed her?"

"There were many vibrations, mixed feelings. Some of them made no sense at all. It happens like that sometimes. Her daughter Billie was part of it, and Gordon. . . . It wasn't clear."

"You said you warned her."

"Yes, suddenly I felt a very powerful feeling of fear. It was overwhelming. It filled the room like a giant demon. I told her then I had great fear for her safety. She told me she was going to her cabin to paint and she would be all right. I should have made her understand how much danger she was in. Perhaps she would still be alive."

"You shouldn't blame yourself," Mario said.

"Did she offer you any information at all about what was going on in her life?"

"There are things I can't reveal. I have an obligation to the people who seek my help."

"The courts might not see it that way," I told her.

"God's will be done," she said stoically.

"I don't know about God's will or the courts, but I do know I'm getting tired." Mario stifled a yawn.

"Just a couple more quick questions. Where were you on Saturday night, Mario?"

"I was right here until three, four in the morning. Then I drove home and I went straight to bed."

"Anybody see you get home?"

"Not a soul. Rosa was sound asleep when I came in, so she can't even give me an alibi. You have any more questions Resnick?"

I took the hint and rose. "If either of you can think of anything that might help, I'll be staying at the Holiday," I told them, heading for the door.

The next morning I was sipping black coffee from a plastic cup and standing in front of the Norville Savings and Loan. The girl looking out at me from inside made a what-can-I-do? face and pantomimed, *I can't open until nine.* I nodded.

Once inside, I bypassed the tellers counter—in the old days, when banks were marble mausoleums, they were called tellers cages—and headed straight for the row of desks. The guy I was looking for was farthest from the door. In front of him was a dirty copper nameplate reading J. SILK, V.P.

I took a seat opposite him on the green leatherette chair and waited for him to look up from his magazine, *The Bank Quarterly Review,* which I figured must make for other, similarly fascinating reading.

"Can I help you," he asked, giving me a professional smile.

He was fiftyish, sporting gray sideburns, the kind that went out with *Yellow Submarine.* He had draped his sports jacket over the back of his chair, and he had his shirt sleeves rolled up to mid forearm.

I introduced myself and told him I was working with the sheriff on the Pat Morgan-Wallace murder.

"Yes, it was quite a shock for all of us. She was a major depositor in this bank," he said grimly.

"I'm interested in the matter of the checks forged with her signature."

He stared at me for a long moment, took a pencil from a rattan cup, and bounced the eraser on the desk. "I'm going to have to call the sheriff to make sure it's all right to discuss this with you," he said.

"Fine. You may also want to call Ms. Amanda Bernard. She was the person who suggested I see you."

"I think I'd rather talk to her, since she's Pat Wallace's attorney. Jack Korn can be difficult."

"To say the least," I offered. We smiled at each other.

He twirled his Rolodex until he came to the Bs and punched in Amanda's number.

"Ms. Bernard? Jack Silk here at Norville S and L. I'm just fine, thank you. There's a detective fellow here inquiring about that business we spoke of last week. . . . I see. . . . Mm-hm. Well, fine, if you say so. . . . Yes, I shall. Just wanted to check. Very well, good day to you." He put the phone down. "Sorry, Mr. . . . ?"

"Resnick. Slots Resnick."

"Well what is it you want to know, Mr. Resnick?"

"How did you become aware checks had been forged?"

"It was last Wednesday. Ms. Howlett—that's Pat's daughter—came in with three checks drawn to her mother's account with what appeared to be Patricia Morgan-Wallace's signature."

"Three checks?"

"Yes, two for ninety-five hundred and one for a thousand."

"Is there any bank regulation that would prevent you from cashing a ten-thousand-dollar check?"

"There's a federal requirement that we notify the government of any single transaction of ten thousand or more. Either Miss Kacey, our president, or I initial any such transaction; otherwise our tellers handle it themselves. On that particular day we had Winslow at the counter. He's new. He didn't know Ms. Howlett, so he informed me and I called her over to my desk."

"You questioned her?"

"You don't question the daughter of the bank's biggest depositor. I gently inquired about her mother, and she told me Pat was fine. I remarked that it seemed like an awful lot of money to be carrying around, and she told me that her friend Ramona was waiting for her in the car outside and they would be heading right home. I told her to be careful, and she left."

"How did you find out it was a forgery?"

"Well, later that afternoon I started thinking about the bank's possible exposure if anything happened to Billie on the way home. You know how it is; you start to second-guess yourself. At the very least I could have asked one of the guards to ride home with the girls. So I called the mansion and Pat answered. I asked her if Billie had gotten the money to her, and she hadn't a clue what I was referring to. A half hour later she and Amanda Bernard stormed in here, demanded to see the checks, and stormed out. Ms. Morgan-Wallace looked to be in shock.

"I don't have to tell you the kind of night I had. I don't think my eyes closed for a second. The next morning Gordon called, nice as can be, said it was just a misunderstanding and we should all forget about it, everything was fine. That's where it stood until you came in. Does this have something to do with Patricia's murder?"

"That's what I'm trying to find out," I said, rising. "Thanks for your time, Mr. Silk."

The detective business, like most others, can be broken down to the basics. It amounts to finding a bunch of loose threads on a sweater and pulling them one by one. Most of the time the thread just breaks off, but once in a while you find one you can pull and pull until the whole case is unraveled.

Billie's foray to the bank was one thread. Her alibi for Saturday night, that she'd been with Ramona, was another one. I pulled up to the first pay phone I could find and got information to give me Ramona Bernard's number. I was hoping she'd have her own phone. Amanda had made it quite clear that she would block any contact I might have with her daughter.

"Yeah," was the bored greeting.

"Ramona?"

"Yeah. Who is this?"

"Slots Resnick."

"What do *you* want?"

"I need to talk to you."

"What about?"

"Your friend Billie is in deep trouble. She's going to need your help if she's going to get out of it."

"My mother is right here," she whispered. "Meet me at the diner in fifteen minutes. Mom," she called out, "it's the record store. Those CDs I ordered came in. I'm going to pick them up."

The Rocky Mountain Diner was fairly empty. The perpetual checker game was going on in back, and one tired-looking waitress and a short Latino counterman were poised to handle the other three patrons. I took a booth overlooking the parking lot and ordered an egg sandwich on a roll with a tomato juice. Anything but the coffee.

I was just finishing the last bite when Ramona pulled up in a beat-up Cutlass that looked as if it had been through desert combat. She was wearing a black T-shirt, two sizes too small, with dangling, ripped sleeves, ripped denim cutoffs, black sneakers, black socks, dangling skull earrings, a straw sombrero, and a pair of black gloves with the fingers cut off. Did I mention she had dyed her hair blue?

The waitress didn't bat an eyelash.

"How ya doin', Ramona. Ya want somethin'?"

"Black coffee and a bran muffin. Like my hair? I did it this morning."

"Bitchin'."

"Thanks."

The waitress retreated and Ramona stared at me. "You look bummed out, man. You're not still pissed? My mother

101

told me you found out. Listen, I just told them to *scare* you, not to beat the shit out of you."

"Well then it's okay."

"Don't start. I get enough of that from my old lady. I'm sorry, okay? I didn't know the real score. We're on the same side, right? We want to help Billie."

"Tell me what happened Saturday night."

"What do you mean, what happened?"

"Billie says she was with you."

"She was."

"All night?"

"All night. It was great. You want a blow-by-blow?"

"Your mother says it isn't true. She says she listened in on the extension and overheard Billie asking you to lie for her."

"That bitch!"

"Give it to me straight, Ramona, it's better we talk about it now."

"Forget about it, okay?"

"I've got to know. A prosecutor will rip you and Billie to shreds. We'll lose the case before we start."

"Okay, I wasn't with her *all* night, but I know she didn't do it."

"How do you know."

"You know somebody. She isn't capable of hurting anyone or anything. She cries at every goofy movie."

"Sounds like a great defense, we'll have to mention it to her lawyer. Tell me exactly what happened from the moment Billie got back to the mansion on Saturday night."

She thought about it while she lit a cigarette and blew out a stream of smoke. "It was her last game, so I thought I'd surprise her. I drove to the mansion and just hung out a while waiting for her. Finally she comes home slamming doors and copping a real attitude. I bought this cake, in the shape of a baseball diamond, no big deal. I figured she'd get a kick out of it. Believe me, she couldn't care less. She says she'll be with me in a second, she's got to talk to Gordon first. So she disappears for a half hour and I'm watching Lucy reruns on the tube and stuffing cake down my throat. After a while I get tired of that shit and I start looking for her. Gordon isn't around, and I find Billie in the kitchen nursing a bottle of tequila. I tried talking to her, but she's all giggly and stupid. Later for this, I say to myself, and I pick up and split."

"Did she tell you why she was so upset when she came in?"

Ramona shrugged. "I don't know. Maybe because it was her last game. Who knows."

"What did she say to you when she called you from the locker room?"

Ramona's eyes started darting. "We just talked," she said.

"She said she spoke to you about leaving home and staying with her."

"Yeah. She wanted me to stay with her."

She was winging her answers. "She told you she wanted to get away from Colorado and take the offer to play on a woman's softball team," I offered.

She nodded. "That's right."

"Bullshit! I just made it up. She never called you from the locker room, did she?"

"You get me confused!"

If it wasn't Ramona Billie had been talking to on the phone when I overheard her—my guess is it had to be Gordon.

"Where was Gordon Saturday night?"

She shrugged. "I didn't see him. It's a big house." She looked uncomfortable, almost like she was ready to bolt. I had to press her. It might be my only chance before Amanda found some way of keeping me from talking to her.

"What can you tell me about the twenty thousand Billie took out of the bank?"

"My mother told you about that too? I hate that woman. You have no idea how much I hate that woman."

"What'd Billie do with the money?"

"She didn't do anything with the money. She gave it to Gordon."

"Why?"

"I don't know why. She told me she had to go to the bank and pick up some cash for Gordon, and that's what we did."

"You had no idea Pat's name was forged on those checks?"

"Nope—and neither did Billie. I would bet on that."

"Why couldn't Gordon use his own money?"

"It was all tied up. Billie told me his money was tied up in loans and mortgages and things. He used to ask Pat for money, and he got like an allowance."

"Did you see Billie hand him the money?"

"Yes."

"You're sure?"

"Yes. . . . Well, I saw her go into the room with the money. When she came out she didn't have it anymore."

"What did you think of Pat Wallace?"

"She was okay. She always seemed like she was in her own little world. She wasn't the friendliest person. She wouldn't talk to you unless you talked to her first, and then it was like yes or no."

"Who'd want to kill her?"

She smiled. "You really want to know? My mother. She's always had the hots for Gordon. With Pat out of the way she would have a clear shot."

Another thread?

7

I called the Morgan mansion and Carla told me that Gordon was away, and that Billie was somewhere on the premises but Carla hadn't seen her since early morning.

When I knocked on the door an hour or so later, the situation hadn't changed.

"Try the stable," Carla told me. "She likes to be with the horses."

She wasn't there, and her pet, Mr. Potato, was AWOL as well. I headed down a manure-garnished path and after three quarters of a mile saw them coming in my direction.

"We need to talk," I told her.

She dismounted and tied up the stallion, and we settled under a shade tree. The boulder we were sitting on overlooked a quiet valley stirring with an undercurrent of insect sounds. In the sun, with the pristine skies and the smell of grass, the thought of a bludgeoned Patricia Wallace seemed unspeakably incongruous.

"You look serious," Billie said. She smiled but got nothing back from me.

"I don't like being lied to."

"I don't know what you mean."

"You're going to finesse yourself right into a murder conviction, Billie. You haven't been straight with me for one minute. I've been willing to believe that you were telling me the truth when you said you didn't kill your stepmother, but now even I have doubts, and I'm supposed to be on your side."

She rose, jamming her hands in her pockets, and stood with her back to me. She was wearing jeans, a red shirt, and boots. She belonged out here in the sun and fresh air, a lithe animal as much a part of the landscape as Mr. Potato or the mountain.

"Maybe you'll beat the murder-one rap, because juries sometimes have soft spots for young girls, but I hope whatever it is you're trying to pull is worth thirty years of your life."

I was hoping for a response, but nothing happened. She stayed turned away from me. That did it. If I wanted to be given the runaround, I could get that in my own backyard, away from marauding rodeo hands, punk-rock whackos, locked freezers, born-again psychics, and tinhorn sheriffs.

"I've got a plane to catch," I told her, getting up and walking back toward the road.

I got about ten feet before she tapped me on the shoulder. I turned. There were tears rolling down her cheeks.

"Please," she whispered. She threw her arms around my neck, pressed her face against my shoulder, and started crying in earnest, big heaving sobs that shook her whole body. I held her until she quieted down, then offered her a handkerchief, which she used to wipe her eyes and blow her nose.

"I don't want Pat to be dead!" she said in a little-girl voice. "Now I've lost both of my mommies. I wanted her to like me, but she couldn't. I wanted her to care about me. I know she only put up with me because of Gordon. It was like I was nothing to her. I only wanted her to like me." That started the tears again, and the shakes. She turned away from me and went and put her arms around Mr. Potato's neck.

"I'm okay," she said, smiling at the horse through her

106

tears. "Don't worry about me. Don't get upset." She patted his nose.

"I want to help you, Billie, but you're not making it easy."

"Slots, I won't lie to you anymore. I didn't want Gordon to get into trouble because of the stupid money, but you know about that anyway. I should have told you everything from the start. I'm sorry. Okay?"

I had to remember this was only a twenty-year-old kid who'd already had her share of disasters. Back off a little, Slots.

"Okay. Saturday night when I first met you after the game, Patricia had called you and told you she was dropping you from her will."

"Yes."

There was the motive Korn was looking for. All he would have to do is question Amanda Bernard. Hell, he wouldn't have to question—Amanda would offer the information herself once she was sure her Ramona was in the clear.

"What else did she say?"

"Nothing. She called me an ungrateful little bitch, and then she hung up on me."

"Then you called the mansion. The phone company's record shows a call going out just about the time I overheard you."

"Yes," she sighed.

"It wasn't Ramona you spoke to was it?"

"It was Gordon."

"You called him gutless. You said if he didn't take care of the bitch, you'd do it yourself. What was that supposed to mean?"

She was silent.

"Maybe you decided that you wanted Pat dead, and if Gordon wouldn't kill her you'd do it yourself."

"That wasn't it! I spoke to him about the money he asked me to get from the bank. He had told me he needed the money fast to close a deal. Pat wasn't around, and he had to stay close

107

to the phone. It was just a minor thing. He was going to return the money the first chance he got. He said he'd tell Pat about it later."

"But he didn't."

"That's why I called him when you overheard me, to find out if he had. He claimed he did speak to her, and it was all over. He had no idea why she was carrying on. I called him gutless because he never likes to confront things. He'll always yes you to death; he just can't stand not to please people. I didn't give a damn about Pat's millions, but I didn't want her to be angry at me, especially when it wasn't my fault. I told him to take care of it, to get her off my back, or if he couldn't, I would do it myself. I was fed up with always doing the right thing and getting shit from Pat. All I ever did was to try and please her. Gordon kept insisting I give her time, not push her. When I said I'd take care of it myself, I meant I'd tell her off once and for all, and the hell with her!"

"Did Gordon explain it to her?"

She shrugged. "Yeah. But he didn't want to get her annoyed, so he probably watered it down. If he had told her before the guy from the bank called, there probably wouldn't have been a problem. The money was no big deal. Patricia used to give away more money than that to schools and hospitals and all kinds of things, for tax write-offs."

"Who forged the checks?"

"Gordon," she finally said.

"Was it possible Patricia thought Gordon was lying to cover up for you, and she was angry that he took your side?"

"Yes . . . I guess so. I don't know, I wasn't there. I can't talk about it anymore."

"I'll need to talk to him."

"You won't find him. He'll be gone at least for a couple of days. He didn't tell me where."

"What do you mean, gone?"

"He called to tell me he was all right and I shouldn't worry about him. He needed to get away. He can't handle things like this. He's a very delicate, sensitive person."

108

"Murder is a very indelicate, insensitive issue. He doesn't mind you taking the heat alone?"

"You don't understand Gordon. He's the nicest, most wonderful man in the world. This could absolutely destroy him."

"What about you?"

She shrugged. "I'm kind of used to taking care of myself."

If she was, she wasn't doing such a good job.

"Tell me everything you can about Saturday night, from the moment you left the stadium parking lot until the next morning. Don't leave anything out no matter how trivial it might seem to you."

She thought about it for a moment. "I got really pissed off after the phone calls. On top of that, I was pissed that you saw me like that. I drove home."

"What did you have with you?"

"It was the last game. I cleaned out my locker. I had my spikes, my glove, and my bat."

"Go on."

"I drove home, and the first thing that happened was that I went up to my room. Ramona was waiting for me. I just wasn't in the mood for her."

"Why?"

"She was just stupid. She was saying stupid things, like how glad she was the season was over, and now I was going to have more time for her. I couldn't believe how happy she was. I mean, I was destroyed, because that might have been the last baseball game of my life, and she was so damn happy about it. She even had this cake she had made up that looked like a baseball diamond, except that it had a big red circle on it with a line through it, like the no-smoking sign or Ghostbusters."

"Then what?"

"She just annoyed me."

"How?"

"Personal stuff, not important. I wanted to get away from

her. I figured I'd talk to Gordon and find out if he'd said anything to Pat. I looked for him, but he wasn't in the house. I could hear Ramona in my room, and I didn't feel like dealing with her, so I got a bottle of tequila from the bar and had my own little party."

"Did you talk to Ramona?"

"I don't remember."

"What do you remember?"

"I woke up in my bed the next morning around ten."

"Did you leave the house at all that night?"

"No."

"How do you know? You said you didn't remember anything."

"Well, I would have remembered that." Her voice quivered. "I'm sure I would have remembered going out."

We looked at each other, and I didn't have to be a mind reader to know what she was thinking. She clutched at my sleeve with a look of terror on her face.

"Oh God no! I *couldn't* have. . . . I couldn't have driven up to the cabin!"

"Take it easy. You don't know anything for sure. The odds are you drank until you passed out."

"But how can I be sure?"

"For now, you can't. That's my job, to try and find out exactly what happened. Things might get sticky for a while."

"What do you mean?"

"Korn may decide to arrest you. You'll have to post bail."

"I have some money."

"How about a lawyer?"

"Gordon has a friend in Denver, a guy named Mike Kelly."

"Call him. Get yourself prepared, just in case. I'll do what I can to hold Korn back."

"Do you really think he'll arrest me?"

Talk about wide-eyed innocence. "He's got your bat, he's got a motive, he's got means and opportunity. I'd say there

110

was a very good chance. Talk to Mike Kelly. He'll have you out of jail in a couple of hours at worst."

We walked back toward the mansion, Billie leading Mr. Potato. "Slots, thanks for not giving up on me," she said as we reached the barn. "Do you want to stay for lunch?"

"No, I think I'd better get back to Norville. I'll call you later."

We went back to the house, and I held the door for her as she stood in the doorway saying good-bye. I made sure to click the button on the inside lock. I needed to find out more about Gordon Wallace, and that was one area where Billie's sense of loyalty wouldn't allow her to be objective or cooperative.

It wasn't the most dramatic way to gain access, but it beat searching around for open windows. And as far as door picks are concerned, sure they work—after maybe twenty minutes. No matter how many you carry, you're always missing the right one.

I doubted anyone was watching, but I pulled the Ford out of the driveway and parked the car on the shoulder about a hundred feet down the road. I doubled back, using the trees as cover, and when I didn't see anyone, I walked right through the front door, ready with my the-car-sounds-funny-I-have-to-use-the-phone excuse in case I ran into someone.

I needn't have bothered. The cool hall was empty. Somewhere upstairs Carla was vacuuming, and Billie was probably soaking in a tub after her ride.

Thanks to Billie's tour the other day, I had a good idea of the layout. There was a guest bedroom, a library, a billiard room, and the living room on the first floor. Upstairs there were some more guest bedrooms, a study, the master bedroom, a solarium, and Billie's bedroom. Most of the bedrooms had bathrooms, each coordinated with the motif and colors of the host room.

I made my way up the stairs knowing that if the steps had the audacity to creak in a house like this, the noise would be covered by the vacuum.

The study was the first room on the right at the top of the highly polished staircase. As was the rest of the house, this room was bright and airy, the center focus being a round granite table. There were also two plump ash-framed armchairs and a trio of low cylindrical tables. Indian blankets on the wall added splashes of bright red and pink. A mahogany desk with matching bookcases rounded out the room.

I wasn't looking for anything specific. Gordon Wallace was beginning to emerge more and more as a key player in the proceedings, and outside of sparkling choppers and a pompadour, he remained an enigma. Learning about people is right out of basic detective training 101. It's not unlike preparing for an acting part. You try to experience the things your subject experiences, wear his clothes, smoke his pipe, see the world through his eyes. Not an easy job when it came to Gordon.

I poked through some magazines that were stacked on a shelf. Not a dog ear in the bunch; they probably hadn't been looked at. There were six pencils in a red clay cup, each the twin of the next, all sharpened to a fine point, never used. A drawer in the desk opened to reveal three decks of playing cards, all with their seals still intact. The bookcase contained about fifty lavishly produced titles ranging from *The Options Trader* to *Mexican Architecture, China's China,* and *Roosevelt.* I wasn't impressed. The collection didn't signify an inquiring, agile mind. I got the impression someone had been given a budget and told to stock the shelves. I doubted if any of the bindings had even been cracked. Gordon was still some teeth and a hunk of hair.

I didn't do much better in the master bedroom. In fact, both of the rooms looked like those model rooms you see in a development: all the trappings but no personality. Everything was neat, functional, and bland.

There was a Trimline phone next to the bed. I lifted the receiver and pressed the redial button. The high and low tones sounded, and there was a pause as the connection was being made. A woman answered before the first ring had ended.

"Hello?" She had a pleasant voice. In the background a baby was crying.

"Oh, dear," I said in my old-codger's voice.

"Hello?"

"I think I may have dialed the wrong number."

"Who do you want to speak to?"

"Is this . . . I can't see very well. I'm supposed to call the daughter of a friend, and I may have dialed incorrectly. What number did I reach?" In New York I would have been cursed and left holding a dead line. Things were different out here.

"This is five five five, three two five two."

"Is this Mary?"

"No. There's no Mary here."

"What's your name?" I asked.

"You have the wrong number. Check the number before you dial, and don't be bothering people!" She hung up.

Well, maybe things weren't so different out here after all. I hunted around a few more minutes, decided my foray had been less than successful, and decided to beat a retreat. The vacuum cleaner had stopped, making things just a little tougher. I opened the door a crack and peered out; the hall seemed to be clear. A green duffel bag lay on the floor. I hadn't noticed it there before. I could hear Carla moving around in Billie's room now.

"Carla, could you bring me a towel?" Billie called out. I had a clear shot to the staircase and then down, but I stopped myself. I only had a few seconds, so I moved fast, crouching over the duffel bag and opening the drawstring.

It seemed to be full of dirty clothes for the laundry and the cleaners. Rummaging through the underwear and socks, I came across a brown windbreaker. It was a man's jacket—too big to be Hector's, but the size and style would be perfect on Gordon. I went through the pockets quickly. There wasn't much, just a bank machine receipt, a book of matches with the cover ripped off, and a Mobil gas credit receipt from a place called Baxter's Mobile Service.

I pocketed my treasures and made it down the stairs just

as Carla's husband Hector walked into the house. If he looked up he would have seen me, but he was talking to himself and shaking his head as he reset the door lock. I froze and ducked behind an archway as he walked right past me.

"Slots, Jack's been looking all over for you," Dan Shelby said, getting up from behind the desk in Sheriff Korn's office. "Where've you been?"

"Around."

"Well he's pretty mad. He says you've been holding out on him."

"There goes my chance for the Miss Congeniality Award," I said, snapping my fingers. I opened the closet door. "Where's that reverse phone directory he used to check the numbers, Dan?" I asked the big man.

Shelby retreated behind the partition and came back carrying the real estate agent's best friend. "Anything I can do to help?" he asked me.

"Yeah, call up information in Boca Raton, Florida, and get the number of a company called Nadco. I'll take it from there."

"Okay, Nadco." He nodded. "Anything else?"

"Yeah, what do you know about a gas station called Baxter's?"

"It's down near the interstate. Nothing very special about it."

"How about Colorado Federal?"

"That's the biggest bank in the tri-city area. It's right in the center of the Silver Brook Mall. Do I get a prize or something?"

"Nope, but you're doing fine, and you're winning my undying gratitude."

He got the number I asked him for while I looked up 555-3252. It was the number of a C. Owens, at 243 Hollingwood Drive, in Hollingwood.

"Thanks operator," Dan said, repeating the number for Nadco Incorporated. "Did you get that, Slots?"

114

"Check," I said, writing it down. "Last question. You know a party named Owens, C. Owens, lives in a place called Hollingwood?"

"Gee, that sounds familiar. I know Hollingwood; it's a kind of run-down area that runs along the train tracks outside of Wesville. Owens . . . I know that name from somewhere."

"Keep thinking," I said, dialing the Nadco number. After many hitches, I was finally put through to the president of the company. It took ten minutes to convince the honcho on the other end that either he gave me the information I needed, or the National Advertising Company would be subpoenaed to testify at a murder trial in Colorado. He grudgingly complied.

Dan Shelby was watching me with a puzzled expression on his face.

"You want to give me a clue about what's going on?" he asked affably.

I tossed the matches over to him. "What do you see?"

"Matchbook without the cover."

"Why does someone go to the trouble of ripping the cover off a book of matches."

He thought about it. "I don't know," he finally said.

"It's been my experience that people rip matchbook covers off because they don't want other people to see where they've been, especially if they're married people playing around."

Shelby nodded. "I see."

I put the other items down on the desk. "These things belong to Gordon Wallace. The bank receipt from the cash machine was for three hundred dollars. The date was two days ago, right after Pat's body was discovered. It's also got the time, thirteen oh six, or six after one in the afternoon. He bought gas at Baxter's service station, which happens to be in the town of Hollingwood."

"The same place where this Owens lives," he said slowly. "Where did you get Owens's number from?"

"It was the last call Gordon made from his house before

he took off to get away from it all. I picked the number up from the redial feature on his phone."

"Do you suspect Gordon?" he asked incredulously.

"How well do you know him?"

"Hell, he's been around town forever. He's always been a good guy, easy to talk to, helpful. I guess you can't say he's close to anybody."

"What's the knock on him."

"Knock?"

"This is a small town. Everybody knows everybody else's dirty laundry. No one's going to tell an outsider like me, but I'll bet you heard a rumor or two about Mr. Wallace."

A half grin crossed Shelby's lips. "Well . . . there is talk he likes the ladies. Just talk, mind you—damn!" He slapped his forehead. "I know who Owens is. It's Carole Owens. She used to be the waitress at the diner. They wear name tags, that's how I know. I knew I'd seen the name."

"A friend of Gordon's?"

"Not that I know of, but I guess he must know her. Everybody around here stops in at the diner."

"How about a place called the Mirage Club?" I asked him.

"They advertise in my paper. It's a nightclub-restaurant a little off the beaten path."

"Maybe a place Gordon might take a lady?"

Shelby looked thoughtful. "I'll tell you this, Slots, they've got a motel behind the place. Where did you hear about it?"

"The matchbook was from there," I said.

"But you said the cover was missing."

I peeled back the striking strip and showed him the tiny print, *Nadco—Boca Raton, Fla.,* and the string of five numbers that followed. "That's the advertising company that printed the book of matches, and the numbers identify the client. In this case, the Mirage Club."

Shelby whistled. "Not much gets by you. It's too bad you and Jack got off on the wrong foot. He's really not a bad kid, you know. He's under a lot of pressure with this case. Just this

116

morning Patricia Wallace's brother, some big shot from Boulder, called and told Jack he better get an arrest in this case, and fast."

"That means Billie."

"Well, from what I gather, the family never really cared for Billie Jo."

"What do they have against her?"

"The usual thing rich people have against those from the other side of the tracks."

The door swung open, revealing a scowling Sheriff Jack Korn. "I thought we had a deal, Resnick! You were supposed to let me know what was going on!"

"So what's your problem?"

"My problem? You're my problem, Resnick! Why didn't you tell me that Patricia Wallace cut Billie out of her will?"

"You heard from Amanda," I said.

"Yeah, and Jack Silk over at the bank. They're talking to me, and I haven't the slightest idea what they're talking about. Finally I had them break it down, and they look at me. Didn't Slots discuss it with you? they ask me. No, I haven't heard from my friend Mr. Resnick. He's running all over the place making me look like a horse's ass."

"Jack, why do you think I came by?"

"You probably came here to make more long-distance calls," he snapped.

Shelby stared at the ceiling.

"Well I'm through listening to you," Korn went on. "I should have picked Billie Jo Howlett up immediately."

"She'll be out on bail in an hour. You won't be able to hold her."

"But I'll be doing my job," he said smugly.

"Your job is to catch a killer. I don't happen to think it's Billie."

"That's your opinion, and right now I'm not interested in it. All I want from you, Resnick, is for you to get the hell out of my office, and out of my town."

"Jack, maybe you're acting a little too hastily," Dan said.

"I know what I'm doing. This guy is nothing but trouble."

"Korn, you're getting on my nerves," I said, getting up. "I'll be talking to you, Dan."

8

Sometimes you get lucky. I looked at my Sunoco tri-city map and found the big shopping mall, Silver Brook, which the guy on the phone at the Mirage Club said was only nine miles away if you head down Route 129.

I clocked the "nine miles," which turned out to be closer to eleven and jammed on my brakes. A white Cadillac, kicking up dust, came roaring out from the motel area and onto the main road. The woman driving looked familiar but I wasn't completely sure until I caught the vanity license plate in my rearview mirror: AB ESQ. Amanda Bernard.

I was pleased I wouldn't have to play the I-vaguely-recall game with the desk clerk. That's the one where I ask the clerk if a guy with a pompadour and shiny teeth registered in the last couple of days. The clerk tells me he can't remember, until I put out enough twenty-dollar bills for him to "vaguely recall" the person I'm asking about. Then we start all over, playing for the woman the guy was with. For once, I happened to be in the right place at the right time.

I pulled into a little clearing and turned off the engine. Either Gordon was going to come driving out in a couple of minutes or he was staying at the Mirage Club Motel. There were nine cabins, and each one had a car parked in front. I wondered which was Gordon's, and then I remembered that I had his gas credit card receipt. The license number on the receipt matched the plates on the gray Lincoln Town Car in front of the third cabin.

I gave him another five minutes and decided he wasn't coming out. Just as I started walking toward the cabin, he suddenly emerged. He was wearing black slacks and a gray short-sleeved knit shirt. He got into the Lincoln and drove off. I hustled back to my car and followed him. I didn't think he'd seen me, and from the relaxed way he was driving I was almost sure of it.

I kept him in sight, never letting more than three cars come between us on the run down 129. He paused for a moment at the traffic light in front of the Silver Brook Mall and then turned into the parking lot. I let him park and waited while he walked in. About fifteen minutes later he came out carrying a large bag with a Kidz Toyz logo. We headed back down the interstate and another fifteen minutes later passed a sign which read HOLLINGWOOD. SPEED LIMIT 25 MPH. RADAR ENFORCED.

I wasn't surprised when he turned down a quiet street, which turned out to be Hollingwood Drive, and parked the car in front of a semidetached brick house that had seen better days. I didn't have to get a clear look at the house number to know it was 243, the house that belonged to the waitress, Carole Owens.

What did surprise me was the four- or five-year-old boy who jumped out of a tire swing hanging from a ponderosa pine and came running toward the street. He ran up to Gordon and hugged him. Gordon handed him the bag, which the towhead ripped open with much delight. After getting to the teddy bear inside, he walked hand in hand with Gordon to the door. Gordon reached into his pocket, produced a key, and let them both in. As the door opened a pretty young woman greeted Gordon with a hug and a kiss, and then the door closed behind the happy couple and child.

I sat in my car and thought about it. Gordon Wallace was a piece of work. A couple of days after the brutal murder of his wife he leaves town and lets the chips fall into his adopted daughter's lap. He then pops up in a fleabag motel, where he has a liaison with the family attorney, Amanda Bernard, and then without missing a beat he scoots off to another family scene with a woman who'd been a waitress in his local diner and, presumably, her child.

I could have turned the Taurus around, checked the map, and headed back to Norville. After all, Gordon had propelled himself to the top of my list of suspects, and what was the sense in tipping my hand? Then I thought about Billie, probably sitting in Korn's jail waiting for Kelly to spring her. I thought about Billie, who was worried that poor Gordon was too distraught to talk to anyone. I thought about Billie, who revered Gordon, describing the man as a cross between Albert Schweitzer and Mother Theresa. Yeah, I could have gone back to Norville, but I decided to knock on the door of 243 Hollingwood Drive and shake up Gordon Wallace's little world.

"Yes?" Carole Owens said, opening the door. She wasn't as young or as pretty as she looked from a distance. Behind her the little boy ran by dragging the teddy bear by its leg.

"I'd like to see Gordon," I told her.

That made her look at me more closely. Her face clouded.

"Gordon, someone to see you," she called out, looking over her shoulder.

Gordon appeared. Maybe his eyes opened a quarter of an inch more. Maybe his tongue touched his lip for a fraction of a second. Outside of that, there wasn't the least reaction.

"Hello, Slots," he said, totally matter-of-fact.

The nonchalance made my blood run cold and brought back a scene I wished I had forgotten. I was a young beat cop called in to check out a domestic disturbance in a tenement in Alphabet City. By the time I got there, the screaming that had been the cause of the complaint had stopped.

I knocked on the door and was greeted by a young

Latino, who smiled and told me yes, there had been a problem with his wife, but everything was okay now. Looking over his shoulder, I could see he had been reading *El Diario* as he was finishing his supper. Everything seemed in order. I told him I'd like to talk to his wife. He told me to go ahead, she was in the bedroom. As I walked into the room off the kitchen he turned on the TV.

His wife was in the bedroom all right—hacked to pieces with a machete. There wasn't any part of her that could be identified. Every inch of the room was splattered in blood and gore. I walked out, gun drawn, shaking. The man was still watching TV, laughing at some comedy show. I asked him what happened to his wife. He didn't bother to look up from the set as he told me, "She forgot to bring home ice cream."

"Carole, this is Slots Resnick," Gordon said. "Slots and I are going to have to talk. Maybe you can take Joey over to Maggie's for a while."

"Okay. C'mon, Joey, let's show Maggie and Samantha your new teddy." She gathered up Joey and ushered him out the door, pausing to give me a polite smile.

"Come on in, Slots," Gordon said, and led the way through the small foyer into the living room, which was only a little larger. The kind thing to say was that it looked lived in, with toys and clothes strewn on the floor and on the mauve sofa. I moved a wooden airplane off a seat cushion and sat down opposite Gordon, who pulled over a pine rocker with a ripped pillow.

"Can I get you something to drink?" he asked.

"Gordon, what's going on?" I asked him, dispensing with the small-talk bullshit.

He shrugged. "What can I say? I can ask you how you found out, but it wouldn't change anything. I can pretend Carole and I are just good friends, but if you've gotten this far you know different."

"Why don't you explain anyway, just for fun."

He leaned back in the rocker. "Well, Carole and I go back

about six years. We just seemed to hit it off. I mean, what is there to say?"

"How about Joey?"

"Yes, Joey." He nodded. "Carole offered to have an abortion, but I wouldn't let her. You know, she was getting close to the forty mark; the old bioclock was ticking. She realized it might be her last chance to have a kid, but she was willing to have an abortion anyway. I admired that a lot, Slots. It showed me what a terrific woman Carole was. Well, I told her to go ahead and have that baby, and I'm sure glad she did. It was the only fair thing to do."

"Was it fair to Pat?"

"Luckily she never found out. That would have caused a lot of complications."

"Gordon, you are aware your wife was murdered a couple of days ago, aren't you?"

"I'm well aware of it. I loved Pat. I'm more heartbroken than you'll ever know. We all show our grief in different ways. I needed to be with someone. Thanks to Carole, I've been able to get through this nightmare."

"Amanda must have been a help also."

"Yes she has, as a matter of fact."

"Did she give you a shoulder to cry on at the Mirage Club Motel?"

No reaction. The guy had ice water for blood.

"I called Amanda for some advice," he said after a few moments. "She's a dear friend, and she came to the Mirage to see me. She cared for Pat too, you know. It was sorrow that brought us together." He made a tent with his fingers. "Mr. Resnick, I've always sought comfort in the arms of women. Perhaps it's a failing."

"What about other people's comfort? What about Billie's comfort, sitting in a cell accused of Pat's murder?"

"I spoke to Billie earlier. She told me that Korn might arrest her. She's hired a lawyer I know named Mike Kelly to defend her, and we both have complete trust in Mike. She'll be all right."

"She'd feel a lot better knowing you were there for her."

"Actually, the thing that made her feel better was knowing I was coping. Quite frankly, I'm not looking forward to having to go back to Norville and answer the sheriff's questions."

"Really? Why would that be?"

"I'm afraid if I told the truth, all I would do would be to further incriminate Billie."

"Run that by me again."

"Look, Slots, this has been a double tragedy for me. I lost both my wife and my daughter on Saturday night. Pat is dead, and Billie murdered her. Sorry if I don't respond to that in a way you feel is morally right. Right now, I need to be away from Billie; I'm not up to giving her support."

"What makes you think it was Billie?"

He sighed. "Saturday night I walked into the kitchen to find Billie half plastered. I knew it was her last college game, and I decided I wasn't going to make a big deal about her getting drunk again. When she saw me, she verbally attacked me. She said I let her take the rap for some financial misunderstanding I had with Pat, and that Pat had called her at the stadium to say she was dropping Billie from her will. Billie demanded I talk to Pat. I explained that it would be taken care of, but she wasn't satisfied. She called me a few choice names and stormed out, saying she'd take care of Pat her own way. I followed her and tried to keep her from going, but she's strong and mean when she drinks. She pushed me, and I stumbled backwards. That was all she needed to get into her car and drive off."

"Financial misunderstanding?"

"Don't be smart with me, Resnick. Billie and Amanda told you everything that happened." The flash of anger was the first spark of real emotion he'd shown.

The front door opened and Carole appeared. "Sorry, I just have to get some chocolate syrup. Joey and Samantha decided they want to make chocolate sundaes." She walked past us to the kitchen.

124

"I'd like to hear it from you," I said. "You always put such an interesting slant on these matters."

He ignored my sarcasm. "A friend needed some money quickly. I had to help. Pat wasn't around, and my accounts are tied up. I wrote some checks and fully intended to tell Pat about it."

"You were looking to invest in some deal?"

"No."

"That's what you told Billie."

"I couldn't tell her the truth."

"Why is that?"

"Because he was protecting me," Carole said, coming into the living room. "He gave me the money so my sister could get good care in the best hospital after her stroke. I swear to God I'll pay him back. Why the hell are you badgering him?"

"Slots is the investigator I told you about."

"Oh really. Well I never had much love for the ice princess. I'm sorry she was murdered, but Gordon had nothing to do with it."

"Carole, you don't have to—"

"Like hell I don't. This is the nicest, most gentle man that ever lived."

"That's what people tell me."

"Yeah, well they're telling you the truth." A mother lion defending her cub.

"After Billie left Saturday night, what did you do?" I asked Gordon.

"I—"

"He came over here and spent the night with me," Carole interrupted.

"About what time was that?"

"Hell, I don't know what time!" she exploded. "What the hell is it to you? I don't think I want you in my home. Do we have to have him here?" she asked Gordon, glaring at me.

"Maybe you'd better leave, Mr. Resnick," Gordon said

to me. "I'll be back in Norville tomorrow morning. Perhaps we can talk again."

"You can bet on it," I told him.

I made two calls once I got back to Norville. The first was to Billie, who told me Korn had come around and taken her in handcuffs to the cell in his office. It was the most humiliating thing that she ever had to go through. Mike Kelly was wonderful and got her out on bail in two hours. She promised me she'd stay put at the mansion, and by the way, Gordon had called her and said he'd be back home that evening. She told me how upset Gordon was that he hadn't been there to help her when she was arrested.

The second call went to a friend who worked for a major credit checking house. I told him to give me the poop on Patricia and Gordon Wallace. I told him I'd call back later.

I left the Holiday and drove over to Mario's place. Barry, the kid who tended bar for Mario, finally came around to stop me banging on the front door. He told me it was too early for dinner, and Mario wasn't in yet. I said that was just fine with me, I'd wait around.

He let me in and went behind the bar. Tuning the radio to a station that specialized in somebody spouting unintelligible rhymes over a bass drum, he continued mopping and straightening up.

"You a native of Norville?" I asked him, taking a chair from on top of one of the tables and sitting down.

"Yeah. Lived here all my life."

"How long are you working for Mario?"

"Mr. Santamaria? About three years, I guess it is." He wrung out the mop and started swabbing again.

"Hard guy to work for I'll bet."

"Nah. He's a good guy. He yells a lot, but he's really a good guy. You're a friend of his, right?"

"We go way back," I said.

"You're the guy that gave him the cologne. I thought he

126

was going to explode when he got that from you. What was it, some kind of inside joke?"

"Yeah, you had to be there. You must have grown up with Billie Howlett." They were roughly the same age.

"Yeah. I knew Billie and her brother Jesse. I was in some of Billie's classes in high school."

"You like her?"

"She's okay I guess. She comes in here a lot. She really likes Mr. Santamaria's lobster dinners."

"Is that right?"

"She and the Moaner—Ramona—come here most every Friday night."

"The Moaner?"

"That's what the kids at school called her."

"Why?"

"It ain't nice."

"You can tell me, Barry."

He smiled. "Well . . . in school she was making it with the Lukas brothers. One day it was Roy, the next day Marty. They had this Iroc with tinted windows, every time you walked by you'd hear Moanin' Ramona."

"I thought she preferred girls."

"Not in high school."

"How about Billie?"

"Everybody says Billie's in love with sports. She never went out on a date with a guy. There's a lot of guys that asked her, too, me being one of them." He shrugged.

"When she comes in on Friday, she's usually with Ramona?"

"Yeah, unless there was a night game at the college. Then she came in with the guys on the team. Billie came in after every night game and had her lobster."

"She didn't come in Saturday night," I said.

"Yeah. That was her last game. It's too bad. Mr. Santamaria made this special Italian cheesecake for her, too. He was real disappointed."

"Really? I didn't think Mario and Billie got along."

"Are you kidding? They're good friends. They can sit till real late at night just talking. You should have seen how nervous Mr. S. was that something happened to her Saturday night. He kept checking to see if the phone was working. He was pacing around. He wound up packing up the dinner and I guess he wound up taking it over to her place."

"Yeah? I figured Saturday was a busy night."

"It is, but I'm talking maybe eleven, twelve. You get the after-dinner crowd, and that's mostly drinks. Hey, listen, you got to excuse me, if I don't finish doing the floor here and in the kitchen, he's going to be pissed."

I nodded. "Go ahead."

When Mario walked in twenty minutes later, he wasn't delighted to see me.

"We're closed," he told me. "The kid shouldn't have let you in."

He was wearing a blue Champion sweat suit that looked tight across his shoulders. He took a chair from the top of the table I was sitting at, placed it on the floor, and sat down across from me.

"I hope he doesn't think he's finished mopping up in here, the floor's still filthy," he said. "Hey Barry, come here!"

Barry poked his head out of the kitchen. "Yeah, Mr. Santamaria?"

"You finished in here or what?"

"Uh, yeah."

"No you're not. When you're finished in there you come out here and do it again."

"Okay."

"And before you do anything, run down to Joe's and get me some Maalox. Now, what do you want, Slots?"

"Stomach bothering you?"

"You live with Rosa, see how good your stomach is."

"I need your help," I told him. "I need someone who knows the town and the people."

"Why should I help you?"

128

"You owe me. You owe me for not kicking your lard ass all over the street after you put me on ice."

"Still a tough cop, huh Resnick?" he snarled.

"Try me."

He thought about it. His hands balled into fists, and then he relaxed, smiling. He touched the spot on his cheek where I'd slugged him the night before. "What the hell, Resnick, I don't want to fight you. You've got a right to kick about the cold storage. What do you want to know?"

"Tell me about Gordon."

"He's the greatest guy in the world. Ask anyone in this town and that's what they'll tell you."

"I'm asking you."

"I can't stand the phony bastard. I've known him since I come out here, when he had a gas station back on the road. I couldn't prove it, but I'd bet he watered the gas he was selling. I do know he used to hustle repairs."

"What do you mean?"

"He would pump gas and pretend to put air in the tires, and while he was under the car he'd use a squeeze bottle and squirt engine oil on the motor and on the ground. He'd scare the suckers by telling them if he didn't repair the leak right away, they might blow their engines."

"That's older than dirt."

"Not around here. They fall for anything. After he fixed their cars people thought he was a hero."

"How did he come to marry Pat Morgan?"

"He's a smooth bastard, you got to give him that. He set his mind to bag the richest broad around and he went after her like a greyhound after those mechanical rabbits at the dog track. She didn't need much chasing, either. Her old man had just died, and she was vulnerable. Gordon lucked out, because the old man had his number. He used to come in here and tell me that if she married Gordon he'd have nothing to do with her. 'I didn't raise my daughter to marry a whoremonger bastard,' he used to say. Where the hell is that kid, I feel like I got a lit cigarette in my belly."

"Gordon liked the ladies?"

"Is water wet? Anything that moved was fair game for Gordon. I've seen chasers in my life, but this guy had them all beat, hands down."

"Pat didn't know?"

Mario shrugged. "She didn't talk to me about it."

"She probably talked to Rosa," I said.

"You know them priests at confession, they take an oath of secrecy, and even if you kill somebody, you can tell them and they can't tell the cops. Well that's the same way Rosa is. Forget about it."

"Billie is crazy about him."

"She's a mixed-up girl. I heard Korn arrested her and a big-shot lawyer from Denver sprung her."

"You heard right," I told him.

Mario thought for a moment.

"I'd of figured Gordon would be right at her side through all of this. I'm kind of surprised he's kept himself out of sight."

I told him what I had seen that afternoon. Mario wasn't surprised.

"Amanda Bernard and Carole Owens, that's some combo."

"You know Carole?"

"Yeah, she worked for me before she went over to the Rocky Mountain. I got rid of her because she'd disappear two, three days at a time. She claimed she had a sick sister."

"She says Gordon gave her sister money for health care after she had a stroke."

"You want to know something, that could be true. Gordon's a crook and all, but then he can do something real nice."

"You mean like what he did for Billie?"

"I still can't figure that out. He and Raymond Howlett never hit it off that well, and I'd be surprised if Gordon ever noticed little Billie."

"Maybe he was close to the wife."

"I wonder about that. She wasn't bad-looking, not that that mattered to Gordon. The thing is, he was going hot and heavy with Patricia Morgan, and she wouldn't let him out of her sight. Matter of fact, the night Gordon and Pat announced their engagement was the night Ray Howlett stabbed Cora and shot himself. Gordon and Patricia were sitting right where you are when we heard about it. Jack Korn senior was there too. Gordon rode out to the trailer with Jack, and Patricia didn't like that very much. Gordon said he knew the family and he had to see what he could do."

"I heard Cora was with someone and Raymond caught them in the act."

"That's what Jack Korn told us. He picked up this fellow who admitted he had been with Cora that night. The guy said that when Raymond came home drunk he hid. Raymond always had a jealous streak, I remember that about him. He beat the hell out of Cora, and stabbed her too, while the drifter hid under a pile of clothes, frightened out of his wits. He ran off afterwards."

"Whatever happened to him?"

"Jack held him for questioning, checked his background and then let him go. It wasn't anything he did. Cora was in heat, so he obliged her."

"Then Gordon adopted Billie?"

"Pat wasn't happy about it, but that's what happened. I told you, Gordon can do nice things."

"Could he have killed Pat?"

"He's no killer," Mario said. "He's a slime, but he's not a killer."

"What if Pat found out about his affairs and decided to cut him off."

"C'mon. He's got his own money. He owns businesses. He's been salting cash away for years. You divorce the broad, you don't kill her."

I figured I'd take a shot based on what Barry had told me. "What were you doing up at the Morgan mansion the night Pat got killed?"

"I told you, I was right here."

"Don't bullshit me Mario! I know you were there!"

131

He got up and walked over to the bar. "Where the hell is that kid with the antacid?" He pulled a container of milk from the refrigerator and poured himself a glass. "Yeah, I was there. I didn't want to say anything. I can't get mixed up in any investigation. You understand that, don't you, Slots? I can't have people looking into my past."

"If I know, other people know. You want to keep things quiet, your best shot is to level with me."

He downed the milk in two large swallows.

"I just went over to bring a dinner I made for her. She usually came here after a game. This time she didn't, and it got me a little worried."

"What's your relationship with Billie?"

"Hey come on. It ain't what you think."

I didn't say anything. I waited for him to continue.

"I mean I'm human, and I think the kid is a knockout, but it isn't like that. I don't know if you're going to believe this, Slots, but I got a soft spot for her. I never had any kids of my own, and I never will. In a lot of ways I see some of myself in her. I lost my folks when I was about her age. I was from the wrong side . . . hey, what the hell, I really like the kid, that ain't no crime. And she likes me to talk to. Maybe I remind her of her real father—at least, the good parts of her real father."

"What do you talk about?"

"A lot of things. You know, sports, school, boys."

"Boys?"

"Yeah, boys. She's no lezzie. She's confused about men. Boys scare her to death, and after what her father did to her mother, who the hell can blame her."

"So you play Dr. Ruth?"

"You think that's funny, Resnick? Maybe I'm having second thoughts about pulling you out of that freezer."

I held up my hand. "Relax. What time was it when you dropped the food off at the mansion? What happened?"

"Nothing happened. It had to be about eleven thirty or eleven forty-five. The door was wide open, so I let myself in.

I called out a few times but nobody came around, so I walked into the kitchen to put the food in the refrigerator. I saw Billie with a bottle in front of her. She was out cold."

"No one was around?"

"That's what I thought, but whoever told you I was there must have seen me."

I nodded. "Go on."

"I figured I had no business walking into the place. Billie was stoned, and who needed any trouble, so I took the stuff and left."

"That was it?"

"Yeah."

"Was Billie's car there?"

He shrugged. "I don't remember. I guess so."

"You're sure you're not leaving anything out this time?"

"Look, Slots, you've got my life in your hands anyway. What am I going to do, be cute with you?"

Barry came walking in and handed Mario a bag with the Maalox in it.

"What the hell took you so long?" Mario said, grabbing it out of his hand. He opened it and took a long swallow right from the bottle. "So what are you looking at?" he asked Barry.

"Nothing."

"So what are you doin' here when there's a kitchen floor to mop?"

Barry retreated.

Mario fixed me with a stony eye. "Slots, what I told you about going to the mansion and seeing Billie, that can't go nowhere. I go on a witness stand and I find out real quick if Rosa's been bullshittin' me about a hereafter. You know what I'm talking about, Slots. I can't afford to have some hot-shot prosecutor digging into my past."

"Take it easy, Mario, it's background info. I'll see your name doesn't come up. Where's Rosa tonight?"

He checked his watch. "She's at the church playing bingo. Somebody reads the card to her and she memorizes the numbers. She should be coming by in a few minutes. She's got this girlfriend that drives her over. You want her to tell you about her session with Patricia, right?"

"It crossed my mind."

He nodded. "You're wasting your time," he told me. He walked off to do some more browbeating of Barry, and I was left to myself to wait for Rosa.

Ten minutes went by and Barry stepped out of the kitchen carrying a plate of clams on the half shell.

"The boss did these for you," Barry said. "He said don't worry, they ain't poisoned." He set the plate down in front of me and went to the bar to pour a glass of wine. "His compliments," he said, bringing me the wine.

I hadn't realized how hungry I was. The clams made me think about Nathan's in Coney Island, and the first time I ate clams on the half shell. That was also my first post as a rookie cop. The CO out of the Six-Oh Precinct was Captain Popofsky, and we were affectionately and not-so-affectionately known as "Popofsky's puppies" by the veterans.

I remember standing on the corner of Mermaid and Twentieth on December 9, 1965. Cops called it "the Hawk"— the winter wind that rolled off the Atlantic and punished every living thing it touched. On this particular night, the Hawk was deadly, freezing the tears right onto my eyelashes.

Three kids rushed up to me, yelling for me to follow them. There was a man standing on the rock jetty. He was threatening to jump, and he was holding a baby wrapped in a blanket.

We stood facing each other, fifteen feet apart. If I came closer, he swore he'd dive into the ocean. The three teenagers who had summoned me took it all in from the sandy beach. I talked to him, reasoned with him, threatened, pleaded. He said he wanted to die. The world was an evil place, he told me. Babies shouldn't be brought into this world.

I thought I was making progress. I told him I'd help him get a job, I'd loan him some money. Let's both get off these rocks and get a hot cup of coffee. He said okay, and began walking toward me—then for no apparent reason he just tossed the baby over his shoulder into the sea.

It was reflex on my part. I jumped in after the scraggly blanket and the tiny infant, and before I hit the frigid waters I heard the howls of laughter and knew I had risked my life to save a doll.

"You learned something important," Popofsky said at the side of my bed in the emergency room of Coney Island Hospital. "A good cop knows how to separate the things that are from the things that ain't."

Popofsky was dead ten years now, and the rest of the old-timers had gone on to policeman's heaven, which translated into a house upstate or in New England, with good hunting and fishing.

Slots Resnick was still eating clams on the half shell, getting his ass froze off, and trying to separate the things that are from the things that ain't.

9

Rosa was guided into the restaurant by an elderly lady who bussed her on the cheek and called for Mario. He came out and sat her down at the table next to me.

"Your pal Slots Resnick is here. He wants to ask you something."

She smiled guardedly. "Good to see you again, Slots. Is there anything new in your investigation?"

"Sheriff Korn thinks he's got Pat's killer. He arrested Billie Jo this afternoon."

"No! That young woman wouldn't kill anyone. What is that sheriff thinking?"

"I happen to agree with you, Rosa, but I'm going to need some help if I'm going to find the person who did do it."

"Mr. Resnick, I—"

"I know. You feel a responsibility to your dead friend."

"There are just some things that must remain private. I owe that to her."

"Outside of her immediate family, you're probably the last person to see Patricia alive. You owe it to her to help catch her killer. You also owe something to an innocent girl who's sitting in a jail cell." I didn't mean for it to come out rough, but I was losing patience fast.

Rosa's jaw tightened. "I have my ideals, Mr. Resnick. The Lord will be my judge and jury."

Mario gave me a what-are-you-gonna-do shrug.

"What if I ask you to confirm what I already know?"

She thought that over. "I'm not promising," she said, folding her arms. "What do you have in mind?"

"Patricia came to see you, and she was very upset; you already told me that. It had to do with twenty thousand dollars that Patricia thought Billie had tried to steal from her account."

"You do seem to know a lot," she said, obviously surprised.

"You also said she was upset with Gordon, probably because he took Billie's side in the business about the money—or was it because she found out about an affair he was having?"

Her lips pursed for a fraction of a second. "That, sir, *is* private."

Her answer told me what I wanted to know: Patricia had found out, or at least had strong suspicions about Gordon's playing around. Korn had a motive for Billie; was there one for Gordon too?

"Perhaps I've talked too much already," Rosa said.

"One last question. Pat told you she was cutting both of them out of the will, didn't she?"

"That shall remain private," Rosa said stubbornly.

"Rosa, this is very, very important. That young woman's life hangs in the balance."

"If you know something, Rosa, tell Slots," Mario said softly. "She's a good kid. Do you want her to go through life with people calling her a murderer? It's been tough enough for me, and I was guilty."

Rosa sighed deeply. She reached out and clasped Mario's

138

hand. "She said she was thinking of writing them both out of the will."

Bingo!

There were three messages for me when I got back to the hotel. The first was from my friend at National Credit Check, who confirmed that the Morgan family were dyed-in-the-wool blue bloods with corporate fingers reaching into most of the pies of major American industry. A good part of Patricia's money was tied up in trust funds, but it was obvious that anyone who inherited her fortune would be set for a couple dozen lifetimes.

When Gordon married into the family, he was immediately elevated to positions of power on the governing boards of a paper-producing company, a lumber company, and a hydroelectric plant. What wasn't clear was whether the board positions translated into any personal financial gain. There were a number of red marks on his report, indicating that he was a slow payer when it came to his credit card balances. There were also two large department stores that had his account over ninety days delinquent. It was a tough call whether Gordon had a financial problem or was just careless about paying, which is a failing you could pin on many of our more wealthy citizens.

The other calls were from Rex, and intriguingly, Amanda Bernard.

I tracked the Mets executive to his daughter's house in Connecticut and gave him a rundown of the situation.

Billie Howlett was a hard-luck kid, as I saw it, who was being set up for a murder rap. I told Rex about the motive, the fact she was being cut out of the will, and about the bat being the murder weapon, and how she couldn't remember exactly what she had done the night of the crime.

"It sounds like a convincing case to me," Rex said.

"All the defense has to do is establish reasonable doubt. Gordon was also being cut out of the will, he had access to the bat, and I'm not sure his alibi would stand up to a hard cross-examination. On top of that, he might have been in financial trouble, and the guy's got the morals of an amoeba."

"You sound like you've made up your mind," Rex said.

"I don't think Billie did it. You can call it intuition or professional instinct, but of the two of them, I'd put my money on Gordon as the person who actually killed Pat Morgan-Wallace."

"I see," the executive said thoughtfully. It was one of those I-know-it-all responses.

"Something on your mind, Rex?"

"Well, Slots . . . I was just thinking that maybe you're identifying too closely with Billie. I mean after all, here's a young person with a lot of skills, all set to be a major leaguer. Then something pops up from out of the blue and turns her world on its ear."

"You mean like a slide into second that breaks a guy's leg."

"I'm not saying that's what's going on, I'm just saying you should be aware of the possibility."

"I don't see it that way, Rex, but your analysis has been duly noted." I promised to let him know how things progressed.

Amanda Bernard's answering machine picked up after the third ring. I started to leave a message but she came on the line.

"Thank you for returning my call, Slots. I'm afraid we got off on the wrong foot. I'm really not the dragon lady my daughter seems to enjoy telling people I am. In addition, perhaps I didn't come off in the best light the time we met."

"We've all had those days," I told her, wondering where this was leading.

"Well, I would appreciate it if we could just get together and talk a little. There are some things I'd like to discuss with you. I'd be happy to meet you someplace, or perhaps you wouldn't mind coming here?"

140

No, I wouldn't mind. In fact, I wanted to get a chance to interview the family lawyer, but I'd been at a loss as to how to accomplish it.

I followed Amanda's directions, happy I didn't have to negotiate the steep mountain roads at night. She lived three miles south of the Morgan place, and I was getting to be a whiz at Norville geography.

The Bernard place wasn't the Morgan mansion, but it was no shack, either. You walked up a garden path of bright-colored stones, past high trimmed hedges and fountains, to a sprawling tan ranch house. The plate nailed to the door said AMANDA BERNARD, ATTORNEY. Off to the side I could see Ramona's Cutlass and the white Cadillac parked in front of the garage.

I rang the bell, which had a tinny little *ping* sound, and eventually Amanda opened the door. Reflecting her informal manner on the phone, she was dressed in casual attire, loose-fitting navy blouse over a pair of khaki slacks, and sandals. Her shoulder-length auburn hair was freed from the severe pulled-back style she usually wore, and on the Resnick looks scale of one to ten, I upgraded her from an eight to an eight and three quarters.

"Any trouble finding us?" she asked.

"No, your directions were fine."

"I'm glad. Why don't we go to my office. I have the walls soundproofed as a protection against Ramona's music. I've given up telling her to turn it down. To young people, 'down' means you can hear someone speaking if they scream at the top of their lungs."

I was about to say I didn't hear anything when the music came on, shaking the house. I say music, but I wasn't sure; the reverberating bass blocked out most of the other sounds. Amanda shrugged and motioned for me to follow her. We walked down a white-carpeted hall, which must have been a bitch to keep clean, and came to a door with OFFICE stenciled on it.

I followed her in, and as if by magic, when the door closed behind us all the ear-blasting noise disappeared.

"Isn't that wonderful! There should be a Nobel Prize for the person who invented soundproofing. Ramona and I had an argument before you got here. She usually runs to her room and blasts the music out of spite." She smiled.

"I'd pull the plug out of that stereo. Get the same results at a much lower price."

"I'm going to guess that you don't have children."

"You're right."

"When you have children you quickly learn that the price they extract in emotional grief is well beyond the monetary price. Can I offer you a drink?"

Behind her desk was a bookcase built into the wall, filled with law journals, reviews, and bound volumes with great titles like *Ranko* v. *Mississippi, 1978–1981. Vol. 2.* There were Kiwanis plaques, golf trophys, a citation from the mayor of Norville, a picture of Amanda with a guy in judge's robes outside a building which looked like the Supreme Court, and behind a false shelf, a well stocked bar complete with a pocket-sized refrigerator.

I pointed to the Johnnie Walker and asked for it straight up. She poured herself the same thing.

"To better understanding," she proposed.

I raised my glass.

"I don't know how well you know Gordon Wallace. Not very well, I presume," she said when we had tasted our drinks.

"Not as well as I would like to," I told her truthfully.

"He's quite a guy, Slots. He's very well respected around here. If he wanted to run for mayor, he'd win in a walk."

"Really?"

"You know, I've worked for the Wallaces ever since Pat's father died. Gordon had a gas station before he married, and I'd done some work for him then. He suggested to Pat that I be their family attorney. Quite frankly I would have quit six

142

or seven times had it not been for Gordon. You have no idea what a bitch Patricia was. I considered her a friend, but she was just an impossible person."

"I didn't know that."

"Oh come now, Slots. Have you found one person who's truly broken up over her death? Don't you find that strange? I'm not saying anyone wanted her murdered, but the fact is that most people found her to be just an obnoxiously cold person. She talked down to people, she insisted on having her own way, she was spoiled beyond belief. I could go on and on."

"Gordon seemed to care for her. Billie told me she was afraid Gordon might be destroyed by Pat's murder."

Amanda nodded. "Yes, I believe that could happen. That's Gordon. He's just a very special guy. Only a saint could have put up with that woman."

"A saint?" I said, letting the skepticism show through.

She swirled the Scotch in her glass. "He told me you found out about us. I'm not going to tell you I don't care, but I'm not going to get worked up about it either. We've loved each other a long time. He wouldn't leave Patricia, but he desperately wanted to. The fact that Gordon and I have had an affair doesn't make him any less wonderful a person. Thank God we live in a more enlightened society."

She waited for my reaction, but I just took a sip of my drink and batted my baby blues.

"The reason I asked you here was to try to dissuade you from pursuing your investigation of Gordon."

"And you think I'm looking to get Billie off by pinning the murder on Gordon?"

"That's precisely right. We both know that Billie killed Patricia. There was bad blood between them for a long time. Not only that, but you are aware of the kind of people she came from."

"Indians?"

"Violent savages. Unfortunately, most Indians and Mexicans are. No matter what you try to do to help them, you can't change their nature. I'm as tolerant as the next person, but it is common knowledge that those people have no compunction about killing."

"Really? It seems to me that most of the Indians and Mexicans are law-abiding hard-working people."

For a flash of a second the laid-back Amanda disappeared and the dragon lady poked through the mask. She forced a smile.

"We don't have to score points off each other. I have something to show you." She reached under the desk and pulled out an attaché case, which she opened and then turned to face me. Staring back at me from neat bundles were the green faces of some of my favorite Americans—Franklin, Hamilton, Jefferson, and Grant.

"Ten thousand dollars," she said. "You can count it if you wish."

I didn't wish. One of the things you learn fast if you want to survive in my business is that when someone dumps money in your lap, you should have your antennae flicking around like those of an ant at a picnic.

"That's all yours if you want it," she said.

"Why do I get the feeling I have to do something in order to get it?"

"Your feeling is wrong. You have to do absolutely nothing. Nothing at all. Can you do nothing, Mr. Resnick?"

"Nothing, as in not lifting a finger to help Billie Howlett?"

"I prefer to think of it as not doing anything to divert justice from its true course."

"Is justice so easily diverted?"

"Of course it is. I see it every day. I'm a lawyer, remember."

"Is this your money, or Gordon's?"

"Gordon knows nothing about this—you'd also have to promise to say nothing."

"You must be very fond of him."

"I'd do anything for him. In fact, I've often toyed with

144

the idea of killing Patricia in order to free Gordon from that witch. I am pleased that Billie did it for me."

"According to you, then, the fact that Patricia was dropping her from the will was enough to make Billie want to kill Pat."

"I think that's obvious."

"Why didn't you tell me that Pat also threatened to cut Gordon out of the will, and that Pat told that to you on the phone?"

"She did no such thing!" Amanda said. "That's an out-and-out lie."

"I have a witness who heard her say it."

She looked at me to see if I was bluffing. My look back at her was as solid as Ray Charles singing "Georgia."

"What of it! It's irrelevant anyway. Gordon didn't kill Patricia. However, perhaps ten thousand is too low a figure; I'm sure I could see my way clear to offering you fifteen thousand dollars to pick up and go home. While you're thinking about it, there's something you should know. Mike Kelly has some important friends in the county prosecutor's office. It's very possible that a deal can be worked out so Billie serves a minimum of time in one of our more comfortable institutions."

"You're a good attorney with a bad brief."

"Meaning?"

"I happen to think Billie is innocent. As far as I know there were three people who had access to Billie's bat on Saturday night: Billie, Ramona, and Gordon." There was also Mario, but that wasn't Amanda's business. "It would seem to me that you have a strong interest in proving that it was Billie who was the murderer. Have you also considered the possibility that you might be the one with the wrong impression of Gordon? Maybe he isn't the saint you think he is."

"Very good, Mr. Resnick. They won't throw you out of the male buddy system. You all band together to protect your infidelities; you managed to imply you've got something on

Gordon without actually telling me about Ms. Carole Owens."

"It wasn't my place. You're a big girl."

"Gordon told me everything about the mistake he made some years back. Do you realize he's supported that child and stood by the mother through everything? I don't feel threatened by a relationship like that, I feel a renewed faith in the man."

"Did he tell you about her before or after I followed him to her house?"

"It doesn't disturb me that he visits his son. There's nothing between him and that waitress."

"You're sure?"

"A woman knows."

"Did Pat know about you and Gordon."

"That's not terribly important at this moment. I'd rather we discussed what's on the table." She nodded at the money.

"It's tempting, but I think I'd rather do things my way."

"You want more, is that it?"

"Amanda, ring up 'No Sale.' "

"You're a fool!" She slammed the attaché case shut, snapped the locks, and placed it under the desk with a flourish.

The door of the room flew open. "I want my car keys now, you damn bitch!"

Ramona stood there, her face twisted with hate.

"You've met my lovely daughter, haven't you Slots?"

"Give me my keys you filthy fuck!"

"The child has a way with words, doesn't she? She has the IQ of a genius, and she's actually quite attractive. I know you can't tell, because she loves to act and make herself look disgusting."

"You're the one who's disgusting! You can't keep me locked up like a prisoner. It's my car. I want the keys!"

"No! You can't go to the mansion. Billie and Gordon don't want you around now!"

"You just want to keep me away from there so you can fall all over your fantasy man Gordon."

"This is quite inappropriate."

"*You're* inappropriate. You're pathetic! Don't you know that Gordon can't stand you. You're such a fool, throwing yourself at him. He *laughs* at you. Now give me my keys!"

"We will talk when Mr. Resnick leaves," Amanda said in measured tones.

"I want to make sure Billie's okay."

"Call her."

"You bitch. You know they're not answering the phone."

"Go to your room. I have nothing more to say to you!"

"I'll go, and I'm going to play my music loud and I hope it gives you one of your migraines and you die!!"

"Behold the joys of motherhood, Mr. Resnick."

"You're never getting Gordon. He despises you!" Ramona said, relishing her mother's discomfort.

"How would you know that?"

"He told me."

"You're a liar. If you must know, Gordon and I are very close. Perhaps this is as good a time as any to tell you, but he's asked me to marry him when this business with Patricia is over."

"You're lying! You're a filthy whore liar."

"Oh am I?" Amanda's eyes shot daggers. "We discussed it just this afternoon at the Mirage Club Motel. Mr. Resnick followed me there, and that's what we were talking about when you barged in here."

In the war of words, that seemed to score a direct hit. Ramona stood in the doorway, her mouth open, her eyes as big as saucers.

"She's lying, isn't she?" she whispered.

"I don't get involved in domestic disputes unless I'm getting paid for it. Good night ladies. I'll find the door my-self."

Before I sacked out, I tried calling Billie. Ramona was right, no one was answering the phone. I started thinking about what Rex had said. Was I personalizing this case? Was I

147

turning a blind eye to the possibility of Billie's guilt because I wanted her to have the chance I'd missed to play major league ball? I fell asleep before I could come to a decision.

I like shaving. I like the smell of Buckley's old-fashioned shaving soap. I like the ritual of mixing the soap in my mug, painting it on my face with the short-bristled shaving brush, and then scraping it off with my barber's straightedge blade. I had just finished my right cheek and neck when there was a tap on the door, actually two taps. Hard decision: do I wipe off the soap and start all over again, or do I answer the door looking like one half of Saint Nick? Another two taps.

"Slots, are you up?"

I opened the door.

Dan Shelby looked me over. "Shaving, huh?" he asked.

"No, it's a yeast infection. Itches like crazy."

I stepped aside to let him in. "Sit down," I said over my shoulder. "I'll be right back." I scraped off the rest of the soap, wiped my face with a towel, went back in and sat down on the bed. There was only one chair in the room.

"I feel funny about being here," he said, shaking his head. "I don't like being disloyal."

"Come on, Dan. You haven't got a disloyal bone in your body. What's Korn up to now?"

Shelby chuckled. "How'd you know I was here about Korn? Don't answer that, I guess it's obvious. You know, I really like the little sucker, and I don't want to see him go off half-cocked."

"Dan, believe it or not, I've got nothing against Korn."

Shelby stroked his beard. "Well, early this morning Jack and I were having breakfast and we got this call. It was from Gordon Wallace. He puts Billie on, and the girl tells Jack that she's going to come into town around twelve."

"Why?"

Dan shifted uncomfortably in the chair. "I heard she's decided to confess."

I didn't react, but it hit me hard.

148

"I feel funny about telling you this behind Jack's back, but the idea that it was Billie who killed Patricia just doesn't sit well with me. I know you were tracking down some other leads, and I thought . . ."

"Maybe I was wrong, Dan. Maybe I was pulling too hard for Billie because she reminded me of someone from my past."

Dan looked dejected. He blew out a deep breath. "It's a damn sorry situation," he said sadly.

I tried calling, but they still weren't answering the phone. If Billie did kill Patricia, I wanted to hear it from her own lips. I took the now familiar roads and headed toward the Morgan mansion on Pecos Hill.

I tried balancing it all out in my head. Both Gordon and Amanda were putting the screws to this kid. Gordon must have spoken to her while Amanda kept me busy. And he'd probably convinced her not to answer the phone, to keep people like me and Ramona from putting any doubts into her head.

The mansion looked beautiful and imposing in the early sun. I pounded on the door a few times after the doorbell seemed to have been ignored. It finally opened, but instead of seeing Carla's pleasant brown face, I found Gordon.

He was wearing a blue silk robe over a polo shirt and gray slacks. I immediately added *robes over clothes* to my list of items I connect to jerks. The rest of the list consists of Playboy decals on cars, jackets with patches on the elbows, Baby on Board signs, pipes, earrings on men, tattoos on ladies, and a love of sushi in anyone.

"Oh, hello, Resnick." He said it as if I displayed more than one of *his* jerk characteristics.

"Good morning, Gordon. I'd like to talk to Billie."

"I'm afraid that's not possible. Billie's very busy this morning, and she won't be seeing anyone."

"She'll see me, Gordon. Why don't you go and ask her."

"I can assure you—"

"I can assure you I'm not leaving here until I talk to

Billie, or until I hear from her lips that she doesn't want to talk to me. There are things I'm going to find out one way or another; you might as well let me talk to Billie now, or who knows what else I might turn up on my own."

He smiled. "Your threats don't scare me, Slots. I have nothing to worry about. If you really have a need to speak to Billie, I'm not going to stand in your way."

"Alone."

"Fine. She's on the back porch." He pointed around the side of the house. I walked around back as Gordon retreated inside.

Billie was sitting at a table on the porch. She was staring off at the mountains.

I took a chair next to her. She tried a weak smile.

"I tried calling you last night," I said. "No one answered."

"No. Gordon and I were talking."

"You must have had a lot to talk about."

"I guess. . . . I'm turning myself in to the sheriff this afternoon." She looked at me. "I don't want you to try and talk me out of it."

"I seem to recall you thanking me for not giving up on you. It sounds like you're giving up on yourself."

"Damn it Slots, I did it. I murdered her."

"What makes you so sure? Yesterday you told me you had passed out and couldn't remember anything; now after an all-night session with Gordon, you're going to confess to a murder."

"Gordon had nothing to do with my decision."

"I'll bet! He told you that little story of how he came down to talk to you and then followed you out when you stormed off, and you pushed him over and drove off to the cabin."

"That's what happened, Slots. I'm remembering it now in bits and pieces. I remember driving to the cabin and talking to Patricia, I remember she argued with me, I had the bat in my hand . . ."

"Billie, you were drunk. Your imagination is playing tricks on you. The odds are you simply slept it off. Gordon has a vested interest in wanting you to admit guilt."

"Don't say anything against Gordon."

"Billie, think about it. He stood to lose two thirds of Patricia's money. He had access to your bat. He—"

"Stop! You're wrong! Gordon would never do anything like that."

"And you would?"

She brought her face close to mine. "I don't know."

"What's that supposed to mean?"

She stared off at the mountains again, and at first I thought she hadn't heard me.

"You know about my parents. You know what happened to them. They found me hiding under the trailer. I blocked out what happened—I have no memory of it at all. Sometimes I wonder if I was the one who killed them. . . . I can't remember anything."

"I was told there was a witness."

"Oh yes, the witness, Ben Wade from Adobe. He was supposed to be my mother's lover. My father burst in on them and Ben managed to hide. My father stabbed my mother and then killed himself with a shotgun." She said it woodenly.

"That's what I understand," I said, wondering where this was leading.

"What if Wade was wrong? What if he only thought my father killed himself, and it was actually me?"

"Why you?"

"I used to walk around with that shotgun. It was mine, a birthday present from Jesse."

"That doesn't prove—"

"It's the nightmares, Slots. I have these nightmares where I see my father stabbing my mother, and I come in and beg him to stop—and then I pull the trigger." She started crying.

"I'm not going to be an armchair psychiatrist, but it seems to me your nightmares stem from your feeling helpless to do anything to stop what happened."

"The dreams are so real!"

"They usually are, Billie, but it doesn't mean you were involved. Billie, you can't admit to something you don't know you did. You have to think about this very carefully."

"What do you think I've been doing? Do you think I want to throw away my life, my career? Ever since you told me that the Mets were interested in me, it's the only thing I've been able to think about. I've worked my whole life for this. I used stay up at night and tell Jesse I was going to be the first girl baseball player. I was five or six at the time. Slots, don't you think I realize what I'm giving up?"

"Then don't do it."

"I've spoken to Mike Kelly; he's gotten a deal from the county prosecutor. They've promised me I'll serve a minimum sentence."

"Gordon talked you into this."

"No!"

"Don't you see what he's doing? He's using you."

"No. You don't understand, Slots. He wanted to confess. He wanted to take the blame himself. He said he'd do it for me. That's why he was away the last couple of days; he had to settle some personal things to prepare himself for a long prison term."

"He knew you wouldn't let him, not after he told you he saw you drive off drunk. Billie, he knows how to manipulate people. He manipulated Amanda into offering me ten thousand dollars if I'd drop the case. He has a woman in Hollingwood who's so mesmerized by him, she'll swear to anything. He's got you confessing to a murder you didn't commit."

"You don't know that! I believe him. He took me in. He gave me everything. Why should I believe you? Please leave, Slots. Please leave now, and stay out of it!"

The ride back to the hotel gave me time to think. I don't like playing Don Quixote. I've tilted at my share of windmills, and experience has taught me that most of the time you wind up on the seat of your pants. Gordon and Amanda had Billie

152

convinced she was the one that went up to the cabin and bludgeoned Patricia to death. As I saw it, all the killer had to have was access to the bat and opportunity, and that gave me four known possibilities.

I discounted Ramona because, as wacky as she was, I couldn't see any motive except to frame Billie, and why would she do that? I also discounted Mario. Aside from having no apparent motive, why would an ex–professional killer do such an unprofessional job? Mario would have gotten rid of the body in a place where it never would be found. I couldn't see a pro using a bat, when a gun was his weapon of choice, and then leaving it under the porch. And why would he want to frame Billie?

Then there was Billie herself. Her motive was the loss of one third of Patricia's money. How much did that mean to a twenty-year-old? I'm not saying kids don't appreciate money, but it takes some maturity to understand the power of wealth. If I took Mario at his word, he had seen her passed out at the kitchen table the night of the murder. Did she get up from the stupor, drive to the cabin, kill Pat, drive back, and go to her room and go to sleep? Possible, yes, but improbable, even if you believed Gordon's story.

Which brought me to Gordon, also known as the Saint, Mr. Wonderful, and an all-round great guy. Gordon stood to lose his two thirds of Pat's money. If Billie was convicted he'd stand to inherit her third also. That was a nice inducement to try to force Billie to confess. He had access to Billie's bat, and the only alibi he had for the night was provided by an old girlfriend who was still very much in love with him and would do anything to protect him.

Sorry Rex, I might be rooting for Billie, but it wasn't because of my own unfulfilled dreams. There were some real problems with this case, and if I didn't find some answers soon, everyone would be happy to oblige Billie with a murder conviction.

I tried calling Mario at home to go over what he'd seen when he brought Billie's dinner to the mansion. After a few minutes of fast talk convincing him that I needed background stuff and I wouldn't jeopardize him, he told me the same story he'd told me before. It wasn't enough to clear Billie. He wasn't sure what time he got there, and he couldn't remember if Billie's car, much less the bat, was on the premises. I couldn't punch a hole in Gordon's story with Mario's testimony. The key was whether Mario had seen Billie before or after she allegedly pushed Gordon and drove off with the car. If he wasn't sure of the time, I had nothing.

"Slots, you've got to leave me out of this thing," Mario said.

"I've got no reason to drag you in," I told him honestly.

I could try to knock down Carole Owens's alibi, but I had a feeling that after Gordon rehearsed her, they would have their story down pat. I tried calling her anyway, and when I told her who I was she hung up on me. I called right back.

"Wait a second Carole don't hang up! Gordon told me to call you," I lied.

"Gordon?"

"Yes. I told him I was going to check on his whereabouts the night of Pat's murder, and he suggested I call you. Look, I don't expect you to believe me. He said you should call him and he'd tell you it was okay. Do you know the number at Pecos Hills?"

"Yeah, I know it."

"Call him. I'll get back to you in a few minutes."

I was counting on the fact that Gordon was still not answering the phone. I called Carole back three minutes later.

"Everything squared away?" I asked her.

"No one's answering the damn phone."

"You'll have to take my word then, Carole. Look, Gordon and I want to wrap this up so I can get the hell out of here," I said patiently.

She hesitated, and I thought I'd lost her. "Well I guess it's all right. I'm just telling the truth, what really happened."

"What time did you see Gordon on Saturday night?"

"I picked him up at ten after eleven. He seemed upset

154

because Billie had driven off and she was drunk. He stayed with me until the next morning." It came out in a rush, obviously memorized.

"Did anybody see you with Gordon?"

"No. We didn't want anyone to see us. You got anything else to ask me?"

"Yeah, do you know what the penalty for perjury is?"

"Screw you!" She slammed the phone down in my ear. Pleasant lady.

It rang almost as soon as I put it down. I wondered if Carole had forgotten some choice expletives and was calling to bring them to my attention. It wasn't Carole, it was Ramona Bernard, and I had to strain to hear her.

"I have to talk to you," she whispered.

"I'm listening."

"Not on the phone. I don't want the bitch to know I'm calling you. It's about the case. Did Billie really confess?"

"She's going to turn herself in to the sheriff this afternoon."

"She can't! She's innocent!"

"I need proof Ramona."

"I can give you proof. You have to come see me. I can't get away from here; Amanda took my car keys. When you drive to my house you pass a little park on your right, it's about a half mile before my house."

"I think I remember it."

"I'll be there in a half hour," she whispered before she hung up.

The park she was talking about was outside a spanking new development, probably built to attract young couples. There were a dozen toddlers in a sand pile as well as kids in swings and on monkey bars and seesaws. I searched the faces of the young women on the benches, but Ramona wasn't there. Fifteen minutes later I started to wonder if perhaps she had meant another park.

I took a drink of water from a fountain, and when I

straightened up I saw her walking down the road. Somehow her blue hair and skull earrings didn't look so outrageous anymore. I was getting used to her.

"The bitch was all over me to clean up the kitchen. Like we don't have help that do that!" she said angrily.

I sat down on an empty bench and motioned for her to sit next to me. "You have some information?" I asked.

"Oh yeah, I've got fuckin' information. I've got information all right, but first I want some information from you."

"Me?"

"What's this shit my mother was saying about Gordon?"

"What do you mean?"

"Come on, Slots, you heard her last night. Did he tell her he was going to marry her?"

"I don't know anything about that."

"But you do know about them meeting each other at the Mirage Club Motel."

I surveyed the playground while I thought about an answer. All the playground equipment had neat rubber mats underneath. I wondered how many little broken arms that saved. "I'm uncomfortable with this, Ramona. Whatever you think of Amanda, she's your mother and—"

"Cut the shit, Slots! You're not telling me anything; I'm asking. Amanda is the one who brought it up, remember. You want to get Billie off, then I have to know more about that slime Gordon."

"You're one of the few people I've met who hasn't told me how great he was."

"Maybe one of the few people you've met that really knows the bastard! Were they together at the motel?"

The hell with protecting Amanda. Ramona was right, I was just confirming what her mother had already told her.

"Yes. Afterward I followed him to another woman's house. Her name is Carole Owens. Gordon told me he was the father of her child."

"The waitress! I don't fuckin' believe it!!" She got up and

156

walked over to the water fountain, took a drink, and then kicked it in anger. Her dark eyes were smoldering.

"I swear to God I'm going to bury that bastard. I'll bury that lying bastard!"

"Ramona, calm down. Come back here and tell me what's going on."

"He lied to me, Slots," she said, sitting down. "He played me for a fool. He's played everyone for a fool."

"Gordon?"

"Yes, Gordon. He told me he loved me. He told me we'd always be together, and I believed him."

She was so wound up, her whole body was trembling. She started punching the back of the wooden bench. I grabbed her.

"Hey hold on! You're going to hurt yourself."

She fought against me for a few seconds and then went limp. "I just want to kill him," she said through clenched teeth.

"I didn't think you were having an affair with Gordon. I was led to believe you and Billie were—close."

She nodded. "It was Gordon's idea. Billie and I were friends, and I used to call for her at her house. After a while Gordon and I started talking when I was there waiting for her to come home after a game. He's the greatest guy to talk to. He's so sincere, so interested. We finally wound up in bed. We started to figure how we could spend more time together. He came up with the idea that I should get closer to Billie. That way I could always be around." She threw her head back and started crying. I waited for her to continue.

"The lesbian thing started when everyone kept seeing us together. You know how people like to whisper, especially around here. Gordon thought it was funny, and then he said it was a great cover for us."

"What about Billie?"

"Billie's funny. Like sex doesn't mean anything to her. She sort of went along with it so boys wouldn't be hitting on her."

"How long did this go on?" I asked her.

She shrugged. "I don't know, close to a year, maybe more. You don't know what he used to say to me. He used to tell me that I was special to him. We laughed about my mother. He always asked me how the 'old lady' was. But now I find out he was with her too. They were probably laying in bed talking about me and laughing about it!"

"Ramona, what can you tell me about Pat's murder?"

She smiled. "I can tell you something very interesting. I'm sure it was Gordon who killed Pat. I just wish I could personally execute the bastard."

She saw the look of impatience on my face. "I got to the mansion early on Saturday night. He told me Pat was going to be away for the weekend and we could be together until Billie got home. So I got there early, and we're getting it on, and then there's this phone call. He gets out of bed and takes it in the study. I don't know what it was about or anything, except he's all flustered and upset. So he tells me something screwed up on some deal he was working on. A few minutes later the phone rings again, only this time it's Billie. He yesses her to death. I'm getting a little pissed, you know? So we finish making love and I know his heart isn't in it. Then he tells me to get dressed, he's got to take care of something. I figure I've got about twenty, thirty minutes before Billie shows, so I take a shower. I start calling around for Gordon but he's not in the house, and I look out the window and there he is, pacing around in real deep thought.

"Right about then Billie shows up, and she's got this attitude, and I don't know what the hell is going on. Frig the both of them, I say to myself, and I start watching TV in Billie's room. After a while I go downstairs, and I see Billie slogging it up with a bottle of tequila. Terrific, I'm like a fuckin' piece of furniture, nobody cares if I'm dead or alive. Later for this, I figure, I'm taking off. I open the door and there's Gordon trying to start his car. It sounds like a stuffed-up garbage disposal. Then he gets out and gets in Billie's car and drives away."

"He took Billie's car?"

"Yes. I'm doubly pissed because the son of a bitch didn't even have the decency to say good-bye to me."

"Which direction did he drive off in?"

"North. The direction of the cabin."

"Would you be willing to testify to that?"

"After what he did to me? Are you kidding? Not only would I testify against him, but I'd do it in a business suit with my hair in a neat bun."

10

X   X   X

Sheriff Korn was impressed. He listened while I related what Ramona had told me. Every now and then his eyes would roll and he'd shake his head in amazement.

"I'm completely shocked," he finally said when I was done.

"I was taken aback also," I agreed.

"You know what shocks me the most Resnick? I'll tell you what shocks me the most. It's how a supposedly professional investigator could fall for such a crock of crap."

"Hold on, Korn."

"How stupid are you, Slots, or should I ask how stupid do you think I am?"

I was going to tell him but thought better of it. "What don't you believe?"

"The whole thing is a complete fabrication. Can't you see what's going on here? That girl will say anything to help her friend. Can you imagine in your wildest dreams a man like Gordon Wallace going to bed with Ramona Bernard?"

"He was having simultaneous affairs with Carole Owens, who used to be a waitress at the Rocky Mountain Diner, and Amanda Bernard. I don't know how many more women he

161

was with. Ramona was around, that was inducement enough for a guy like Gordon."

"No way! It doesn't make any sense. I'll grant you Gordon got around, but how do you compare those women with Ramona, and Amanda is Ramona's mother, for God's sake. It's just too sick. Ramona is trying to help her friend and spite her mother at the same time, and you fell for it."

"Why are you so sure?"

"Why? Because I know, that's why. Billie Howlett called me up and told me she did it."

"She doesn't know what she's saying. She's being manipulated by Gordon."

"I've got a sworn affidavit from Ms. Owens stating that she picked Gordon up at the mansion at around eleven and they spent the night together."

"What makes her word better than Ramona's? Ramona will swear to what she saw."

"She's got no credibility. Everybody knows she's gay. If I took what you told me seriously I'd be laughed out of town. Now, I don't mean to be rude, but I've got an appointment at the county prosecutor's office in less than an hour. As far as I'm concerned, we got Patricia Wallace's murderer. If there isn't anything else I can do for you, why don't you let me get back to my job."

It was getting close to two in the afternoon. I stopped in at the Rocky Mountain, had an onion omelette and a Coke, and wondered about Carole Owens.

My waitress was a tired, matronly woman with sagging breasts and heavy jowls. She looked ridiculous in the short brown waitress uniform and sneakers. I got the impression she knew it too.

"Anything else, honey?" she asked me.

"I could go for a cup of coffee, but the last time I drank that mud I thought they were going to have to pump my stomach."

"You're probably from back east, right?"

162

"New York."

"That's it. I hear that about the coffee, and it's always the people from back east. You're not used to our water, that's all. We got hard water out here. It's better for you. You look at your statistics, less heart attacks, less cancer, less ulcers even."

"I didn't realize that."

"People always complain about the coffee. It's the water. You take a look over at my station. They got that state-of-the-art Braun coffee machine. It does everything for you automatic, you can't make a mistake if you wanted to. So it ain't the coffee machine, and the coffee is Mountain Peak, that's one of your big premium coffees out here. Got to be the water. Like I say, I hear about it all the time. Then you got the truckers come in, all they want is our coffee. They bring in big giant thermos jugs, want them filled for cross-country runs."

"Maybe you're right."

"Now, take your beer. You people back east can't get enough of Coors. Everybody comes to Colorado wants to get some of that cold Coors. I tell them it's the same water they got in the coffee but somehow since it's beer it seems to go down better."

"You must be a native."

"I am."

"Work here long?"

"September it'll be four years."

"Did you know Carole Owens?"

"Carole, sure. She's a friend of yours?"

"I met her recently. She's living over in Hollingwood with her son."

"Yeah. She was here before I started, and then she used to come in part time and holidays.

"You know her boyfriend Gordon Wallace?"

"I never messed into her personal business. So you want to try our coffee again?"

Her tone let me know the subject was closed.

"No, make it a Coors."

* * *

Dan Shelby hadn't been at the sheriff's office, so I reasoned he was at his home-office. I reasoned right. For once someone seemed happy to see me.

"Hi Slots, come on in," he greeted me warmly.

I followed Shelby into the living room and he motioned for me to sit down on the sofa. I wedged myself in between three of his cats and sunk into the cushions.

"Any luck?" he asked me.

I liked Dan Shelby. He'd been straight with me from the moment I met him. He didn't have to give me the tip about Billie turning herself in. I also realized that he reminded me of Paul Bunyon, who is a favorite folk hero of mine.

"Things are simmering," I told him. "I thought I'd find you with Korn at the county prosecutor's office."

He shook his head. "Not me. I've got bad feelings about what's happening here."

"Well, let me pour a little kerosene on those feelings of yours." I told him what Ramona had told me and about my afternoon following Gordon to his motel rendezvous with Amanda and then to Carole Owens's place.

Shelby shook his head. "Pat, Amanda, Ramona, Carole—when does this guy get a chance to sleep?"

"Those are just the ones we know about. He told me he always seeks comfort in the arms of women."

Shelby laughed. "He must be a pretty comfortable guy."

"Except for Ramona, they'll do anything for him. Owens will perjure herself in court, and Amanda offered me fifteen grand to leave him alone."

Shelby whistled. "What did Korn say when you told him all this?"

"He told me to peddle my papers elsewhere. Ramona is just trying to protect Billie and hurt her mother. Everybody knows Ramona is gay."

"Tell you the truth, Slots, I always wondered about her and Billie. She had this hot and heavy thing going with these Lukas troublemakers. They used to call her Moanin' Ramona, and she was with a lot of guys."

164

"I saw her, Dan. If she was lying, they better get a movie producer down here, because this girl will win an Oscar."

"I tend to believe it too, Slots. So now what?"

"We've got to nail Gordon. There's really very little I know about the guy. I know you newspaper people usually have a morgue; maybe we should look through the stuff and see what turns up."

"Are you prepared to go down into the cellar and pull out bundles of old brittle papers and thumb through each one for the last ten years or so?"

"It's not my idea of a fun couple of days, but dig we must, then dig we must."

Shelby smiled. "Relax. Follow me, Mr. Resnick, and I'll show you a miracle of modern computing."

Shelby took me into his little computer room, which reminded me of the cockpit of a 747. He stationed himself behind the keyboard, typed some instructions, and stared intently at the screen, blank except for a tiny icon of a watch, which seemed to be spinning off the seconds.

"There's a program that indexes every single word on your hard disk. I've asked it to come up with every article from 1976 to the present on Wallace, Gordon. . . . There you are Slots!" he said triumphantly. He was Paul Bunyon with a Mac instead of an axe.

Six separate listings came up. Each provided a date and the headline of the article in which Gordon's name appeared.

"Okay, I've got an index; now how do I get the articles?"

"For that we use the CD Rom."

"I know all about CD Rom. She's that country singer who tells people not to eat meat," I quipped.

"Not even close," Dan said, all business. He entered the first listing and the line vanished; in less than a second the article was on an adjacent screen. The head was BARNEY SMOOT TO RETIRE.

Smoot had owned the Shell station in Norville for eighteen years before he decided to pack it in and move to California. The last line of the article mentioned that he'd sold his station to Iowa businessman Gordon Wallace. The second and third articles had appeared a year apart in the early eighties. They had to do with a contest Gordon sponsored for the "Most Adorable Norville Baby."

"Probably a great way to meet women," Shelby commented.

The next article appeared in May of 1985: PATRICIA MORGAN TO WED GORDON WALLACE.

It was a typical society fluff piece: Patricia Morgan, daughter of the late industrialist Leroy Morgan, blah blah blah, will marry Norville businessman Gordon Wallace, formerly of Des Moines. The happy couple, blah blah blah, will formally announce their engagement at a private dinner party to be held on Sunday, June 3. The wedding is planned for late summer.

"June third; that must have been the night they had the party at Mario's. That was the night Billie's parents and brother died," I thought out loud.

The next article had a June 11 dateline. Shelby's paper was a weekly, so it had a few articles on the Howlett murder-suicide. The article mentioning Gordon wasn't really about him at all, it was a background article about Sheriff Jack Korn, Sr., who "was called away from the engagement party of his friends, Gordon Wallace and Patricia Morgan, to investigate the evening's events at the Howlett trailer."

An accompanying article quoted Norville businessman Gordon Wallace as saying, "It was the most horrifying thing I had ever seen. There was blood everywhere. It was fortunate for the fellow who was hiding that he got out of there alive." The last piece of Gordon memorabilia came in an article about Billie two years later: "Her father Gordon Wallace stated that he would be proud of Billie even if she had struck out."

"Dan, can you bring up the whole issue for June eleventh of 'eighty-five?"

"Sure." He tapped in a few commands. "Here you go, page one."

The headline screamed out GRISLY NORVILLE MURDER-SUICIDE.

The tri-city area woke the morning of June 4 to a horrific tale of murder and suicide. According to Sheriff Jack Korn, Sr., Mrs. Cora Howlett, a Norville resident, was murdered by her husband, Raymond Howlett. He is alleged to have stabbed her fifteen times with a kitchen knife. Raymond Howlett then took his own life with a shotgun, shooting himself in the head.

Sheriff Korn said that Cora Howlett was accused by her husband of having an affair with an Adobe resident identified as Ben Wade, 44. Wade was said to be passing through Norville when he decided to buy native jewelry from Mrs. Howlett. Mr. Howlett appeared at the trailer and accused his wife of being unfaithful. An argument ensued, and Mr. Howlett murdered his wife and then took his own life. Ray Howlett had a history of drinking and assault charges.

Sources tell the Post *that Mr. Wade was hiding inside a closet in the trailer and heard what transpired. Fearing for his own life, he was unable to come to the aid of the victim. He was questioned and released without any charges being brought against him.*

As a tragic aftermath, Jesse, the Howlett's son, an all-state athlete in track, basketball, and baseball, was found dead in his car after colliding with a bridge abutment at the junction of Route 96. After being told of the deaths of his parents, he was seen driving off at high speed. The car smashed into the concrete structure and caught fire. It is believed that the young man was knocked unconscious or killed instantly as he made no effort to escape. Evidence on the scene sug-

gested that he had been drinking (see more on Jesse Howlett, the Colorado Jim Thorpe, pg. 9).

The family is survived by Billie Jo Howlett, 13, daughter of Raymond and Cora Howlett and sister of Jesse, who was found wandering near the trailer in a state of shock.

I read through the rest of the articles. Most of them were written by Shelby, a few of the others had a J. Norris byline.

"J. Norris?"

"A stringer who used to work with me. He's out in Denver now. I think we did a follow-up the week after." He brought up the next week's paper.

This one had the "Howlett tragedy" on page three. There was a brief rehash of the story, and a quote from Korn about how Raymond Howlett had a reputation for brutalizing his wife. A human-interest slant told how a prominent Norville businessman—Gordon—had promised to provide for Billie Jo's education. There was a picture of the inside of the trailer, and another picture of Jesse Howlett's accordioned car. A broken bottle, the label showing two roses with their stems crossed, was circled, and the caption was *Jesse Howlett's car on Route 96, bottle found at scene.*

"Anything else?"

"I don't think so. Don't forget, we're a weekly. By the time people around here get the newspaper, the story's a week old."

"Why the hell was Gordon at the scene? I thought he was having an engagement party."

Dan thought about it. "Probably because his gas station was right down the road from the Howletts' trailer. I believe he knew Raymond."

"Convenient."

"What are you thinking, Slots? I see those wheels turning in your brain."

"I just find it interesting that there's a woman within

168

shouting distance of Gordon and he's not having an affair with her."

"But he was engaged to Patricia."

"I doubt that would stop him. I'd like to know more about Ben Wade."

Shelby ran his fingers through his beard. "I don't recall too much; he was just some fella that came by. He was a truck driver, I believe. Here, wait a second."

Shelby went into the other room and came back with a phone book. On the cover was an advertisement for the Silver Brook Mall. It was the phone book for the three towns, Adobe, Wesville, and Norville. "Let's see. . . . Yup, here it is, the only one in the book: Benjamin Wade, one-thirty-two Lake Street."

I went to his phone and dialed the number. It rang three times and then a woman answered.

"Hello?"

"Hello, may I speak to Mr. Wade please?"

There was a long pause. "May I ask what this is about?"

"It's a confidential matter. It's very important I speak with him."

"I'm his wife Rita. Perhaps I can help you?"

"I don't think so. I really need to speak with Mr. Wade."

"I'm afraid that's impossible. My husband passed away last year."

"I'm sorry to hear that," I said, the disappointment coming through.

"Who is this?"

"My name is Resnick. I'm a private investigator from New York City. I'm in Colorado working on a case that he was involved in about six years ago."

"The Howletts?"

"That's right."

"You've come all the way from New York to talk to Ben?"

"Not exactly. The case just took that turn."

"I see."

169

"Perhaps you'll be good enough to allow me a few minutes of your time."

"I don't know what I could tell you. It—It was a great source of embarrassment to me. I think you can imagine."

"It won't take long. It's very important."

She gave it some thought. "Well, I don't think so. I'm really not up for company these days."

Shelby saw my face. "Let me try," he said. I gave him the phone.

"Hello, Mrs. Wade. This is Dan Shelby. . . . Dan Shelby, of the *Tri-City Post*. That's right, I'm the man with the beard. Read the *Post*, do you? . . . Glad to hear it. . . . Yes, well, we intend on making those low-sodium, low-cholesterol recipes a regular feature. Look, Mrs. Wade, this fella is a friend of mine. He's come all the way down from New York. I'd appreciate it if you'd give him just a little time. We've got an unsolved mystery, and you could be a big help. . . . Well I should think you can trust what I say. Hold on, now." He handed me the phone.

"Thank you, Mrs. Wade. I should be there in about . . ." I looked at Shelby.

"I'll give you directions. Figure thirty-five, forty minutes."

"I'll be there within forty minutes."

"Okay, then," she said.

The sky was turning an ominous metal gray, and an orange rim of setting sun played peekaboo with a far-off mountain in the west.

The Wade place was down a dirt road that a wooden street sign indicated was Lake Street. I doubted there was a lake within twenty miles. When the road forked, another wooden sign saying WADE pointed the way down the left fork past some heavy brush. A rustic-looking mailbox with its red flag sticking up also had WADE painted on its side. I followed the fork a hundred yards until I saw the house.

It was an unimposing, solid frame house. Behind it was a

170

forest, which was taking on an eerie look with dusk settling in. A dog lying in front of the door barked at me a few times but decided I wasn't worth getting up for.

There was a heavy brass knocker instead of a bell. A woman answered the door.

"You must be Mr. Resnick." She said in a voice that I recognized as the one on the phone. "I'm Rita Wade."

"I hope I'm not being too much of a bother."

"No, no none at all," she assured me. She asked me in, and I followed her into the living room. "Can I get you something to drink?"

"A cup of coffee would be just fine," I told her.

The house was done in Early Americana. There were old-fashioned muskets on the wall, carved eagles, and pictures of Civil War generals, some in blue uniforms, some in gray, sporting long beards and stern looks. On the mantel next to what looked like a wooden loom were models of the *Merrimack* and *Monitor*. Other ships, full-masted ones, could be seen riding white-crested waves in large oil paintings hung about the room.

Mrs. Wade came out of the kitchen carrying a tray. There was a pot of steaming hot coffee, sugar, milk, and an assortment of doughnuts.

I sat down in an overstuffed easy chair covered with a floral print. Rita Wade took the rocker across from me.

"I was admiring your Civil War items," I told her.

She smiled. "That was all Ben's stuff. He said he was related to one of the generals who fought at Richmond, Calvin Cooper Wade. Did you ever hear of him?"

I shook my head.

"I'm not surprised; no one else has either—except Ben." She said it with a shrug and a good-natured laugh. She was about fifty, with a friendly face, glasses, and gray hair. Dying it would have taken five years off her. She was wearing a plain pink housedress, oversize even on her ample frame.

She poured us both coffee. "Now, how can I help you?"

"First I have to apologize for bringing this whole matter up again. I'm so sorry about your husband."

"Thank you. In spite of what happened that day, Ben was a good man."

"How did he die?"

"He had diabetes and never paid no mind to it. He was very headstrong. He got an infection, then blood poisoning." She turned her hands palm up. "That was it."

"Do you have any children."

"Yes, I have a son, Leonard. He's a veterinarian over in Adobe."

I took a sip of the coffee and it was delicious. So much for the waitress's theory about the local water. "The reason I'm here is because Raymond and Cora Howlett's daughter Billie Jo has been accused of murdering her adoptive mother, Patricia Morgan-Wallace."

"I see."

"Do you know Gordon Wallace?"

"I don't think so."

"His name comes up both in what happened back in June of 1985 and in today's case. I wanted to ask Ben about Gordon."

"Well, I don't recollect him ever mentioning anybody by that name," she said after giving it some thought.

"I have to ask you to tell me what happened that day. What was Ben doing in Norville?"

"To be quite honest with you, so much about that day doesn't make any sense. I know in my heart that Ben was faithful to me for twenty-two years up to that day. He said he couldn't explain it, and didn't want to ever talk about it." She sighed. "He left early that morning to go fishing. I was away the whole day working at the church for this Fourth of July picnic we have every year. We do the early phoning, the mailing, and straighten up the building and, well, you know how those things go. I called home a couple of times in the afternoon, and he hadn't come back yet. About nine I got home, expecting to find him, and instead the phone's ringing and it's the sheriff over in Norville telling me they're holding Ben for questioning. Well, I almost died when he said murder. Then he told me that Ben wasn't involved, he was just a witness. Later I found he witnessed it all right—from inside that woman's closet."

"You're saying that it was the first and only time he was with Cora Howlett?"

"He swore to it, and I believed him. He told me he didn't even do anything with her. He said they were together talking when the husband came in, and she hid him on account of the man's temper. I guess you could say she knew her man.

"Well it didn't make me feel that much better, because no one around here believed it except the people who knew Ben and me, and I guess if you're attempting to do something like that, it's just as bad as if you did it. When I'd get mad he'd say, 'At least if I did something, then it'd serve me right you being angry.' The point was I found it hard to show my face, with all the publicity. There were reporters from all over the state coming in here."

"How did he meet Cora?"

"He said he stopped off at the trailer to pick me up a present. He wanted me to have one of them Indian bracelets they make. I guess you could say that little stop changed our whole lives."

"Did he ever talk about what he had heard when he was hiding in the closet?"

"No. He never wanted to talk about it. I think maybe he felt funny about not helping the woman. I told him at least that was one smart thing he did. I would have been a widow five years earlier. Poor Ben only weighed about one fifty soakin' wet. Tall as a weed, skinny as a reed, we used to say." Her eyes clouded. "I miss him," she said simply.

I gave her a moment to compose herself. "The coffee is great," I told her.

"You wouldn't have liked it before I put in the water filter. The water is so hard around here you can't even get your clothes washed right."

My apologies to the waitress.

"I understand your husband was in the trucking business," I said.

"Yes. Ben had his own rig for ten years, a big Peterbilt eighteen-wheeler. He had to give it up and work for someone else. When we first got married, before Leonard was born, I'd travel with him all over the country. Those were some good days. You know what killed it for him, what killed the whole trucking business?"

"No idea."

"Taxes. Every time you turned around, Uncle Sam would hit you with something else. That and the high price of gasoline. You couldn't make a profit because the government killed it for everyone, and the ones that could pay the government got killed by the Arab oil prices."

"So what did Ben do?"

"Well, Ben said if you can't beat 'em, join 'em. He got a job with Backer Trucking, driving their rigs. He got straight salary and let them have the headaches."

"Are they a big outfit?"

"One of the biggest. They've got trucks for every industry from hospital waste to tankers, like what Ben was driving."

"You mean Ben drove gasoline tankers?"

"Sure."

"Was Shell Oil one of the companies Backer supplied trucks for?"

"They sure were. That's what Ben meant when he said you can't beat 'em so join 'em. It was the big oil companies that put him out of business when he had his own rig, and here he was supplying them."

"That fellow I told you about, Gordon Wallace, owned the Shell filling station in Norville."

"He did?"

"Is there any way we can find out if that station was one of Ben's regular customer's?"

"I know it was. He'd make the Norville station his last

174

call. Except . . . oh damn, it was a friend of his, but his name wasn't Gordon; what was it? Oh yes, Ben called him G.W."

"Gordon Wallace."

"Why, I guess that's right. What does it mean?"

"I'm not sure. After the bodies were found, Gordon was quoted in the paper as saying how lucky the fellow who was hiding was to get away alive. He certainly didn't say that he and Ben knew each other and were friends. Maybe Ben never really was in the trailer. Maybe he lied about being with Cora Howlett."

"Why? Would would he put himself and his family through that?"

"Money. Probably a great deal of money."

"Mr. Resnick, I don't understand any of this. Are you trying to tell me that Ben. . . ." She placed her hand over her mouth. "Oh dear. No, that can't be."

"What is it, Rita? You just thought of something."

"Oh Mr. Resnick, I think you're right. I think Ben lied."

"What happened?" I asked her gently.

She was deep in thought trying to put the pieces together. "About a month after all of this happened," she began slowly, "Ben told me that our luck had changed. He said we won the lottery. I never knew Ben to play the lottery, but he insisted we'd won. I wanted to see the ticket. I said where is the ticket, and he told me he had some elderly man who wasn't working cash it for us. This way we could beat the taxes. Lord did that man hate taxes."

"How much?"

"He said ten thousand dollars. We used the money to help put Leonard through school, and my mother was ill, and we spent some on nurses. Ben said we couldn't tell anyone about the money since we didn't pay the taxes. It had to be more than ten thousand though. He was always getting me presents, I thought it was to make up for—oh he was such a sweet fool. He was always worried about what would happen if he died. He was worried about how I would get along. There was some money in a strongbox. . . ."

"It wasn't from the lottery."

"No. I suppose he lied to cover for this Wallace fellow. But why?"

"Wallace didn't want the true story to come out. Somehow he was tied in to the lives of Raymond and Cora Howlett. He was engaged to a very wealthy woman who would have broken off the engagement at the first sign of scandal. Paying Ben was a sound business decision."

"Will they ask me to give back the money?"

"You don't have to worry. That money belongs to you and Leonard. You earned it."

11

The rain held off until I got back to Norville. It was dark enough for Mario to have his big pink and blue neon sign on, flashing MARIO'S to the world, and underneath, AUTHENTIC ITALIAN CUISINE, and if that didn't grab you, STEAKS—SEAFOOD.

It was still early. Two couples were having pasta and sipping wine at tables near the door. A middle-aged man was sitting at the bar talking to Barry.

I poked my head into the kitchen, and an olive-skinned guy in a chef's uniform looked up from a skillet.

"Yes?"

"Mario?"

"He went pick up Rosa. He back soon."

I hit Barry for a glass of Black Label and brought it over to a back table. The bartender finished his conversation with the fellow at the bar and came over to me.

"Mario went to pick up Rosa. He'll be back soon. Anything you want?"

"Who's the chef?"

"That's Tony, he comes in when we get busy. He's a good chef. I think he's better than Mario, but don't tell Mario I said it. You want something, Mr. R.?"

"Maybe later. Thanks, Barry."

"Okay. Let's see, it takes ten minutes to get to his house, another ten to get Rosa moving, and ten to get back. He should be walking through the door"—Barry looked at his watch—"right about now."

On cue, the door opened up, and Mario and Rosa walked in. Mario was wearing a bright yellow rain slicker and shaking an umbrella.

"You got a pretty good act there, Barry," I said, "but it would be more effective if I hadn't seen Mario's headlights when he pulled up."

Barry laughed. "We won't even charge you the cover for the floor show."

I nodded to Mario, who acknowledged me with a short nod and immediately went behind the bar to check the register receipts. Rosa sat down at what I imagined was her customary table near the kitchen. I went over to her.

"May I join you, Rosa?"

"Oh, Mr. Resnick. Yes, of course." She waited for me to be seated. "Mario told me that Billie Howlett confessed."

"Yes, she did."

Rosa shook her head. "I don't feel it. I don't feel that she was the one. I'm getting altogether different vibrations."

"You bothering my wife again, Resnick?" Mario asked playfully as he joined us.

"I was out of town this afternoon. What happened with Billie?" I asked him.

"They had her down at the prosecutor's office, and she signed some papers. A little while after that, Gordon and that attorney from Denver came out, along with Amanda Bernard, and they were looking very solemn. I mean everyone had their heads down, except for Sheriff Korn, who looked very pleased with himself standing next to Mitchell."

"Mitchell?"

"He's the prosecutor."

"He was the guy they were supposed to make a special deal with."

178

"Well they had something going. They're talking about granting her bail based on her ties in the community and her clean record. It may take a while till the paper work is completed, but it's still pretty unusual when you plead guilty to murder," Mario said. "But I'm not surprised. They want to be done with this case, and pin medals on each other's chests."

"I gave Korn some new information, but he didn't want to be bothered with it." I told Rosa and Mario about my conversation with Ramona and Rita Wade.

"Can we do anything about it, Slots?" Rosa asked me.

Mario probably thought I was going to ask him to testify about what he saw Saturday night. He suddenly got very interested in the ceiling.

"If we can find out more about what happened the night Billie's parents died, we might be able to use it as leverage against Gordon. I need you both to help me."

Mario seemed relieved that that's all I wanted. "Just name it, Slots. I told you I really like the kid."

"Will I be able to help too?" Rosa wanted to know.

"How good is your memory?" I asked her.

"Like a steel trap," Mario responded.

Rosa smiled shyly. "He always says that. The Lord has blessed me with good recall. It's a comfort when I'm listening to the psalms of the Good Book."

"I want you both to concentrate on that Sunday evening in June of 'eighty-five. Try to remember the engagement party for Gordon and Patricia."

"That was over six years ago. I can't even remember what I had for breakfast this morning," Mario said.

"You had cold cereal. I know because you left your plate on the table again," Rosa told him.

"How do we do this, Resnick?"

"Peg your memory on something you wouldn't forget, something that you'll associate other things with. Who was invited that night?"

"Mayor Citron; Dan Shelby was supposed to come but

he had to work at the paper; Jack Korn, Sr.; Patricia wanted Rosa to be her guest."

"There was that woman from Las Vegas, Pat's friend. I think her name was Edna or Eleanor," Rosa added.

"Steel trap," Mario said appreciatively.

"Do you remember how the party started? Who came in first? What were they wearing?" I got blank expressions. "Okay, let's work backwards from the moment you were told that something happened at the trailer." Over twenty years of conducting interrogations had taught me a few tricks when it came to triggering people's memories.

"That was that fellow, his name was Louis Howard. He was Korn's deputy for a while. He came in and apologized for having to disturb the party and said he had gotten a report that something had happened at the Howlett trailer," Mario said.

"Did he say how he knew it?"

"I don't recall. Do you, Rosa?"

"It was a tip. He said he got a tip from someone who called and said something was going on—no, that there was a shooting."

"What was the reaction?"

"I can't recall," Mario said after a while.

Rosa shook her head.

"What do you remember about Gordon that night?" I asked.

"I'm trying, Slots, but Jesus, it was years ago."

"Please don't take the Lord's name in vain, Mario," Rosa chided.

"Rosa, can you remember anything about Gordon?"

"I just remember he was late. Patricia took me aside and told me she was worried he wasn't going to show up. She was so nervous she made me nervous. I told her not to worry, and a few minutes later he came in. We said we would forgive him if he didn't do it again on his wedding day."

"Wait a second. I got something in the back that may help," Mario said. He got up and went into the kitchen.

"Are we doing okay?" Rosa asked me.

"Excellent. Mario is right, you do have an extraordinary memory."

"When I lost my vision, it seemed the good Lord compensated me in other ways. Mr. Resnick, do you think Gordon Wallace had something to do with the Howlett tragedy?"

"I'll answer that question with two more questions. Why did he pretend not to know Ben Wade? And how did Ben Wade suddenly come into a great deal of money?"

"I see what you're saying. There was a cover-up of some kind."

"Gordon wanted the Howletts' deaths to be found to be a murder and a suicide. I have to believe there was a reason for him to pay Wade well over ten thousand dollars."

Mario returned and sat down at the table. He was wearing small wire-rimmed reading glasses, which just didn't fit his macho image. As if reading my mind, he hastily folded them and shoved them into his shirt pocket. He handed me a brown card with gold lettering.

"They asked me to come up with something special, so I pulled out all the stops," Mario said with some pride.

The Engagement of Patricia and Gordon
June the Third, Nineteen Hundred and
Eighty-five

Sausage in Pastry With Honey Mustard

Herb-Marinated Mozzarella

Braised Veal Roast With Vegetables
Provençale

Steamed Rice

French Bread

Boston Lettuce and Radicchio Salad

With Orange Vinaigrette

Cream Puffs With Vanilla Ice Cream and
Cherry Sauce

Les Roses Croisees '83

"I'm impressed, Mario. I thought all you did was take the Ronzoni out of the package and boil it."

He chuckled. "You know, I remember I was angry because I had so much left over. The mayor had to leave early, Shelby never showed up, and then Korn and Gordon ran out to the trailer."

"Why did Wallace go?"

"I'm not sure. Maybe he gave Korn a ride," Mario said. "Yeah, Korn had walked over from his office, and to save time Gordon offered him a lift."

"Was it because he knew the family, or because his gas station was near their trailer?"

"I don't recall exactly," Rosa said, tapping her forehead.

"Pat didn't go along?"

"No, she stayed. She had her friend here. I don't remember much else," Rosa said.

Mario looked at me and shook his head. "I can't recall anything else either," he said.

"How can I contact Mayor Citron?" I asked them.

"He lives in Palm Springs now. He had a stroke, didn't he Rosa?"

"Yes, he did, that unfortunate man. He's living in a nursing home. He lost the power of speech, I'm told. One of the ladies from the church went to visit him about three months ago, and the poor soul didn't even know she was there. He just sat in front of the TV all the time, staring at the game shows."

"That leaves Pat's friend, who we don't know how to contact, and Jack Korn senior, who's passed on, and Gordon himself," Mario said.

"There's one other person who was around that night."

"Who?" Rosa and Mario said it at the same time, sounding like owl impersonators.

"Billie."

"Slots, that girl won't be able to help. Good Lord, what she went through that night. In a few short hours her whole family was wiped out, practically right before her eyes. It's no wonder the child blocked everything out."

"I don't have many other options."

"I can't see her going against Gordon, Slots. I've had lots of talks with her, and she worships him."

"I know. She's taking the fall on the murder thanks to his loving advice. I've got to try to see her alone, without him around."

"She's probably still in Korn's lockup. Will he let you talk to her?"

"No chance. Let's find out if she's still there. Where's your phone?"

"Barry, bring the phone over," Mario called. "And bring over my address book."

The bartender came over carrying the portable phone and placed it on the table. He handed Mario a small leather address book.

"Okay, right here. Jack Korn, Jr." He read me the number.

I dialed it and waited.

"I thought you said he wouldn't talk to you," Mario said.

I put my hand over the mouthpiece. "He won't, but he will talk to a TV newsman." I put on my country western nasal twang. "Hello, may I speak to Sheriff Korn please. . . . Hello there, Sheriff, this is Mike Thompson of Western Features, that's the cable feed out of Denver for your local news spots. . . . That's right, we take the shots and air them on your local stations. We want to congratulate you. We heard you've done a first-rate job there in police work. . . . Uh-huh. Well, I think you're being modest. Our producer sent us down to get some coverage, but we've been tied up with a fire and a jewelry store holdup. We're about ten miles from you, and we were hoping we could get some shots of you at the scene of the murder. . . . No sir, it has to be today. As a matter of fact, within the hour. We've got to get to the satellite feed office in Denver and send it out, or we're in big trouble."

Korn bought it. He couldn't wait to get his pompous ass on TV. The problem he had was that he had to release a prisoner in about a half hour.

"Well, Sheriff, can't you get somebody to do that for you? I would imagine the hard part is getting them in, not letting them out." I gave a laugh worthy of any performer on "Hee-Haw." Korn joined in.

He decided he could have his deputy, Mr. Shelby, release the prisoner. He gave me directions to the cabin and hung up, presumably to wax his moustache for his big TV spot.

Mario rolled his eyes. "The man's dumber than dirt. Jesus, what a moron."

"Language, Mario!" Rosa warned him.

It was only a couple minutes from Mario's to the sheriff's office. I parked across the street and watched. Within fifteen minutes Shelby pulled up, and Korn was waiting for him at the door. A bantam rooster puffed up with his own importance, he patted Shelby on the back and headed off in his Land-Rover to his appointment with the TV crew.

I gave Shelby a minute to settle in before I walked across. He was sitting at Korn's desk reading a computer magazine. He looked up at me.

"Slots, how are you? You just missed Korn."

"Yeah, I saw him leave."

"Did you get to see Mrs. Wade?"

I gave Dan a rundown on my conversation with the widow. He gave a low whistle. "It's looking more and more like Gordon was somehow involved with Cora Howlett."

"I need to talk to Billie about it."

"Well I'm going to let her out in . . ." He looked at his watch. Fifteen minutes."

"I want to see her before Gordon picks her up."

"I can understand that. Would you want me to let you inside?"

"I'd appreciate it, Dan."

I followed him into the cell block. Billie was the only prisoner. She was wearing jeans and a denim shirt and watching a small TV.

"Someone to see you, Billie." Shelby said.

"Slots." She looked tired and a little scared.

"I came by to see how you were."

"I'm okay," she said with little conviction.

"I thought we could talk for a few minutes."

I could see her mouth harden. She didn't want to be hassled. "I'm going to be leaving soon, Billie, and this might be the last chance for us to talk."

She thought it over. "Okay. Sure."

Shelby opened the cell and then slammed the door behind me. "I'll be back in about ten minutes," he said.

There was a bunk bed and a chair. I took the chair. Billie turned off the TV.

"What happened today?"

"They questioned me, asked me to sign some papers. I just told them the truth."

"What's the truth?" I asked gently.

"I really don't remember exactly what happened. I seem to recall talking to Pat, and there was a fight." She shrugged.

"What did your lawyer, this Mike Kelly, have to say?"

She made a down payment on a smile. "He reminds me of you. 'Are you sure you want to do this? Are you positive that's what happened? Is there any other possibility?' "

I shrugged my shoulders. "There's not much more I can do to convince you that there are other scenarios."

"Slots, please don't."

"Did you talk to Ramona?"

"Gordon told me all about what she's trying to do. I appreciate her trying to help me, but she shouldn't be doing it at Gordon's expense. I was furious, but Gordon said that she's just trying to be a good friend. That's the way he is. He always sees the good in everybody."

"Maybe I don't really understand the man."

185

"You really don't, Slots."

"Tell me a little about him. Did you know him before the night your parents died?"

"No. I met him the next day. He visited me in the hospital. He was very kind and told me not to worry, he felt very bad for me and he was going to help me. I'll never forget that. It was like having a guardian angel. He brought me presents . . . it was just such a nice thing to do."

"Why were you in the hospital? Shock?"

"They found me walking on the side of the road." She sighed. "I was in a daze and couldn't remember anything. I still can't."

"What's the last thing you can remember of that day?"

"Walking with my father back from Norville to the trailer. We had gone to town to see a movie, but the picture was so bad we walked out on it in the middle. The next thing I knew I was waking up in bed in the hospital."

"That's why you think you killed Pat? If you blacked out once, maybe it happened again?"

"Let's not talk about it."

"Tell me what you remember about Jesse."

"He was my idol. I worshipped him. One of the things I loved to do was clean his spikes when he came back from baseball practice. Do you know he was probably the best all-around athlete to ever come out of this state? He might have been the best athlete in this part of the country. He could do anything, Slots. He even thought about training for the decathlon in the Olympics. When he was fourteen they were calling him the Colorado Jim Thorpe."

"I had heard that."

"Jesse was totally committed to being a great athlete. He never smoked, and the only time I ever knew him to drink was the night he wracked himself up."

"Where had he gone that day?"

"He had practice at the high school. He was always running off to some practice. When he visited me at the hospital, he still had his uniform on from football practice. That's how

I remember him, with those exaggerated shoulders, telling me he'd take care of me and I shouldn't worry."

"I thought . . ." I was trying to remember the article I had read on Shelby's computer.

"What?"

"I was under the impression that he came home and was told what happened by the police, and then he got drunk and—"

"No."

"The paper said he sped off."

"Well, I guess he sped off to see me in the hospital. He was fine when he came to me."

"I see. Did he know Gordon?"

"He used to hang out at the gas station and work on his car. He liked Gordon, until they had some kind of fight. It wasn't anything important, just some misunderstanding about something. Jesse never spoke about it. Gordon was very upset that Jesse died before they got it straightened out. He said if he had seen Jesse that night, Jesse would have had someone to talk to and he wouldn't have gotten drunk. He always felt bad about that, as if it was his fault."

"What did Gordon do after he went with Korn to the trailer?"

She stared at me. "Why are you asking me these questions?"

"Billie, I'm sorry. I would really like to share your feelings about Gordon, but I can't. I think Gordon had something to do with the death of your parents. He paid Ben Wade a great deal of money to come up with a story. Did you know that he and Ben were old friends? Wade used to deliver gas to Gordon's station."

"Slots, I'm not going to listen to this."

"Billie, I don't want to destroy your hero, but I can't let Gordon use you like he's used so many other people."

Billie's eyes flashed in anger. "If he's so evil, so rotten, why did he take me in? Why did he adopt me? Why did he look after me and care about me?"

"I can't answer that. Maybe there's a piece of him that is decent. Maybe it was out of guilt, or maybe there's another reason that we don't know yet. All I'm saying is that based on the facts, Gordon is a lot more likely to be Pat's murderer than you are."

She turned her back on me. "Shelby!" she called. "Isn't it time yet?"

Dan walked in jingling the key ring. He opened the door of the cell. "Gordon is waiting for you outside in the car," he said.

She walked out without turning around to say good-bye.

"You got a call," Shelby told me. "Mrs. Wade didn't have your number, so she called me at the paper. I just called my answering machine with the remote and there was a message for you to call Dr. Wade, and the number. She said he'd wait at his office until you called."

I thanked Dan and dialed the number. A young woman answered with "Dr. Wade's Animal Care."

"Can I speak to Dr. Wade please?"

"May I ask who's calling?"

"Slots Resnick, returning his call."

"Hold on, please." I heard the click and was treated to a string ensemble playing "Can't Buy Me Love." John, Paul, George, and Ringo would have loved it.

"Hello, Dr. Wade here." He had a rich baritone voice. "Could you hold on for a moment, Mr. Resnick, I want to take this in my private office."

I waited. In the background I could hear two or three dogs barking.

"Hi, that's better. I understand you went to see my mother earlier."

"Yes."

"Perhaps you can tell me what this is all about?"

"Well I think you know what it's about, Doctor. The case where your father was a witness to a murder-suicide has been closed for quite a while. There's recently been another murder

188

in Norville. That led me to check some of the facts of the Howlett murder, and after talking to your mother, I found out that one of the suspects in the case, Gordon Wallace, knew your father. That in itself isn't a big deal, but at the time he seemed to imply that he and Ben were strangers. It just opened up more questions about Mr. Wallace and the actual role he played in the Howlett case."

"I see."

"My feeling is that your father didn't witness anything. He was paid to say what he did."

"By Mr. Wallace?"

"Yes, that's my guess. It doesn't sit well with me that for no apparent reason your father leaves his Adobe home after a fishing trip to travel a half hour to buy his wife Indian jewelry you can get in any curio shop along every other road. I don't buy it.

"The man had never been unfaithful, but for some reason on that day he changes his whole life-style and beds Cora Howlett, whom he'd never met before. It's the one time in his life they're together, and her husband barges in in a jealous rage and confronts his wife but neglects to open the closet where your father is hiding. Run that story up a flagpole and see who salutes it."

"Then you think it's possible that Mr. Wallace was the man who actually saw the murder and suicide, and not my father."

"Doctor, I think Mr. Gordon Wallace is implicated in the double murder of the Howletts."

There was a long pause.

"Are you still there, Doctor?"

"Yes. Mr. uh, Mr. Resnick. There's something I have to tell you. Actually, show you. Something that may be relevant to the case."

"What is it?"

"I'd prefer you see it rather than having me tell you about it over the phone. Could you possibly come out to my office? I'll be here until ten."

189

"I could be there at about ten."

"Fine. I'll give you the directions."

I wrote them down. Shelby was scribbling a note, which he handed me: *Can I go with you?*

"Would you have any objections if I brought a friend with me whose been involved with the case?"

"That would be okay. But I would want this to be kept confidential. You'll understand why."

"Don't worry about that Doctor, we wouldn't do anything that could jeopardize the apprehension of Ms. Morgan-Wallace's murderer."

"All right, then."

"Ten o'clock."

It was fortunate that Dan came with me; I was lost ten miles out of Norville. The roads that seemed so easy to follow during the afternoon became a labyrinth as soon as the sun went down. I got so balled up, I finally stopped the car and let Dan drive the rest of the way.

"Don't feel bad," he told me. "You should see me travel the subways in New York. I'm afraid I'll be like that guy in the Boston song who got on a train and never came back."

We arrived at the vet's office at five to ten. It was a white stucco building, low to the ground, with a wide, well-lit entrance. A shingle hung outside saying LEONARD BERSON WADE, VETERINARIAN.

There was a little black plaque on the door that said RING BELL AND ENTER. I followed orders and stepped into a small hallway with an umbrella stand in the corner and dog and cat lithographs on the walls. This in turn opened onto a small waiting room. There were benches around the walls and magazines on the coffee table in the center. There wasn't any carpeting on the floor; the animals wouldn't have appreciated it, and neither would the person who cleaned up after them. Instead, Wade had red stone tiling. A high-school-aged girl sat in a square office behind a sliding window, working with filing cards. She slid the window open.

"Can I help you?" She was the same girl who answered the phone.

"We're supposed to see Dr. Wade."

"Your name?"

"Resnick."

She pressed a button on her phone and announced us. A garbled message that seemed to make sense to her came back.

"Please have a seat. He'll be with you soon."

I sat down, and Shelby went to a wall rack and took one of every pamphlet having to do with cats.

"With your brood you could keep this guy in business by yourself," I told him.

"You know, all my cats are healthy. Except for shots and to have them spayed or altered, I never go to a vet."

The window slid open again. "Dr. Wade says to please come in," the girl said. She pointed to a door.

Wade had a pretty nice setup. As we walked in, a woman carrying a small poodle in her arms walked past us. "Soon you're going to be all better," she said in baby talk, snuggling her face next to the animal's.

Leonard Berson Wade was standing in front of his private office, which was past the examining rooms. He ushered us in and closed the door.

It was more of a nook than an office. There was a desk and a couple of leather chairs. This was the place he would check his mail, go over accounts, and grab a quick smoke. There was an ashtray on the desk with the remains of five or six cigarettes.

"Thanks for coming," he said.

He was a young fellow with a short, well-trimmed black beard, which I guessed he'd grown to make himself look older than his twenty-five or so years. He wore glasses, tortoiseshell, and had brown eyes and a full face. The beard gave his cheeks a puffed-out look, like a squirrel hiding acorns. He took after his father, in his mother's words, "tall as a weed and skinny as a reed."

We sat down, made some small talk about finding our

191

way there, and declined his offer of a cup of coffee. He poured himself a cup from a Mr. Coffee he had on the desk, pulling out the powdered milk and packaged sugar from a drawer.

"I need to talk to you a little bit about my father," he said, taking a deep breath. He seemed to be thinking about where to begin.

"You were right, Mr. Resnick. My father never was one to chase after women. I wouldn't be surprised if my mother was the only woman my father ever went to bed with. He was basically a very honest and decent man, who in his later years became embittered after a series of financial failures. He had his own trucking business for years and had been doing very well, but then the oil embargo and subsequent price rises put a big strain on his cash flow. Suddenly the price of fuel tripled, and the people who used him switched to the big outfits, who bought their fuel in larger quantity, which kept their costs lower than Dad's. He might have survived that, but his accountant, my mother's brother Howard, screwed up his books. The government sued for back taxes and penalties and toward the end, all he was doing was working to pay back the IRS.

"Well, I'm in my second year of vet school, and I get a letter that I may have to come home at the end of the semester because there isn't any money to pay the tuition. I'm disappointed, to say the least. All of a sudden at the end of the school year, my father tells me not to worry, I should make arrangements to continue at school next fall. He'll take care of the money. The money isn't a problem anymore."

"This was June of 'eighty-five?" I asked.

"That's right."

"Did you ask him about it?"

"My mom told you the lottery story, which I never believed. My father playing the lottery was as ridiculous as me shooting elephants for their ivory. He preached against gambling his whole life. He used to say that buying lottery tickets was like throwing your money in a river—worse, even, because when you threw it in a river at least you got to watch the dollars float away.

"He said he had some business deal in the works. He came up with the lottery thing about a month later. I'm telling you all this because I don't want you to get the wrong idea about my father. He wasn't an evil guy, he just got burned by the system, and it was a system whose rules he'd always played by. It didn't make sense to him that after all his hard work and fair play he had less than nothing to give us. It broke his heart that I wasn't going to finish school.

"Okay, look. I've been holding a secret inside ever since my pop passed away. I never would have told anybody about it if you hadn't shown up, Mr. Resnick. I'm not happy about what my dad did, and I was very content to let this thing die with him. As you will see, my dad was under the impression that Wallace was the person hiding in the closet. He never dreamed—and until now I never did either—that Gordon Wallace was anything but a reluctant witness in the case. The idea that he might have committed the murders is what's driving me to share this with you. I hope I'm doing the right thing."

He reached into his pocket and pulled out a small key. He used the key to open the bottom drawer of the desk, from which he took an envelope. He placed the envelope in front of him.

"My dad gave this letter to me and made me promise I wouldn't open it unless he was found murdered or was the victim of some accident. I remember trying to make a joke out of it, but I've never seen him more serious. I had to swear an oath that I would follow his instructions. I locked it up, and as the years passed I forgot about it. When he died, my curiosity got the best of me. I read the letter, and now I want you to read it."

He handed it to me, and I pulled the handwritten page out of the envelope. Shelby pulled his chair closer to mine and looked over my shoulder.

If your reading this here that means I'm dead. If I was murdered by someone or if I died in some accident it was not no accident. I was killed by Mr. Gordon Wallace of Norville Colorado who I warned that I would write this letter to protect myself. You didn't believe me Gordon and now you will pay for what you did. The reason Mr. Gordon Wallace of Norville Colorado murdered or had me killed was because I was blackmailing him.

I'm not proud of what I did but I did it for my boy so he could get an education which was something I never had which was why I wound up in the bad shape I was with money. I never want that to happen to him and neither do I want it for my wonderful wife Rita, the only woman I ever loved or ever will love to the grave and beyond.

On June 3, 1985 at 5:45 in the afternoon Mr. Wallace called me. He sounded very upset. He said I got to meet him. It was urgent. He said he had a business deal to talk about. All I had to do was to hustle over and talk to him and he would give me one thousand dollars. He said to meet him at the trailer near his station. I got there at six twenty and he spoke to me. He said that a very rich friend of his saw a terrible thing, he was with the lady in the trailer and her husband came and killed the lady and then he killed himself. This rich man called Gordon and asked him to tell the police what happened. He didn't want his wife to know that he was with the lady in the trailer, Cora Howlett. He offered Gordon ten thousand dollars if he would pretend to be the witness. Gordon said that he was going to do it himself but he realized that he lived in town and had a business so it wasn't a good idea. If I did it he would give me the ten thousand. He said that if there was any problem his friend would

194

come forward because he wanted justice done but this way he wouldn't have to ruin his marriage.

I didn't want to ruin my marriage but Len needed the money and I didn't want to die having nothing for Rita so I agreed. He told me what to say and he told me what his friend told him happened. He said I would have to look in the trailer and see what it looked like then I could stay outside and make like I was in shock when the police arrived. I stuck my head in and saw so much blood I thought I would be sick.

Mr. Wallace drove away. I practiced my story and then I thought I would look inside the trailer again. I walked around and looked. Then I saw a blue windbreaker jacket on the back of a chair. It was a Shell gas station jacket that I recognized belonged to Gordon. I noticed it had his name Gordon sewed over the pocket. I realized it shouldn't be there and he must have left it when his friend was explaining what happened. I took it out and hid it behind the trailer in a spot where I could find it.

A little while later the sheriff came with Mr. Wallace who pretended not to know me. I told my story to the sheriff Mr. Korn who was very kind to me and then I went home. Mr. Wallace met me at the Mirage Club Motel and gave me ten thousand dollars in cash the next day after I was home. I was so excited about the money that I forgot to tell him about the jacket.

I then read in the newspaper about a week later that Mr. Gordon Wallace was getting married to Patricia Morgan. She was RICH! I THEN REALIZED THAT IT WAS MISS MORGAN THAT HE WAS AFRAID WOULD FIND OUT—AND HE WAS REALLY THE MAN IN THE CLOSET!!!

I saw where he was going to get millions of

dollars. For marrying her and I was getting nothing in my life and I worked all my life. I was mad. I was mad that he took me for such a fool. I was mad to get ten thousand dollars and he was getting millions.

I went back to the hiding spot and found the jacket. I told him I had his jacket and it would prove he was at the trailer that day and I wanted more money. He argued but finally agreed. I will get another ten thousand, and more later if I need it. I deserve it. It was people like the Morgans who hurt my business. They took everything from me. I want to get some back. I am not ashamed of what I did and now you killed me Gordon even though I told you I had wrote this letter and it was in a safe place and now you will pay for doing that.

Ben Wade's signature was on the bottom of the page, along with a date in 1986.

"You were right, Slots!" Shelby said, finishing the letter a few seconds after I had. "Gordon *was* involved in the Howlett murders."

"You can understand that I didn't want anyone to know about this," Leonard said. "I thought that when my father died that would be it. Like I said before, I thought the only thing Mr. Wallace was guilty of was not sticking around to tell the cops what happened. If I ever for a moment thought he was implicated . . ."

"I would have done exactly what you did," I told him. "I appreciate the fact that you came forward now. What happened to the jacket?"

"He had me keep it in a locked closet. I had no idea what it was or why it was important until I read the letter." He opened a closet behind his desk and put a blue sateen windbreaker on the desk. When I was a kid they went for five dollars at Pushkins on the corner of Delancey. Today the same jacket sells for eighty-five. Over the right breast pocket there

196

was the old-time Shell emblem, looking like some prehistoric fossil you'd find at the bottom of a tar pit. On the left side in neat yellow script the name *Gordon* was sewn in. The front of the jacket was clean; the back had some dark tobacco-colored stains.

"Oil stains?" Dan asked.

"What's your opinion, Doctor?" I asked him.

"It looks like coagulated blood to me," he said.

"I'd bet on it," I told them.

Dan wanted to talk on the way back; I just wanted to think things through on my own. In spite of my one-word grunts, he didn't get the hint. He was driving, so we talked. In my pocket I had a copy of Ben Wade's postmortem letter. The jacket was safely folded away in the trunk.

"What I can't figure is, why did he kill Cora? I mean, what did he have to gain?"

"If he didn't kill her, he figured he had everything to lose."

"I don't follow."

"Look Dan, Pat's father had Gordon's number. He called him a whore-mongering bastard. Gordon's working his butt off to show Pat that Big Daddy Morgan is wrong. Pop does him a favor and dies. Now Gordon has a clear shot, only one trouble spot: he still has this thing going on with Cora Howlett. Now, I can't swear to this, but your paper had that little article saying there was going to be an official engagement party on June third, and I'm sure Cora could read."

"Right! She must have been upset."

"More than upset, because part of Gordon's game is to make the women think that they're the most special thing in the world to him. He did it with Amanda, and Ramona, and probably with Carole, and who knows how many others."

"So the fall is that much worse."

"Gordon never gave anyone an even break. Here's Cora thinking about her dream guy who's a hundred light years from her abusive jealous husband, and from out of nowhere she finds out he's getting engaged."

"Bad situation for Gordon," Dan mused.

"How about an ultimatum? If you go to the restaurant tonight I'll go in there and tell your little rich bitch what you've been doing with me the last who knows how many months."

"Would she do that?"

"Why not? As desperate as Gordon was to marry Pat, Cora might have been just as desperate to escape Raymond. She might have figured she had nothing to lose."

"He had his back to the wall."

"That was something he wasn't used to. Don't forget, Dan, this is a master manipulator. He knows how to deal with women, you've got to give him that much. He would have been better off being a kitchen appliance salesman. Maybe he tried everything to calm Cora down but she just got more hysterical and obstinate."

"The knife?"

"Cora probably grabbed it and told him to get out of there and go to his whore. Or maybe as a last-ditch attempt he tried to make love to Cora, but she pushed him away and got the knife to keep him away. He knew it was getting late and people were waiting for him at Mario's, and everything he tried to do to calm Cora down wasn't working. Maybe he just lost it. Maybe he took the knife away from her and started slashing. In his mind, he was cutting away the obstacle to his fortune. For the first time he found a woman who wouldn't cosign his bullshit."

"Then he just sat tight and waited for Raymond to come home," Dan said.

"Don't give up your day job, Dan. Stay in the newspaper publishing business. Gordon had no reason to kill Raymond. He probably was going to set it up as a robbery that led to murder, but Raymond walked in on him. Raymond and Billie were supposed to be at a movie in Norville, but they left the theater early. Raymond might have heard Cora screaming and come running down the road. When he got into the trailer, there was Gordon."

"And the shotgun?"

"It was Billie's shotgun, and Raymond probably tried to get it. They struggled, each man with one hand on the barrel and one on the stock. Gordon wrenched it away and shot Raymond right under the chin. Maybe he did it because he figured he'd be able to make it look like a suicide; maybe it just happened that way. He knew there'd be lots of questions, so he decided there should be a witness to answer them. Ben Wade was the perfect sap. In his rush to call Wade, meet him, and brief him, he forgot his jacket, which was draped over a chair. That's why only the back has blood on it."

"So that's it. Now we just take the letter and the jacket over to Korn and we reopen the case. Is it too late to reopen the case?"

"No statute of limitation on murder, Dan. But we can't do anything yet."

"Why not? There's physical evidence that Gordon was there. The letter proves that he hired Ben. He lied to everybody. He had a motive, and—"

"Dan, all we really have is my version of what happened. It's all guesswork, based on conjecture, based on intuition. The facts are that Gordon hired Wade, paid him off, and there's blood on Gordon's jacket. I painted one scenario. An equally plausible one could be that it was Gordon in the closet and Raymond did kill his wife, although I don't believe that."

"Why?"

"You're Raymond. You come home early from a movie. You're suspicious that your wife might be fooling around in the trailer. What do you do?"

"Raymond would beat her up."

"Before that."

"I guess . . . I guess I'd look around for the guy."

"Okay, and the second place you'd look after you checked under the bed is the closet."

"You know, you're exactly right."

"Dan, did you know Jesse Howlett?"

"Yes I did. I found him to be a nice kid with a good head on his shoulders."

"He have a drinking problem or a drug problem?"

"Not that I ever heard. What makes you bring him up? You don't think Gordon had anything to do with his death, do you?"

I shrugged. "Whenever you have an investigation, some things don't fit right. Sometimes it's significant and other times it's nothing. Billie told me her brother came to visit her in the hospital and he was stone cold sober. He tells her that there's just the two of them and he'll be there for her, and the next thing he does is get so drunk he smashes his car into a bridge."

"Well, it could have just started working on his head, you know, about his parents, and he did something dumb. Maybe because he hardly ever drank it hit him harder."

"Maybe. How far is the bridge abutment from the hospital?"

"The bridge is a few miles past the trailer, in the other direction from the hospital," Dan said.

"So he went home before he got drunk." I ran that around the cranium. "Billie told me he'd had a fight with Gordon. They used to be close and then something happened."

"You know, now that you mention it, I remember that anytime you pulled into Gordon's station you'd see Jesse working on his car."

"I wonder if Jesse found out about Gordon and his mother. Billie tried to talk to him about the fight, but he got sullen."

"It's possible. But what has that got to do with anything?"

I smiled. "Probably nothing."

"So what happens now?"

"I try to put some doubts in Billie's mind about Gordon

and the advice he's giving her, and we keep digging. We keep asking questions."

"Until?"

"Until we find the famous smoking gun. Without it, we're only spinning our wheels."

Cops call three to four A.M. "hammer time." It's the time when you resolve a hostage situation, it's the time when you storm a house, it's the time you make any dangerous bust.

It wasn't a matter of coincidence or custom. There was a study at Rockefeller University back in the early sixties that showed that the human biological clock slows at precisely that time. The senses are dulled, and people are less able to react to surprise. It's the time when there are the most accidents, and when most surprise attacks throughout history have been successful.

By all rights then, I should have been asleep, with all systems operating on minimum cylinders. The brain should have been cotton candy, and any thoughts I did have should have been no more than foggy fleeting sparks of sound and fury signifying nothing. So go figure I would have a eureka-type idea pop into my consciousness.

It was precisely three eighteen when I sat up in bed, rubbed the sand out of my eyes, and fumbled for the phone. I dialed Mario and Rosa Santamaria.

It rang six or seven times before a gruff-voiced Mario answered, "Yeah."

"Mario, it's Slots."

"You drunk? You know what time it is?"

"I know. I've got to ask you something."

"You got to be kidding—just a second. . . . It's Resnick, he says he has to ask me something. Yeah, what the hell do you have to ask me? Why the hell couldn't it have waited?"

"Tell me about the wine."

There was a long pause. "Are you out of your fu—freakin' mind? You call me up at three in the morning to ask me about wine? It's made from grapes. What're you, stupid or somethin'." He followed up with a string of Italian curses.

"No, the wine at the engagement party. Les Roses Croisees. I saw it on the bottom of the menu."

"What about it?" He put his hand over the phone, but his voice came through anyway: "He wants to know about the wine at the engagement party. You know the wine I got for Pat and Gordon's party? Hello, Resnick? What do you want to know?"

"Who else sells that stuff around here. I never heard of it."

"What is this? You have a broad over and you're settlin' a bet? Go read a wine book, for chrissake—hold on." Again the hand over the mouthpiece. "I'll say chrissake if I want to. I didn't say Christ, I said chrissake, like crisis. Resnick, I got her yapping in my ear."

"Mario it's about the investigation. I need to know if it's easy to pick up a bottle like that around here."

"Easiest thing in the world," he said.

"Damn! I thought I had something."

"All you got to do is write away to a wine supplier three weeks in advance. Wait for him to ship it to you from New York, maybe that takes another week to ten days, and shell out two hundred twenty bucks for a magnum. Only that was five years ago; it's more now."

"What happened to the wine at the dinner party?"

"What are you talking about? We drank it."

"How many bottles were there?"

"Resnick, you are nuts. I said I paid over two hundred bucks for that wine. I got one bottle. What the hell did you think I'd get?"

"You finished it?"

"Why, you want some? Of course we finished it! . . . He asked me if we finished it. . . . Hold on, Rosa is telling me something. . . . Yeah . . . Yeah. . . . Oh, that's right, I got real pissed. . . . Yeah I'll tell him. Hello, Resnick, here's what happened. We didn't get to finish the bottle. We all had one little glass. When Korn's deputy came in to get him, he got up and Gordon picked up the bottle and—what did he say? . . . Right, right. Gordon picked up the bottle and said something about he was going to take this home for later to share with his bride-to-be. I got pissed because I wanted to at least have another shot of the thing."

"Mario, I could kiss both you and Rosa."

"Just let us go to sleep," he said, yawning.

I hung up the phone feeling very pleased with myself. I thought of Gordon. "Gotcha you bastard!" I said aloud. "You and the smoking gun."

12

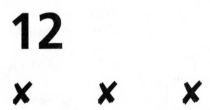

It was almost nine in the morning when I drove by the mansion and got a look at Gordon's newest employee. Even sitting on the rocker on the porch he looked big. I knew he was there to keep me out of Gordon's hair and away from Billie.

I circled back and parked next to his car, which was about twenty yards from the house on a grassy knoll. I knew it was his car because there was a Joe Weider muscle magazine on the front seat. I read his name off the mailing label: Herb Unkel.

I got out and waved at him and he got up from the rocker and stood with his hands on his hips. He reminded me of something back in New York—the Chrysler Building. Except the Chrysler Building was smaller and didn't have a red flat-top.

I waved for him to come over, but he just stood there watching me. He had a Chevy Iroc with tinted windows and an irridescent Playboy decal on the rear window. I walked over to the left front tire and kneeled down. He was watching me with a perplexed expression on his face. I held up my ballpoint pen, made sure he saw it, and started letting the air out of his tire. He cocked his head to one side with a look like politicians give you when they're pretending to be listening to you.

When I kneeled down next to the right front tire he finally made a move. He lumbered off the porch, all three hundred muscle-bound pounds of him. He was wearing the same kind of black knit shirt and pants set that Jack La Lanne sported back in the seventies. He filled the clothes to the bursting point with lats, deltoids, and pecs that looked as if they were pumped up with helium. This guy had forearms that made Popeye's look like twigs.

"What do you think you're doing?" he asked me. He sounded like he gargled with razor blades.

"Trying to get you off the porch," I said standing up. "I've got to see Billie Howlett, and I didn't want to cause any commotion in front of the door."

"Nobody gets in to see Billie or Mr. Wallace. I keep everybody out. You get in your car and get off this property. Hey! You let the air out of my tire!"

"Only halfway. I wanted you to be able to drive away without too much trouble."

He moved toward me menacingly. "I'm going to make you blow that tire back up with your mouth!" he said.

"Take it easy, Herbie."

He stopped, his head cocked again. It was obviously a permanent part of his repertoire. "How do you know my name? You see me wrassle?"

"Sure. Look, whatever Wallace gave you to play dragon and guard the castle, I'll double. Sounds like a good deal, right?"

"You never saw me wrassle. You're that wiseass detective Mr. Wallace told me about. I'm going to break you in half."

"I don't think I'm getting through, here. I'm offering twice the bucks you're getting from Wallace, and you don't have to get hurt."

"You think you can hurt me?" he actually chuckled.

"Yup. But I'd rather give you the cash."

I wasn't kidding. I had seen tough guys all my life. Skinny

206

Latinos with pockmarked faces, shanty Irish with shoulder-length hair, black guys with eyes so hollow you think you're looking into a cave, big fat Italian guys with bellies so big you wouldn't think they could move, let alone fight. They laughed at body builders, black belts, and boxers and took them apart just for fun. Forget the arena and the rules of competition, the most dangerous men in the world are the street fighters.

I didn't survive being half Jewish and half Irish in Hell's Kitchen and Alphabet City by not learning how to take care of myself.

He reached out to try to grab me but I stepped back and he snatched a handful of air.

"Last chance, Herbie, three times what Gordon offered you if you jump into your car and drive away."

He gathered a fist, crouching slightly.

Maybe it was better this way. I had no idea what Gordon was offering, and I'd hate to have to blow my retainer on the big goon.

He took a swing at me. I ducked the punch by pivoting to my left. Herb's wild punch left his whole right side open. I countered with an uppercut that landed flush on the big man's jaw. His head snapped back, but he stayed on his feet. He charged again, but I wasn't in front of him anymore. I used his forward progress to slam him into the car. He bounced off the door and crumpled to his knees.

"Just go home, Herbie. You don't have to do this for Wallace."

He got up, shaking his head to clear it. "I'm going to kill you," he growled.

I let him get a step closer to me before I snapped a jab to his nose. There was no barbell that could build up that part of his anatomy, and I could feel the soft cartilage give way. The blood came pouring out like someone had turned on a faucet.

It looked a lot worse than it was, but it finally dawned on Herbie Unkel that he was in trouble. He held his nose with his left hand and telegraphed a roundhouse right, which swept harmlessly over my head. From my crouched position I was face to face with another part of his anatomy that didn't benefit from weight training. I straightened up, connecting with my knee.

He made a sound between a gasp and a dry heave and slowly sunk to the ground, one hand on each of his aching parts in a variation of the *September Morn* pose.

I lifted his head. "We don't have to do this anymore, do we?" I asked.

He vigorously shook his head. I helped him to his feet and opened the door of the car. All the fight was out of him. He gingerly felt his nose.

"Have a doctor set that for you and you'll be as good as new," I told him.

He got into the Iroc, gunned the engine, and drove off Wallace's property.

Nobody had told Carla I was persona non grata on the Morgan estate. She cheerfully told me to come in and said she would get Billie for me. I waited in the hall. A few seconds later Carla came down carrying a pocketbook.

"I leave now, but Billie will be down soon. I tell her you here."

I thanked her and gave my best to Hector, who was home with a cold. I spent the next couple of minutes looking at Pat's painting hanging on the wall. Murder is a terrible waste of talent.

"What the hell!" Gordon walked out of the downstairs drawing room. "How did you get in here, Resnick?"

He gave me the kind of look you reserve for your dog when he does something on the living room floor. He walked past me to the door and stared outside, looking for his muscle.

"Herb took the day off," I told him.

Gordon verified it by going outside and looking for his security man's car. Satisfying himself that I was telling the truth, he came back and glared at me with renewed anger. "Get out! I don't want you here!"

"I'm sure you don't. I'm not here to see you, Gordon. I

have something to show to Billie." It was only then that he noticed what I was wearing. It was a nice blue windbreaker with the old Shell emblem over one breast pocket and Gordon's name over the other. His jaw dropped.

"What is this?"

"It's your jacket, Gordon. Don't you recognize it? Here, take a look. Here's your name sewn over the pocket."

"I can see it's one of my old jackets—I mean, it looks like one of my old jackets. . . . Where did you get it?"

"Where did you leave it?"

"Resnick, just what is it you're up to?"

"I'm going to see you go to prison for at least one murder, maybe four."

"You're crazy!"

"Am I, Gordon?"

"I'll take my jacket, if you please," he said, making a move for it.

I gently brushed him away. "I don't please. Possession is nine tenths of the law. Ask your friend Amanda about it."

Gordon's mouth twisted into a vicious sneer. "Give me the jacket, Resnick."

"Make me an offer," I told him.

He nodded, giving me a knowing grin. "Fine. Let's say one hundred dollars."

"Come on. Ben Wade got one hundred times that."

"I don't know what you're talking about. I'll raise my offer to five hundred."

"You're not even close."

"What's going on?" Billie was standing on the stairs looking down at us.

"Gordon is trying to buy his jacket back from me. He's offered me five hundred for it, which is a lot less than he gave Ben Wade to keep it hidden."

Gordon glared at me. If looks could kill . . .

"Don't listen to him, Billie, it's some kind of lying trick."

"The reason he wants it, Billie, is because it's the jacket he left in the trailer the night your parents were killed."

"Give me that jacket and get out of here!" He made a grab for my throat, and I let him get both hands around it. A hard punch right under the rib cage made him release me fast. He deflated like the Macy's Parade balloons on the day after Thanksgiving. I stepped back, anticipating whatever he'd had for breakfast ending up all over my shoes.

Billie came running down the stairs to his side. "Gordon, are you all right?"

He was gasping for air.

"How could you, Slots?" Billie said. "Have you gone insane?"

"He's just had the wind knocked out of him."

Gordon straightened up and took a couple of deep breaths. The color started returning to his cheeks. "I need a drink," he wheezed.

Billie supported him as they went into the living room. She sat Gordon down and went behind the bar, where she found a bottle of brandy and poured some into a glass.

"You better go, Slots," Billie said looking daggers at me as she gave Gordon the brandy.

"I intend to, but first I want to give you a letter that you might find interesting."

"Billie, don't read it," Gordon said. "It's got to be a trick of some kind. He's been out to get me from the minute he came to town."

"I don't want to read your letter, Mr. Resnick. I'm going to ask you again to leave."

"Billie, this is Gordon's jacket. He left it in the trailer the night your mother and father died."

"That's a lie! I wasn't in the trailer. I was at my engagement party at Mario's."

"This happened two hours before your engagement party."

"Gordon, what is he talking about?"

"Don't listen! It's just a pack of lies."

"It's a pack of lies all right, and he's the one telling them." I took out the copy of Leonard Wade's letter from his father.

210

"Read this Billie. If you want me out after that, I'm on my way to New York."

"Let me see that." Gordon struggled up out of the chair, but I pushed him unceremoniously right back.

"It's a letter Ben Wade wrote in case something should happen to him. He was blackmailing Gordon."

Billie looked shocked. "Blackmailing? Why?"

"Wade was hired and coached by Gordon. He didn't see what happened in the trailer that night, but Gordon did."

"Billie, I forbid you to read that letter. Resnick wrote it up himself."

"It was given to me by Wade's son Leonard. Dan Shelby was with me when we visited Leonard Wade's office in Adobe. Did I make this jacket myself and stitch his name on it? Billie, I'm sorry to have to put you through this, but you have to know the truth."

She looked down at the letter hesitatingly.

"Billie don't! He's playing mind games with you. He knows you're vulnerable and confused."

"He's the one who plays mind games. He's done it to Ramona, Amanda, Carole, and lots of other women. He's trying to get you to take the blame for a murder you didn't commit. Gordon is no hero Billie, he's lied to you and he's using you."

"Resnick, if you don't leave I'm calling the police!"

Billie weighed the letter in her hand. She looked at me and then back to Gordon.

"I'm just going to read it and then he'll go," she said.

Gordon tried to get up but I stared him back down into his chair.

Billie read it through, and when she was finished she handed it to Gordon. "You were there in the trailer?" she asked him. "I can't believe you lied to everybody about that."

I took off the jacket and handed it to her. "There are bloodstains on the back, Billie. I don't know whose blood, but a jury might conclude that Gordon was in the trailer the night of the tragedy."

"Gordon . . ."

"Billie, you would believe the word of this hired bedroom peeper over your own father? I took you in. I gave you everything."

"Why would Ben Wade write this if it wasn't true. You paid him blackmail money?"

"Billie, it's a trick. Sweetheart, I wouldn't tell you a falsehood."

"The phone's right there. Call Dan Shelby, or better yet call Leonard Wade in Adobe," I said.

Billie looked at the telephone.

"You can't possibly be taking this seriously," Gordon said to her. "The whole thing is preposterous."

That seemed to make the girl's mind up. She walked over to the phone, dialed Adobe information, and asked for Leonard Wade's number.

Gordon waited for her to dial the first four numbers.

"You don't have to call him," he said in a voice just barely above a whisper. "It's true. I was the witness that night in the trailer."

"I don't understand this, Gordon. Then what the letter says about the jacket—"

"That's true too. It's my jacket. But Billie, it's not what you think."

"It was you who was having an affair with my mother." Her voice was soft, but there was accusation in it.

"Billie no! Let me explain." His tone was desperate. "All I was guilty of was being a good neighbor. I just came over to bring your mother some cigarettes from the machine at the station. She liked those Newports with the menthol, remember? Well, no sooner do I get there than Raymond comes in, and he's in this vile mood. Cora had seen him walking down the road, but there was no way of me getting out of there without him seeing me. She didn't want a scene because—well, you know how jealous Ray could be over nothing. So she had me hide in the closet."

"Why did you have that man, that Ben Wade lie?" Billie wanted to know. "Why couldn't you just tell the truth?"

I answered that one. "Because he didn't want Pat to know. The fact of it is, Gordon, that you were having an affair with Cora. She was going to tell Pat about it if you didn't break off your engagement. Rather than risk losing all that money, you killed her."

Billie eased herself into one of the wing chairs. She was trying to compose herself but her hands were shaking.

"That's a damnable lie, Resnick!" He rose and went over to Billie, taking her hand. "Your mother and I were friends, Billie, nothing more. After what your father did, I was so ashamed that I hadn't tried to do something to help Cora. I admit it, Billie, I was a coward. I stayed in that closet and heard the fighting, but I was too scared to move. I didn't know that he was stabbing her. I just thought he was hitting her. I guess I should have stepped forward, but it just would have looked that much worse. I'm sorry now. I'm so sorry now that I didn't do anything. I never wanted to tell you, because I didn't know if you could ever forgive me. I'm glad it's out. I've been carrying this around in my heart for so long now."

He was good, I had to give him that much. If I were on a jury I might have bought it. Billie had tears running down her face, and so did Gordon. It was the finishing touch. She reached out and took his hand. "You wouldn't have been able to stop it," she said.

"I swear Billie, the next thing I heard was a shotgun blast, and when I finally worked up enough nerve I walked out of the closet into . . . I can't . . . They were both dead. There was nothing I could do. Yes, Resnick is right. I didn't want Pat to know anything. I was afraid that if I told the truth, some people would be like Resnick and try to make it out to be a scandal. I took the easy way out, Billie. I called this fellow I knew who needed the money, and I told him what I saw, and he repeated it. It happened just the way Ben said in the letter. Much later, I realized I didn't have my jacket. Ben figured out that I was the person hiding. You read the letter; he used the jacket to blackmail me. I didn't care about the money. It was more important that you didn't think badly of me."

"I don't, Gordon. I don't," Billie said tearfully.

"It was more important that Pat didn't get the right idea," I said. "Where did you get the money to pay the blackmail? You didn't have money of your own, so you skimmed it from Patricia's accounts. The money you gave to Carole Owens was just the tip of the iceberg."

I went over to Gordon, who was looking at Billie and shaking his head.

"He knew that Pat was on to his scheme. The check you cashed got her to start paying attention. There were too many withdrawals of large sums for him to explain. That's why Pat wanted you both out of her will. She didn't know who was the real thief. She told Rosa Santamaria that she thought you'd both betrayed her."

"How did you pay the blackmail?" Billie asked him.

"I have money of my own."

"You were always arguing with Patricia that you needed money in your own account. You said you felt embarrassed that you always had to come to her like a kid coming for his allowance."

"Billie, I was able to get the money. I borrowed, I sold things. It's not that important."

"Sure, it's important," I said. "It's his motive for killing Patricia."

"All right, Resnick, that's enough! You've done all the damage you're going to do. You think you have a case, go and prove it in court. Everything you've got is pure speculation and conjecture. You want the world to know I was a coward and hid when I should have come forward, fine. You want to accuse me of paying off Wade with Pat's money, well go ahead and try to prove it. You've got nothing at all. You think I care about the jacket now that Pat's dead and Billie knows the truth? You can wear it, with my compliments. Now use the phone and call the sheriff, or get out of our lives, once and for all."

"Gordon, where did my father get the shotgun? Jesse gave it to me." Billie had a funny look on her face. She seemed to be far away.

"I don't know, Billie. I was in the closet, remember? So what's it going to be, Resnick?" he said to me.

"I thought you'd put on a good show, Gordon, but you did even better than I expected. The little bit about the menthol cigarettes was perfect. I think you're right. I think if you were tried in a court, you'd twist the story around just enough to create doubt, and you'd walk. You might have actually gotten away with everything, except you slipped up with Jesse."

"Jesse?" Billie questioned.

"I'm not sure how, but after Jesse visited you in the hospital, he ran into Gordon."

"Wrong, Resnick. But continue. Maybe I'll get a good laugh out of this." Gordon took a sip of his brandy. He had his old confidence back. He was in control again.

"My guess is, Gordon went back to the trailer when he realized the jacket was there. He ran into Jesse. You remember the fight they had, Billie, the fight that Jesse didn't want to talk to you about? My feeling is that Jesse found out about Gordon's affair with your mother."

"We argued about him leaving a mess in the garage. I told him to come back when he learned how to put away tools," Gordon said disgustedly.

I ignored him and concentrated on Billie, who seemed to be only half listening.

"I think Jesse threatened to expose Gordon, and that would have put you in the same position you were in with Cora. Only this time you had already murdered someone. If Jesse came forward, that would put doubt on the whole story, and there would have been a more thorough investigation. You couldn't have that, Gordon, so you killed Jesse too."

"I see. And how do you propose I did that? The kid was stinkin' drunk."

"Gordon!" Billie yelled.

"I don't mean it that way. Who could blame him for getting drunk?"

"When he visited Billie in the hospital, he talked about sticking together and taking care of each other. He didn't use booze. It was a big personality change for him."

"Your personality changes when you lose your parents like that," Gordon interjected. "So you're saying that I got him drunk?" He looked at Billie. "Can you believe this guy?"

"Slots, I don't see—"

"We don't know if Jesse really *was* drunk. They couldn't do any kind of autopsy because of the fire that destroyed the body. The assumption is that he was drinking, because of the bottle they found."

"Why else did he smash into the abutment?" Billie wanted to know.

"He was unconscious or dead before he hit the bridge. Gordon probably hit him with the bottle. Then he drove Jesse a hundred feet or so from the bridge abutment and lined the car up to hit the concrete square center. My guess is he put the shift in neutral and wedged Jesse's dead weight against the gas pedal, flooring it. With the engine revved at a high speed, he just had to get out of the car, reach in and shift the gear to drive and watch it crash. After that, he hiked back to his own car."

"I'm not going to listen to any more of this." Gordon got up, his face flushed.

"Billie, it was Sunday. Ask him where Jesse got whatever he was drinking. All the liquor stores were closed."

She thought about that. Her eyes went to Gordon.

"How the hell am I supposed to know?"

"Witnesses at the engagement party remember Gordon taking a bottle of wine from the restaurant. He told them he was going to save it for himself and Pat for later. It wasn't just any kind of wine, it was an expensive French import called Les Roses Croisees. The chances of Jesse picking up a bottle of that specific wine from another restaurant in this area were one in a million.

216

"Shelby ran a picture of the so-called accident scene in the *Post*. The picture showed a bottle on the ground with two crossed roses on the label. That's the translation of 'Les Roses Croisees': 'crossed roses.'"

"You told me you hadn't seen Jesse," Billie said to Gordon. "You said you wished he had, and then you would have spoken to him and he wouldn't have been killed." Her voice sounded hollow, mechanical. Her eyes were open wide in horror.

"I can explain," he began.

"This one you're not going to explain away," I said, tapping him hard on the chest with my forefinger.

"Move away from him, Slots!"

I turned to see that Billie had gone behind the bar. She was holding the gun that was kept there. It was the same one she had pulled on me when I first told her that the Mets were interested in signing her.

Gordon smiled broadly. "Good work, Billie. Let's get him out of here. I forgot all about that gun."

"Billie, what are you doing? Are you all right?" I asked her. She was holding the gun with both hands and the pistol was shaking, she was shivering so hard. Her face was blanched, and the tears were streaming down her face.

"She'll be fine once you're out of her hair. I'll take the gun now, Billie." He reached for it.

"Don't, Billie! If you give it to him we'll both be killed!"

"That's crazy. Give me the gun Billie!"

Billie's face twisted into an expression of cold hatred. "Gordon, I remember about the shotgun," she said softly. She raised the pistol. "I was walking down the road with my father, Slots, and we heard screaming. I heard my mother screaming. My father hid me behind a tree and told me to stay there no matter what happened. He asked me for my shotgun. He asked me, 'Billie, where's the shotgun Jesse gave you. Someone is trying to hurt Mommy. Where's the shotgun?' I pointed to the place under the trailer where I kept it. My father got it and went into the trailer. *And he yelled, 'Gordon, what*

217

are you doing? You're killing her!' There was a struggle then. I heard the two of you fighting and cursing. I heard my father groaning in pain and he screamed, 'Don't! Don't do it Gordon!' And then the gun went off and then you came out covered with blood. I saw you. You dirty murdering bastard I saw you."

Gordon remained frozen, then he shrugged and sat back down in the leather chair. He picked up the brandy and took a sip.

"So you got your memory back. I knew that was a mistake. I should have made sure that you didn't."

"That's why you adopted her, wasn't it, Gordon? You were never sure if she saw anything. By taking her in, you were presenting yourself to the world as a great guy, but in reality you were keeping close tabs on her to find out how much she might know."

"Something like that," he acknowledged. "The fact is, Billie, I got to like you. That's what happens when you let your emotions get in the way of business."

"You're a monster!" Billie hissed.

"Maybe. I don't care what you call me. I know what I want, and I know how to take it."

"You're finished now, Gordon," I told him.

"Not hardly. I'll beat this too. I'll come up with something. Maybe I'll have a friend give me an alibi."

"That's why you were so nice to Carole and the boy. You knew you might need her someday."

"It was a long-term investment, and I was using Pat's money, so I didn't mind. Women are so easy, you know. The key is to be a good listener and repeat back to them what they want to hear. If this ever gets to a jury, I'm going to have some fun." He threw his head back and laughed.

He was still laughing when the bullet from the .357 Magnum blew a fist-size hole in his right temple, passed through his head, and gouged a hunk of plaster out of the wall ten feet beyond him.

13

We stood frozen, Billie still holding the gun straight out with both hands in the classic shooting stance, still aiming at the spot where Gordon had been standing, me off to her left, and Gordon himself sprawled over the back of the sofa, arms and legs akimbo, lifeless eyes staring up at the ceiling.

The retort of the big gun was echoed by the ringing in my ears. I moved very slowly, going to Billie and taking the gun from her hand and placing it on the bar behind her. She didn't make any move to stop me. She was shaking almost uncontrollably now. I drew her close and held her until she calmed down.

"I'm okay," she finally said, moving away.

"You sure? Maybe I should call an ambulance for you."

She didn't say anything, just stared at Gordon's corpse.

"Why don't I feel anything, Slots? I don't feel bad or good or anything. It's like it isn't me."

"You're in shock," I told her.

She sat down in the same wing chair Gordon had taken just a few minutes before. "It all came back to me, everything I had suppressed for all these years." She shook her head.

"They told me it would happen like that, that one day I'd remember again."

"You had to be ready. Your mind protected you by blocking it out, and now maybe you feel you're strong enough to look at it."

"Slots, he would have killed me years ago if I had regained my memory and let on I knew what happened."

"I know. How do you feel now?"

She looked at me and managed a sad smile. "Calm, resigned. I guess I always felt that Gordon didn't really care about me. Maybe that's why it hurt me so bad that Pat was angry at me too. I wanted someone to like me."

"I'm going to have to call the sheriff," I said.

"I know."

"Just for the record, I think you're very likable. You could be my kid anytime."

She nodded. "I appreciate that. When I go to prison, maybe we'll write to each other."

"Yeah, sure," I growled.

This all stunk! I called up Korn and got Mr. Pompous himself. I told him there'd been a fatality at the mansion and he better get his ass up there right away. He asked me for details and I told him he'd see when he got there.

"He's coming?" Billie asked me.

"On his way."

"You know, I don't know how to say this, but I don't feel bad at all. I feel a great weight has been taken off my shoulders. I don't think it was good for me to bury what happened. It made me afraid. I was always questioning myself. I feel . . . I feel better, freer, for the first time I feel in charge of myself. Don't look so sad, Slots. I'm prepared for whatever happens."

It wasn't right. I had busted my butt to keep Billie from being nailed for a murder she didn't commit only to have her murder someone else.

The slimeballs, the Gordons of this world too often seem to be able to break all the rules and reap all the benefits. And

220

even if they don't, they hurt a lot of good people when they try to get away with something. This kid would be in jail until she was an old lady, and why? Because she knew that Gordon would have gotten away with everything. We would have played by the rules, and Gordon would have laughed at us at every step while he spent the inheritance that came to him from the woman he murdered. The shame wasn't that Billie had killed Gordon, it was that she could only do it once. I walked over to her and took her face in both of my hands, forcing her to look into my eyes.

"I want you to think very carefully about what I'm going to ask you. It's very important."

"Okay."

"Can you live with this? Can you live the rest of your life knowing that you shot Gordon? Think carefully, Billie. A lot of people before you have had to pull the trigger, and then they spend the rest of their lives going nuts, haunted by what they did."

"Slots, look what he took from me. I would only regret it if I didn't kill him," she said softly.

I nodded. "I'm not going to let you lose everything because of this bastard. You do exactly what I say, no questions. We haven't much time."

I saw a flicker of hope behind the quiet resignation in her eyes. "Okay," she said.

"Find me another bullet for the Magnum," I told her.

She went behind the bar, ducked down, and came up with the box of ammo. She opened it and handed me a bullet.

"Now find me a handkerchief."

"I've got one in my room."

"Go, fast!"

I grabbed Gordon under the armpits and dragged him over to the far wall. There was very little blood; the power of the caliber actually fuses blood vessels as it passes through the tissue.

I propped him up as best I could against the windowsill, then went back to the bar and placed a bullet in the one empty chamber of the gun. Billie rushed back into the room with a fresh white linen handkerchief. She saw Gordon had been moved to the window but was smart enough not to say anything to break my train of thought.

I wiped the gun down with the handkerchief and then, still holding the gun in the hankie I went and placed the pistol in Gordon's right hand. I opened the window, stuck Gordon's hand with the gun outside, placed my finger on top of Gordon's, and squeezed a shot off out the window. Then I took the gun out of his hand with the hankie and put it on the bar again.

"Help me drag him back," I said to Billie.

We got him back to where he had originally fallen. I stood up and measured the line of sight where the bullet plowed into the wall.

"A three-fifty-seven leaves powder burns. That's why we shot one out the window, so Gordon would have burns."

I doubted Korn would know enough to look for them, but the boys from the Denver ME's office were sharp.

"Gordon killed himself, Billie. I came by and showed you the evidence I had found, and he got remorseful, grabbed the gun from the bar, put it to his right temple as we looked on in horror, and killed himself. Do you have that?"

"Yes."

Using the hankie, I put the gun back in Gordon's hand, squeezed his fingers around the pistol to set the prints, and let the gun fall from his cold grasp onto the floor next to him.

We heard Korn's Land-Rover screech to a stop, and moments later he came running into the room. He saw me with my arms around a weeping Billie Howlett, and then he turned his gaze to the corpse in the center of the room.

"Holy Mother of God! Is that Gordon?"

"It was Gordon," I said.

"What happened?"

"Come on, Sheriff, it should be obvious even to you," I goaded him.

He stepped over to the body. "He shot himself?"

"It was so horrible," Billie said, sniffling.

"I think he's dead," I said.

"You think! You mean you didn't even check? You idiot, he could still be alive." He bent over the corpse.

"I was trying to help Billie," I explained. "She went to pieces."

I watched as Korn turned Gordon around, putting his head to the dead man's chest. His knee landed on top of the gun, which he reached down and moved out of the way. It was beautiful. It would be almost impossible now to prove Gordon hadn't committed suicide. The angle of entry was distorted, and the prints would be useless. Korn was a disaster. The people of Norville really had themselves a winner.

"He's dead all right." He ran his hands all over Gordon's skull. "One shot to the temple. That did it." As if for the first time, he noticed the Magnum lying on the floor. "He used a Magnum, and if I'm not mistaken, the bullet entered here in the wall where the plaster is knocked out. Look, you two, sit down over there and tell me what happened. Just don't touch anything."

I did most of the talking. I had found some new evidence having to do with the deaths in 1985 of Jesse, Cora, and Ray Howlett. I wanted to talk to Gordon about it before I brought it over to the sheriff's office.

"What kind of evidence?"

I gave him the jacket and the letter, which he read very slowly. When he was finished he tilted his oversize hat toward the back of his head.

"This legitimate?"

"Ben Wade's son Leonard gave it to me. He's a veterinarian in Adobe."

"Well, it doesn't really change anything in the case. It just means that Gordon himself was the witness and not Wade."

"He admitted he killed my mother and father, and while he was telling it to us I remembered everything," Billie said.

"You mean all the stuff you had blocked out?"

Billie told him about the shotgun and how she remembered hearing her father call out Gordon's name.

"Well, damn!" Korn said.

"He also killed Jesse." I told him about the wine, and about how Jesse couldn't have gotten it from anyone but Gordon.

"Listening to all this makes me kind of wonder if he wasn't also involved in Patricia's murder," Korn said, discovering America.

"You're absolutely right, Sheriff. He admitted to that, too, before he killed himself. He said he'd been taking large sums of Patricia's money for a long time, and she finally got wise. She was going to cut him off and he couldn't allow that to happen. Ramona was telling the truth."

"Well, I'll be. . . . You know, I had my suspicions." Korn's brows knitted. "So why did he decide to admit it and take his own life all of a sudden?"

"Guilt. When I talked about what happened to Cora and Jesse, he couldn't stand it. The reason he adopted Billie was to assuage the guilt he had for killing her family."

"He apologized for trying to put it on me," Billie said. "He was glad it came out in the open. He told me he'd been carrying it in his heart for too long a time. We were just talking, and he asked if I could ever forgive him, and then he got the gun, and put it to his head, and—"

"Okay, okay, I get the picture. Why don't you get yourself freshened up, Ms. Howlett? You're going to have to come down and sign some papers. I'm going to need you there too, Slots."

"I guess this clears Billie as far as Patricia Morgan-Wallace's death is concerned," I said.

"Well, a death-bed-type confession carries a lot of weight. I guess if what Slots says about the accounts turns out to be true, Gordon had a pretty good motive, and based on what happened in the trailer . . . The only thing is the sworn testimony from Ms. Owens that Gordon was with her all Saturday night."

224

"Now that Gordon is dead, I'm sure she'll recant. She was lying. I'm sure I don't have to tell you that though, Sheriff."

"I had my suspicions."

The idea for the party was Rosa's, Mario said. It was in celebration of the county prosecutor's dropping all charges against Billie based on lack of evidence and on the new evidence implicating Gordon Wallace. It was also a good-bye-Slots party.

Mario did it right, closing the restaurant except for our little shindig.

Dan Shelby of course was there. I had spent much of the previous afternoon giving Shelby the exclusive story of Gordon's admission of guilt in four murders and of his "suicide." Shelby was very excited.

"I bet I could do a book on this," he said. "It might make a great movie."

Ramona and Billie were sort of shy with each other at first, but as the evening wore on, they were giggling and whispering together. Billie had grown up a lot in the last few days, but she was still only a twenty-year-old.

"Listen, Slots," Ramona said, cornering me. "There's something I got to ask you. I want you to tell me the truth. Don't worry about sparing my feelings."

"Okay."

"When Gordon was about to kill himself, he was doing a lot of talking, right?"

"Yeah."

"Well . . . he didn't, like, say anything about me, did he?"

"Like what?"

"A special good-bye of some kind."

"No Ramona, he didn't. He was kind of concerned with himself, to tell you the truth."

"Okay, I can deal with that." She lowered her voice. "He didn't mention Amanda, right?"

"Not a word."

"Good!" she said with a large measure of relief.

It was Rosa's idea to invite Leonard Wade and his mother. Mario told me he had asked Rosa if it was a good idea, since Rita and Leonard wouldn't know anyone, and she said Leonard was going to get to know Billie very well.

"You going to tell me there's nothing to this second-sight stuff? Look at them. He's falling all over her, and if she doesn't dig guys, you'd never know it from the way she's hanging on every word he says. I seen him take her number, for chris—I mean, for gosh sakes. Will you listen to me? That woman is making me nuts."

Two people Rosa insisted on inviting but who didn't show were Amanda and Sheriff Korn. Amanda said she felt it improper as the Wallace attorney to be at a party, in light of recent tragic events. Korn said he had to work but he would stop off for a few minutes.

After the scallop mousse and shrimp appetizer and the main course of deviled roast rock cornish game hens with french-fried sweet potatoes and green beans vinaigrette, Shelby started tapping his glass with his spoon.

"I want to hear from our two guests of honor. Speech, speech, we demand a speech."

"What for, you need to fill in some space in that rag newspaper of yours?" Mario kidded him.

"Don't knock my newspaper, goombah. If it weren't for my paper, you'd have nothing to wrap your fish."

Everybody laughed at that, particularly Mario, who bellowed, "He's right, he's really right. I use it for the fish."

"Speech, speech!" Rosa started in, and the rest of them took up the chant. Billie looked at me, and I nodded for her to go first.

She stood up and waited until everyone quieted down.

"Mario, this was quite a party. I don't ever remember food tasting this good, except for the last time I was here. Rosa and Mario, thank you. Actually, I just want to thank you all.

"I don't really have a family anymore . . ." Her eyes filled and the tears spilled over. "Excuse me." She dabbed at her eyes, sniffling. "I don't have a real family anymore, but I will always think of you as my family. I want to thank all of you for not giving up on me. I know that wasn't easy, because I had given up on myself. I'm going to try not to make that mistake again.

"I wouldn't be standing here tonight if it wasn't for Slots Resnick. I can never say enough about what Slots did for me. I'll never forget it." She was crying harder now.

"Slots told me I could be his daughter anytime, and I'm going to take him up on it. I want him to know and I want all of you to know that I'm going to do my best to make you all proud of me."

After the applause, it was my turn.

"Look, I'm not one to make speeches. Some of you made arrangements to have my face rearranged"—I looked at Ramona, who cracked up—"others of you tried to freeze me out"—I stared at Mario, who stretched nonchalantly in his chair—"but in the end I think it all worked out for the best. Billie Howlett is a fine athlete and a fine human being. If I was there to lend a hand at the right time, I'm very pleased. In one way or another, you've all made a big difference in this case. I think justice was done in Norville." That brought more applause. Korn appeared in the back of the room. He held his stetson at his side and nodded to me.

"Now I've been told that I can make a special announcement, an announcement that as we speak will be made to the major news media in New York City. The New York Mets Baseball Team has invited Ms. Billie Jo Howlett of Norville, Colorado, to a special press conference at the Waldorf-Astoria in New York. The press will be invited to meet the Mets' number-one draft choice, Billie Jo Howlett, who will be signing a professional baseball contract. Included in the contract will be a provision for a one million dollar signing bonus.

"Ms. Howlett will become the first female to be signed by a major league club, and she'll begin her minor league career with the Tidewater Tides.

That brought a new round of cheers and Billie got hugs

from a bevy of well wishers. Then Mario brought out the pièce de résistance, rum zabaglione with strawberries and amaretto. The party lasted well into the night.

Sometime later I said my good-byes. I was headed for the door when Korn pigeonholed me.

"Resnick, got a second before you leave?"

"Yeah," I said warily.

He stuck out his hand. "I guess you and me got off on the wrong foot. I just want you to know that I'm sorry if I went off half-cocked with you."

I shook his hand. "All's well that ends well, to coin a phrase."

"You know, I'll never be the lawman my dad was, and I guess I won't be the lawman Slots Resnick is. I'm young, and I'm going to make some bonehead mistakes. But I'm going to keep trying. Maybe someday we can even get to be friends. Maybe I can call on you to be a real partner."

"Korn, I think I might like that. Take care of yourself," I said, turning to the door.

"Slots," he said, putting his hand on my shoulder, "take a look at this." He held out a slug casing. "It's the casing from a three-fifty-seven Magnum. I found it in a funny place, right outside the window of the room where Gordon killed himself."

"No kidding. What do you make of that?"

"Well, I heard of cases where people try to make a shooting look like a suicide by having the corpse fire a gun to get powder burns. You shoot the gun out the window and replace the bullet with another."

"Seems a little far-fetched to me," I said.

"Yeah, to me too. Why don't you take this as a souvenir of Norville." He placed the shell in my breast pocket. "Like you said, all's well that ends well."

"You know, Korn. I might have underestimated you. I think your dad would be real proud."

Epilogue

✗   ✗   ✗

A month later to the day found me standing in the back of a cadre of reporters who were trying to question the beautiful young woman sitting on the dais.

Rex Thompson and Bucky were sitting next to her, Bucky as uncomfortable in his tux as a nun at an orgy. In the front at a special table was Dr. Wade, with whom Billie had flown up to New York. I was going to see the kids later at a private little dinner at a place in Soho.

Yeah, I saw myself up there. I thought about how a twenty-year-old Slots Resnick would answer the questions of the fourth estate.

Yeah, I was jealous. Just for a moment. There was also a sense of pride, a fatherly sense of pride that felt damn strange.

You don't look back in life. Not for too long. As Satchel Paige once said, "Don't look back, somethin' might be gainin' on you."

I helped myself to a glass of the free booze, took a little canape off a waiter's tray, and then flung my elbows around and fought my way to the door. A wag from one of the dailies nodded hello. He followed in my wake until we were outside on the cool New York sidewalk.

"So what do you think, Slots. You think she'll make it?"

"Pal," I said, smiling, "she already has."